THE
DARKNESS
RETURNS

A Lythinall Novel, Book One

GREY SHELTER

TIR-LARAH

SILVERSWORD
PASS

SNOW PEAK

MOUNTAINS

THE TOR
HILLS

THE WINDING
RIVER   HAVEN

VALLEY OF

THE DARKNESS RETURNS

A Lythinall Novel
Book One

MICHAEL D. NADEAU

SKULL GATE

THE DARKNESS WITHIN

Copyright © 2017 Michael D. Nadeau

"Skullgate Media" and associated logos copyright © 2021 Skullgate Media LLC

www.skullgatemedia.com

ISBN

Ebook ISBN

Third Edition: 2021

Second Edition: 2019, Kyanite Press

First Edition: 2017, Michael D. Nadeau

Cover design and internal layout by Chris Vandyke

ACKNOWLEDGEMENTS

To my wife, Sheila, for always being patient with me, even though you want to smother me in my sleep sometimes.

To all of my friends for always having faith in me and reading my stories.

To my gaming group for inspiring me with our escapades. You all made this possible. But wait...there's more.

To Gwen and Lexi Gagne, who were the inspiration for my faeries.

Last, but definitely not least, my kids and grandkids: Amber, Gabriel, Connor, and Jackson —Widdle Dood—.

THE DARKNESS RETURNS

A Lythinall Novel

MICHAEL D. NADEAU

MAP OF LYTHINALL
And Surrounding Regions

S'REN-SELLERE

NORTHERN BELT

TIR LANAN

SILVERSWORD PASS

SNOWPEAK MOUNTAINS

THE WATCHING WOODS

THE TORN HILLS

LYTHINALL

WYNDRAL

THE BELTFLOW RIVER

DAELYN

HAVENAR

NORHIL HOLD

THE WINDNG RIVER

NORTHERN RUN ROAD

THE HIDDEN VALE

SHEILD MOUNTAINS

THE MISTY WOODS

END OF THE WORLD

KERAGAN HOLD

EVERKNIGHT

RIVER VALE

CAERLYN HOLD

ALRIN

TERAFAR

FOREST OF THE LOST

WHITELEAF LAKE

SOUTHERN RUN ROAD

THE SERPENT RIVER

BARRIER MOUNTAINS

CONTENTS

❧ I ❧

TO LIVE AGAIN

He starts to come around. Slowly at first, then more and more as memories start to filter into his mind. If only he could remember his name. The damp earth shifts as he flexes his arms, filling in the space where they were. Those elves buried him deep this time. Very deep. Not at all like when his brothers and sisters had done it. He gathers his strength, pulling power from the soil packed in around him, and moves still further; little by little. He chuckles inwardly, thinking how impossible this would be if he were only human; but he isn't even close to human. He wonders briefly, as he moves the heavy earth around him, why he awoke. They surely had placed powerful wards around him, to keep him slumbering and docile. Perhaps something had weakened them. He would find out soon enough.

He pulls more power from the earth around him and swivels his head back and forth to dislodge more of it. He strains his legs and pulls them up towards his body slowly as it fills in under him. When he finally feels the ground under him settle, he tests it by gently pushing back down with his feet. It should hold. With one more draw of energy from the very substance meant to be his prison, he builds power within himself, shoves down with his legs, and springs through the soil and roots towards the surface. He feels his legs break with the exertion but shrugs off the pain. It will heal. He bursts through the ground with a mighty explosion and his unnatural body comes to rest waist-deep. He immediately feels the wind whipping through his dirt-crusted hair, temporarily deafening him. With a thought he shuts out the sound; he knows that his hearing will adjust soon. He doesn't dare open his eyes yet; even moonlight could blind him at this point.

Then the smell hits him. Nauseated, he refuses to ignore this sensation. Instead, he revels in it. It must be early spring, his least favorite time of the year. He can smell the budding leaves, the healthy branches of the tree nearby, even the chill in the air that reminds him of a coming storm. It's all so disgusting. Life was springing up all around him and it made his skin crawl, but that would change soon. He braces his arms against the sod-covered ground and levers himself out of the gaping wound left in the earth. Already his legs are healing, bones knitting in a rapid pace that still amazes him to this day.

When they are strong enough to support him, he stands on unsteady legs and laughs, coughing rich dirt out of his long-unused mouth. He shakes the loose soil free of his long mane of black hair, opens his mud-caked black eyes, and takes a careful inventory of his appearance. His clothes have all but rotted away, except for the cloak bestowed upon him by his lord and sovereign on the day he was transformed into this vessel. Otherwise, he was in good shape for being in the ground for gods-above-know-how-long. His tall, seven-foot frame is thinner than he remembers, yet he feels strong. At least his long imprisonment hadn't taken that away.

He opens his mind to the forest surrounding him, flexing his mental muscles, and tries to get a feel for this world around him.

He can sense the smaller animals already fleeing for the farther reaches of the wood, knowing instinctively that something unnatural has appeared. Smart creatures. He shakes his head, thinking that these tiny beings were smarter than some of the so-called greater races he had known in his many years. Farther and farther out his consciousness goes, *seeing* the slopes and valleys of this great wood. There. He spies a familiar landmark deep in a recess, almost covered by the forest floor. The *sight* staggers him. It would have taken the woods at least two-hundred years to grow over the statue he was *seeing*.

He brings his *sight* back, memorizing the way there from his current location, and breathes deeply. Now he has a destination. Gathering his cloak around him, more out of habit than any need to shelter himself from the elements, he begins the long walk. He needs to move to work out any remaining kinks and limber up his muscles in case he needs them, but it may be a while before anyone comes for him. As he walks through the ancient, quiet forest, he notices that his other powers have not slackened in the slightest, though he has less than some of his brethren.

Glancing over his broad shoulders, he notices that his passing still withers the smaller vegetation not hardy enough to withstand his presence. He slows his pace and reaches out to brush his fingers against the bark of a mighty oak tree. The effect is immediate. The bark darkens, the blight spreading outward around the trunk and spiraling down towards the roots in the span of two slow steps. He hears the slight groan of the tree as its life slips away, rotting from within. He knows that in twenty paces, the tree will collapse and decompose. He walks back to the gaping hole in the ground and looks down at where he was imprisoned for so long. He can now see the rotting roots that he broke through, and feel the wound in the earth from his very presence. He smiles to himself. *Still got it.* He turns once more and restarts his journey.

In two hours' time he stands in front of the figure, or what is left of it anyway. Moss, earth, and roots engulf the massive marble sculpture, only revealing its huge face protruding from below. The statue of his lord and master was thrown down when they dragged him through here. He still remembers that fateful day, many years though it has been, as it was only yesterday. His name comes to him then; a moment of clarity in a hectic morning. *Dar'Krist.* Now he feels complete.

He is eager with hunger to walk the land, destroying the crops, animals, and even people with his touch, bringing his lord's will to the people of Lythinall whether they want it or not. As he prepares for his journey, he wonders briefly who will oppose him this time. Will it be the elves again, throwing their human slaves at him in the hundreds, or will his brothers and sisters come for him again? He was weakened the last time or they never would've brought him low. No, this time he will know his limitations. Let them all come. He will see even his fellow incarnations lay at his feet, broken and bleeding, if it was the last thing he would do. Letting his *sight* spread out before him, Dar'Krist begins his walk thinking how good it felt to be back among the living once more. He spies a distant castle, hundreds of miles away, and knows instinctively that a ruler of people resides there.

He laughs, his mighty voice echoing off of the trees and scattering the few animals that had thought they were far enough away. No, this time he would not be sent into sleep again, the only prison that could even hope to hold him. Yes, this time he would be victorious. This time he would bring suffering and decay to the world, and his master would be most pleased. Dar'Krist moves towards a boulder blocking his path and places his hand upon it. In moments it splits down the middle with a resounding crack that echoes through the solemn forest. Stepping over the rubble, he wonders if the elves are even in power still. That castle doesn't look like anything an elf would build. He needs to know more. He orients his *sight* once more and finds a new destination; his first stop among the people of this land, whatever they called it these days. The village seems like a frontier town, full of . . . humans. No elves. Even better. He strides through the forest, and tuning his *sight*, he gauges the town to be about eighty miles . . . *that way.*

The Village of Wyndral

RHOE SAW the land below him as if he were flying. The packed earthen road flashed by beneath him rapidly; this had to be a dream. He recognized the area, being from the north country himself. This was the road to Wyndral, some sixty miles north east of Daelyn. The bridge over the Belt Flow River came and went in a blink. Then he saw the town coming up fast, and he could feel himself begin to slow. Flashes came to him as he soared over the town and spiraled downward, seemingly on invisible wings. That was when he heard the screams. His first thoughts were of a dragon, rampaging out of the northern Watching Woods. Dragons hadn't attacked a settlement in over seventy years, but no one was dumb enough to outright dismiss the thought. When his *sight* turned quickly in the direction of the horrible cries, however, he saw only a man. The man was almost seven feet tall and walking slowly towards the center of town. Bodies of the town's guardsmen surrounded him on all sides, both the dead and the dying.

It looked like the man was taking a stroll through a summer's field, meandering as if nothing concerned him at all. He was dressed in rotting black traveling clothes and a great billowing cloak that seemed tattered around the edges. His whole stance and demeanor screamed violence. Rhoe watched in utter horror as more men came running from buildings, carrying the tools of their trades as weapons: hammers, pitch forks, and even ice tongs. What these people thought they could do when the guard had obviously failed was beyond him, but he was unable to look away as they closed within striking distance of the strange man. He needed to see how dangerous he was.

The first to reach him was a smith, a huge bear of a man with more hair on his arms than anyone Rhoe had ever seen. He swung a heavy hammer straight at the wandering man in an overhead chop, his muscled arms bringing the weapon down with awesome force.

The stranger reached up, grabbed the hammer out of the air, and redirected the momentum of the off-balanced man to the far left. The man tumbled for a good twenty paces, his shoulder cracking under the force of the impact. The stranger had barely turned to face his next foe, an old grandfatherly-type wielding a pitchfork, but he already had his foot up to stop the charging old man. Rhoe heard the cracking of bone as his chest caved in; the foot carried the body down to the bare ground. He heard the solid whump, as the man's entire chest cavity was crushed under the force of the stranger's follow through.

The stranger casually batted the fork aside as the remaining two men scrambled to a stop just outside his reach. They both looked as if they would empty their stomachs at the sight, but seemed bolstered by some unseen motivation. Even though Rhoe couldn't see what it was that was giving these men courage when braver men would have turned and run, he certainly knew that they had given something away to the stranger . . . or whatever this *thing* was in front of them. The stranger's black-cloaked arm shot out suddenly behind him and his seven-foot frame hardly moved at all as he grabbed the huge man coming up behind him by the throat. With a slight smile, almost as if to acknowledge their failed ruse, he brought his arm over his head completely, still holding the huge man by his crumpled throat, and slammed him down into the ground at their feet. The wet, sickly crunch was enough that time, and both men turned to the side and emptied their breakfasts onto the packed street. The man walked on, watching the fleeing people, and chuckled quietly to himself.

But then he stopped suddenly to spin in Rhoes' direction. He looked around, up, even back the way he came before settling in on where Rhoe was hovering. His eyes burned with a dark spirit that seemed to have a life of its own, the kind that would suck your soul down, chew it up, and then swallow it . . . slowly. Rhoe was petrified. *This had to be a dream*—he thought —*a really bad dream.*

He could see the bodies behind the strange man already decaying, a black rot spreading over them like some kind of death mist. The strange being—for no man could be capable of this much suffering and death all by himself—was staring intently at him now, and he began to feel a pressure in the back of his mind. The man wasn't even breathing hard. Rhoe saw him bow slightly, turn his back, and continue walking towards the center of Wyndral. Somehow Rhoe knew he was still concentrating on where he was, even without eye contact.

The man's voice came to Rhoe from across a vast emptiness then, and even though the man was too far away to be heard, Rhoe could understand him completely. "I know you are there elfling, and you can't stop me." The voice paused, as if searching for the right words. "No man, woman, elf or even the very incarnations of the gods will be able to stop me, not this time. This is the Dark One's final plan--no one will silence the cries of the suffering." Rhoe felt a mental pull, and he was hurtling backwards then, dragged out of the town by a force that hurt everywhere at once and yet nowhere that he could define. His very bones seemed to throb with cascading pain, but he used that pain and focused it down. Rhoe had learned from his mother how to channel pain, and even a novice like himself had to be proficient in this life-saving technique. He grounded enough of the pain to save his body from going into shock, but he still felt himself slipping away into blackness.

Least it's only a dream, he thought to himself, and then the darkness swam up and engulfed him.

2

AND SO IT BEGINS

The deep verdant green of the spring leaves swaying in the breeze always made him smile. The cool air filled his lungs as the bard walked slowly on the Northern Run Road, humming a merry tune. He hadn't traveled this far north in years; the last time being when he went to see his family. That had been over ten years ago and hadn't gone at all well. But now he was here once more in the crisp Northern lands. He had felt the presence of something horribly bad, malevolent, and downright evil, and so of course had to come right away to see it. He had packed his things, donned his best clothes, and went off one more time to fight the bad guys. *Maybe even write a song about it,* he thought. *A nice one, not one of those gaudy ballads that women swoon over.*

It was then that he noticed the ruffians waiting to ambush him, a lone traveler out of his depth in the wilderness. He had to laugh. He put a light bounce in his step and started to sing a little ditty. It was a horrible song, going on about how to swish your sword to impress the ladies, but all the while it gave him an excuse to draw his own slender sword in mock challenge to his invisible foes.

He was at least twenty miles from the last village, and there was no one to help. Poor guys. He wasn't much to look at as an opponent, at first glance. He stood a hair above five feet with long auburn curls draped over his slender shoulders. His clothes were finely made, especially the burgundy longcoat that he was quite fond of. He had a ruffled shirt with tiny pockets, and his black pants fell down to his black polished high boots, decorated with tiny charms. But it was his mannerisms that most people found disturbing. It was that look that said he had seen everything and still wasn't impressed. It helped that he wasn't bluffing. He almost giggled when the first Jake jumped out of the bush he was hiding in.

"Drop your weapons and stand fast!" The man had to be all of twenty years old, and none too bright. "You men circle 'round and get his purse . . ." The bard still held the sword. "Hey! I said drop your sword."

The bard could see this was going to be one of those days. *Well,* he thought with a grin, *let's get on with it.* "Actually, you didn't. You said to drop my weapons, and since I had only the one, well, I didn't think it applied." He ended with a flourish and spun on the balls of his feet just for show. "And 'stand fast' what does that even mean? I mean if you wanted me to stand *still,* well that's one thing, but 'stand fast' how does one even *do* that?"

"I... uh... well that is... drop that sword so we can take your money!" He was plainly losing the respect of his men, and now he was going to have to prove himself... pity.

"I most certainly will not drop my sword! It could scratch up the shine on the blade. And it doesn't matter--I have no money anyway. Now we can do this the easy way, in which the two of you behind me walk away with your lives, the two behind the trees with bows get to run away into the woods, and only this young man loses his head... or you can all die here in the dusty road. Well?"

The gathered men laughed a nervous laugh, but it was five-to-one odds. Their leader looked even more nervous; he could see the resolve in his supposed prey's eyes. It never wavered. In the end there was little he could do, and he knew it. "You leave me n—no ch—choice then." Drawing his sword, an overly long and callous blade, he took two steps in the bard's direction and had the life taken so quickly he didn't even scream.

He never saw the bard's hand move, but the blade went through his chest and out his back. He had time to mew softly, then slumped down to the hard earth. The others cried out, but the bard was already amongst them, slashing and spinning with a grace that defied nature.

He took the two behind him cleanly, swinging his slender blade through the neck of one and running the other through before they could even raise their blades. He could hear the whoosh of the arrows fired with haste, not accuracy, and threw his legs outward. He slipped down into a split as the arrows flew harmlessly over him, and mumbled under his breath calmly. The two archers screamed their defiance at the sight of their comrades' deaths but as they fired again a terrible wind tore across the road. It turned their arrows wide and threw dirt into the air in small funnels of swirling dust. As they scrambled out into the road, drawing their small knives, the bard went to meet them with death in his eyes. Seeing the look on his face was enough for them. They threw down their feeble blades and scrambled away, falling down and hopelessly flailing on their back sides.

"Don't, please mister, don't kill us!" One was crying now, just a scared little kid with long hair and a baby's face; the other was hiding behind a tree praying quietly to . . . Syll? He stopped his advance and let the fury drain out of him slowly with a cleansing breath.

"Why, dear thief, do you offer prayer to the goddess of nature?" He let his gaze drift over the crying boy while he used his *sight* to look at the praying one behind the tree; the boy was even younger than the others, barely sixteen, and had ragged features that spoke of a farmer's son. "Why don't you pray to the skulking god of thieves, Norar?"

"I've always loved nature mister, and I'm not no thief, just tired of being poor is all." He sounded frightened, knowing that death had come for him and there was nothing he could do. The crying one sniffed and drew the bard's attention once more.

"We weren't going to kill ya, just take your money." He smiled a little through his tears, so the bard put some of the edge back into his eyes until the young one quailed once more.

Can't be seen as soft, or they'll be all over me in every town and city from here to G'harr, he thought. Still, they were so young. He'd been that young once, and just as stupid too. "Listen, I'm going to let you two go for now, but if I ever hear that you have been waylaying people on this or any other road ever again, I'll come for you. Personally, I would go home and find work in the fields; it might improve your overall survival." He smiled now, letting his anger fade as he turned to once more wander up the road to the north. They were still scared stiff. Good. Let them run all the way home to their mama's teats.

"Who are you?" One of them called out as the bard was leaving. It was the other one; the quiet, praying boy. "That wasn't natural. The way you killed those men... you were everywhere and..."

He stopped and turned, giving them a look that silenced them both before they really began to ramble. *Might as well tell them,* he mused, *might even do me some good for a change.* The bard spun in a lazy circle, pirouetting on one foot. His longcoat spinning with him added to this effect. He tossed his auburn curls over his shoulder and turned to look at them once more as he walked backwards down the road. "I am known as Karsis the bard," He paused for dramatic effect. He always did. "You may have heard of me?"

Karsis the bard: legendary rogue, warrior, and general hero of the downtrodden. His name had spanned centuries, his deeds the stuff of legend. His auburn curls were as recognizable as his one-of-a-kind burgundy longcoat. He had played for kings, slain tyrants, even won the heart of an ancient dragon. That's what all the songs had said. He should know; he wrote most of them.

People had been trying to figure his legacy out for decades, since he never seemed to age or even look like he was slowing down in the slightest. So they made up their theories and invented stories. Rumor had it that the title of Karsis was passed down to his heir once the child became of age, others hinted at a pact with demons from the hells. They all made him giggle. He wished he had come up with one as good as that last one himself. Every child in the country of Lythinall had heard of Karsis the bard, but these two young ones had evidently assumed that he was a fairy tale. Not very likely. He was more like a 'monster in the closet,' or a 'be good or the bard will get you' type of person. But fame will do that for you. He put a little more bounce in his step, whistled a merry tune, and continued on up the road to Daelyn, leaving Piss and Pot to scramble to their feet and run for the sun with all haste. It was time to look in on a few friends, and maybe save the world. Gods above he was hungry.

Village of Daelyn, Northern Lythinall

THE DARKNESS WAS all that he knew for a long while. How long he couldn't say, but finally his thoughts turned towards faint voices that were vaguely familiar. It was like fighting through quicksand, but Rhoe struggled towards the sounds, inch by inch. He couldn't hear what they were saying so much as hear the emotion in the tones, but it gave him an anchor. There was a woman's voice; melodic and sweet, and suddenly he felt secure knowing that voice was there.

The other voice, a deep, husky tone, also made him feel safe, if only because he got the feeling that any danger would have to get through that voice first. His thoughts swam with hints of memory and visions. *Almost there.*

"He's coming around." The sweet voice purred softly. He recognized it now. It was his mother, Tierra. He giggled. He did that whenever he thought of her.

Tierra Whiteheart had a slim build and long flowing hair that gave an almost dainty look to her short frame, yet Rhoe knew that her prowess with her hands and feet would be a match for any knight in the king's service. She always kept her platinum blond hair in twin braids, straight back, and set with two-inch steel balls that would click and clack whenever she was about. Once, he saw her turn around so fast that the deadly steel almost laid Tomas the Baker low; she had shot her hands out fast enough to catch them scant inches from his sweating face. Rhoe slowly opened his eyes, fluttering them against the flickering lamp light. He tried unsuccessfully to put his arms underneath and brace himself up, but was pushed back down by a huge meaty hand. *That would be the other voice,* he thought with a kind smile to match the giggle that greeted his mother.

"Stay down lad, you've used up all of your reserves coming

back to us, and I'm not for letting you leave us over getting out of that bed." The deep voice was reassuring, but cold fear clenched Rhoe's gut as he heard the voice of his father Gareth. H remembered the dream, and how that great bear of a man was thrown about like a mime in a wind storm.

"Rhoven? What's the matter son?" His mother sounded worried. She only used that name when she worried. Rhoe carefully cleared his emotions from his face and forced a bright, but weak smile. *It's nothing,* he tried to tell himself, *just a lingering fear of that awful nightmare.*

"Nothing mother, just a bad dream. And you needn't worry father, I won't get out of bed with that arm of yours holding me down anyway." He flashed his best 'Who me?' look, and instantly regretted it.

Gareth Whiteheart was not the type of person that liked sarcasm. In fact, the man had been rumored to have had his own sarcasm ripped out of him with a spoon, just so he could throw it off a high cliff. The man was well over six feet tall, and his corded muscle stood out prominently through his woolen shirt.

He had shoulder-length brown hair that always looked like it could use a combing, but no one dared to get close enough to try it. His hard face was lined with age, but you wouldn't be able to tell his stamina that. The man could still do the work of three men, even well into his late forties. In essence, the man hit things for a living--preferably with weapons, but he didn't need them. "Don't get smart with me pup, if you've got the energy to be witty, then it's to work with you." His father winked before Tierra went into her tirade about her son needing rest.

Rhoe let his gaze drift out the window while his mother was poking her finger against his father's massive chest and telling him where he would be sleeping if he didn't like it. The green grass swayed easily in the spring breeze, and children ran about the fields like the world was ending tomorrow. The village was getting bigger every year as more and more people came north to settle the northern reaches. Even north of the Belt Flow River, called the Wilds, were being settled now. Eighteen years ago, Daelyn was the farthest north that people had gone, but in recent years they had moved ever northward, seeking peace and solitude with nature.

He heard his parents arguing again and was shocked that he had forgotten that they were pioneers themselves once. They settled this very town with a small following of friends over eighteen years ago, when his mother had found out that she was with child. He never did ask why they moved way up north to settle a small town of their own. It never occurred to him till now. A thought gnawed at the back of his consciousness, something about their companions, but he shook his head to clear it.

"How did I get here?" Rhoe murmured aloud. He couldn't remember anything except that frightening dream. The sun had already sunk far lower than he would've thought possible. He must've been out for hours.

"What?" His mother stopped berating Gareth to spin towards her son. Gareth ducked just in time. The vase of flowers didn't. Rhoe winced as the vase shattered under the metal ball's impact, but was even more worried about his mother's reaction. He had never been able to catch her off-guard before. Something had her on edge. Something to do with him, he knew it.

"I said, how did I get here? I don't remember..." He said, carefully studying his mother's serene face. The worry lines were there, but it was something deeper than that, like a buried secret that had never seen the light of day. Rhoe turned his gaze back out the window. He didn't like how this was going. He was getting that feeling in the pit of his stomach that always warned him of something awful. Like that one time that De'enna had taken that potion from the local Herbalist when they were seven... she thought it was a growing potion and finally she would be a big girl.

Rhoe had had that feeling then, really bad, and then she drank it before he could warn her. Had he been but a second faster... It was poison, fast acting. She was gone before he had screamed her name. He had carried her to the herbalist, but there was nothing he could do. He shook his head at the somber memory and tried to focus on his mother.

Tierra took a deep breath and sat down on the floor lotus-style. "Alright," she started reluctantly. "The twins heard your screams up on the hill where you had been reading. They thought something had crept out of the hills and was tearing you apart. Rhoe, we could hear you down here!" She paused and closed her eyes, gathering her will to steady her voice. "Gareth ran up the hill with his axe in one hand and met them, ready for anything. They were hysterical with a fear that they couldn't name." Tierra stopped and Gareth put his large, comforting hands upon her delicate shoulders. He had always been her rock to hold onto.

"You didn't stop screaming till I grabbed you, son." His voice was thick with worry. "Then you started to ramble off things. Like things that were happening far away." There was something in his voice then. They both knew something about all this.

They'll tell me sooner or later, Rhoe thought tiredly. He finally got up and stared out the window. "Well, I'm all right now. Just a bad dream is all." Rhoe turned back around and saw them staring at him. Their faces were lined with worry and . . . pity? He had finally had enough. "Alright, I'm getting changed. You two go relax and fret in the other room if you like." He pushed them out his door with some effort, not letting them have any more words till they wanted to be honest about what they knew. It was an old family trick, one that they taught him early on. "I'll be out in a little bit. Maybe go for a walk or something. Let the twins know that I'm fine." With that he shut the door and sank to the floor with his back against the door.

It was going to be one of those days. He knew it. Rhoe finally got off the floor and went to the closet to pull down one of his grey robes. He threw it on, stopped in front of the mirror, and studied himself. He was a little over five feet tall with a solid, but wiry frame. He had trained all of his life as a warrior, like his mother, and had kept his body in shape. But the most striking feature of the young warrior was his long, flowing, white hair. It reached down to his lower back and was as white as bone. The village acolyte had worried when he was born, thinking he had some disease or such, but didn't say much about it. Mainly because his mother would've heard, and the acolyte wasn't that keen on seeing his goddess in person just yet. People still whispered various things when they thought she wasn't listening, things that often made Rhoe laugh. He had never done anything that disgusting to a farm animal in his life, and he was pretty sure his mother had never even met a demon lord.

He let them say these things because he knew that he was different; this way he didn't have to worry about it, he let them do his work for him. He had endured the stares and whispers most of his life, until about three years ago.

He had saved a young girl from a falling tree, damn near dying himself. Another of those bad-feeling days. In fact, the whole thing was pretty much a blur to him. He remembered charging towards the girl and wishing that the tree would miss. That was the most vivid memory, praying that the tree would fall the other way, or maybe fall slightly askew (he remembered that because it was the first time he had ever used the word askew). The next thing he remembered was his father lifting the both of them out of the mess of branches. The tree had missed them by a foot, but the heavy branches still beat him bloody. He had covered the girl as he rolled with her, so she was only scratched here and there. He had taken two days to heal up after that.

The townsfolk all visited him as he recuperated, bringing him food, gifts, and anything else that seemed plausible for an apology. Since that day not one person said anything about his hair. Unfortunately, the tree jokes started soon after that.

He smoothed his robe and decided that he needed a walk. Rhoe swept up a few books, grabbed his leather strap to tie back his hair, and headed out. He needed to relax and think things through. His parents tried to stop him, but he wasn't listening to them at the moment and they both knew it. He dodged his father's arm, ducked under his mother's hands, evaded her flailing hair as she turned—father wasn't so lucky—and went out the door. He soon sprinted around the village until he was sure his parents had let him be. He looked around suddenly and thought, *How flimsy these huge wooden palisades look.* It was such an odd thought that he wondered why he should even care. These walls had kept the people of Daelyn safe for years. Rhoe shook his head to clear it and kept going.

He went out the gate and trudged up the hill, and was surprised to find that his fatigue had nearly disappeared. He found the twins, Innal and Rythal Summerleaf, sitting by his favorite reading tree, all but chewing the nails off their fingers with worry.

"Hey guys!" Rhoe called out to the two boys, and almost instantly regretted it. They burst up off the ground and rushed him in screams of glee. He dodged one, then the other, and soon it was a game of "catch the warrior." The twins lost. Again. Big surprise. Both boys were fourteen years old, with sparkling blond hair and golden eyes. Their darker complexions stood out when they spent too long in the sun, but the mischievous smiles never faded. They were tall, thin, and full of way too much energy.

"You're all right!" Innal exclaimed, dusting himself off, and ignoring his brother with practiced ease. The other boy glared at him for a moment, then gave up and got up on his own with a harrumph.

"Of course he's alright you ninny, it's Rhoe." Rythal looked at Rhoe with a cocky smile, "I wasn't worried Rhoe, it was him."

"ME!" Innal lunged at Rythal taking him down in a flurry of punches and kicks that went wide more often than not. Rhoe laughed as they tumbled down the small hill towards the town well. *Least they might leave me alone for a bit,* he thought to himself. The twins never ceased to put a smile on his face and he had been hoping they might be up here. They were the closest thing to brothers that Rhoe had growing up, and he liked being a big brother to them whenever he had the chance. He sat next to the tree where he always sat, opened his book, and lost himself in reading again. At least till they wore themselves out and traipsed back up the hill to find him.

Rhoe was fascinated with books. Any book. He'd read anything just for the knowledge inside, no matter how trivial. He particularly loved books on the history of the world. Books on Lythinall were rare, but he'd read every one of them, including the *Ancient Rule of the Elves.*

He wasn't supposed to read those, but he had found them in the basement of the church dedicated to the goddess Syll. He had read every book in the church library and had stumbled on a loose board in the wall that had stored volumes of books on the subject. He read one at a time, sneaking them out to his tree and slipping them back at dusk--when no one was looking of course.

The elves of ancient times had enslaved humankind. They were made to be workers, playthings, even traded amongst the royal houses in bets sometimes, and all because the elves could.

The elves' magic kept the humans from fighting back. Eventually, some of the humans learned a crude form of magic and retaliated. Every child in Lythinall knew the story, told mostly at bedtime or when parents wished to remind their children of how far they had come in the world. But seeing the words written and preserved for all time in something treasured by the church made it seem more real to him. Gone were the fantasies that the humans had decided one day to rise up and be free like so many children thought. No, these books told the gruesome history of the oppression and the breaking of the human spirit.

If only he could find books on how they finally did break free. But nothing remained of the times that humans and elves made war on each other. That dark time was lost to human history. Of course, one could always ask the elves, but you would have to live long enough to get the answer.

He looked up from his book at the sound of the twins racing back up the hill towards him and sighed heavily. Some days you just couldn't get away. But then he saw the way they were running and he snapped the book closed and was on his feet before the pages had finished rustling. Their faces were tight and the grim set of their mouths were shouting volumes to him. He covered the remaining distance easily, and stopped them with one cold glare.

"What's the matter, is someone hurt?" He noticed that dusk had fallen. He couldn't have been reading for more than a couple of minutes, so where had the time gone? Did he fall asleep? He didn't feel like he had.

"Rhoe come quick... your pa said to hurry... smoke on the horizon." They were winded, and still in concert. If he wasn't worried to high hells he would be impressed. He left them behind with the speed his training allowed, and moved easily over the grassy hills and small rocks that the children often played on. His long hair whipped in the evening breeze as it slipped out of its leather strap.

He *felt* more than saw the smoke. How, he didn't know, but it was there. That spurred him on faster. As he skidded into town, he almost ran headlong into his father, who was standing outside their home, not fifty yards from the north gate.

"So what if you think he saw it happen Tierra, he won't come for him, it was just . . ." His father's voice trailed off into the quiet. Gareth stood facing the northern gate, his arms on Tierra's shoulders. "Just... Well try not to worry too much, even though it is your specialty."

Rhoe could see the great column of smoke on the horizon. It was Wyndral. He knew it. He knew who, or what had caused it too, though he didn't want to think about that man again right now. He felt an acute feeling rise in him, and could almost feel what his mother was feeling, but it slipped away like a leaf caught in a strong wind. He couldn't speak, and his father didn't even seem to know he had almost run into him.

"I'm telling you Gareth, He has awakened—" His mother broke off keeping anything she was going to say to herself as she sobbed quietly.

Rhoe could feel icy fingers gripping his heart. He had only seen his mother cry twice in his life, and both times she had thought he was dead. He stepped out suddenly, trying to be obvious so they wouldn't suspect that he had heard their turmoil.

"Are there refugees yet?" he asked quietly. He never took his eyes off the column of thick black smoke that drifted on high like some omen of impending doom.

Gareth wiped his sleeve over his face once then turned to smile sadly at his son. "No Rhoe, but they should be here soon if they were coming."

"They will come, my husband... I know they will."

"Hush, Tierra. We have to be realistic. There was no one there who knew the wilds like we did, and even if they did, they have sixty miles to travel before getting within these safe walls." Gareth looked over at his son to quietly dismiss him, but the look in Rhoe's eyes gave even him pause. His boy was becoming a man, even if the boy didn't know it yet.

IT WAS two days later when the stragglers arrived at Daelyn in the bright light of a full moon. Rhoe was sitting at the north gate, dozing off and on, and heard the first hoarse yell of approach. At first he thought they were under attack, but the sound came more as a surprise than alarm. It was joyful and mournful at the same time. Then after a few minutes, it was accompanied by strange flute music. The people were shouting their joy at finally reaching what they thought was safe haven, but he still didn't know where the music was coming from. To his knowledge there were no bards of any accomplishment out this far north. Surely, they would've stopped at Daelyn first on their way to Wyndral. *Mom will know what to do,* he thought. *She knew a bard once. What was his name again?* His parents hadn't talked about their companions much, but he knew who a couple of them were. Especially Tanan.

Tanan Norhil was Lord of Norhil Keep, and was a typical lady's man. Tall and lean, with a shock of black hair that brought out his stark blue eyes, the man could talk a barbarian into buying a lace frock coat, and still swindle him out of all that he owned. This wasn't common knowledge mind you, but Rhoe had many long conversations with the man, and learned the hard way. Rhoe had met him numerous times before. But on the whole, his mother and father had never wanted to bring up who they had traveled with all those years ago. He assumed that they were saddened by loss, or maybe they'd had a fight, but suddenly it mattered.

Rhoe was snapped out of his reverie by the music. It was eerily beautiful, and he found his spirits lifted just hearing it. Then he saw the flutist and couldn't help but stare in astonishment. It was none other than the great bard Karsis! The man, the myth, the legend. Karsis the bard was his favorite hero of all time. Rhoe liked him even better than King Arian the Brave. He wasn't much from a distance; his long auburn curls bouncing across his slim shoulders, but it was how he held himself that made the difference. He was a warrior, a fighter, and a general pain in the ass and gods above he knew it. His long burgundy coat hung loosely for maneuverability, and his feet were perfectly balanced with his every step. He projected an air of confidence that, if half of the stories were to be believed, was right on the money.

"Don't stand there with your mouth hanging open like that young one." Karsis called out to him teasingly as he passed him into the town. "You might make these poor folk think you mean to swallow them whole." He stopped then, spinning around with a grand flourish. His flute was away before Rhoe even saw his hands move, and he was leaning with his head cocked to one side, almost examining the young warrior.

Rhoe turned to call out to his father, if only because he could think of nothing else to do. This was Karsis the bard after all. He started to yell when he heard the bard all but whisper to himself. Something about... awakened. *That's what mother said to father.* He thought quietly to himself, though he had the sneaky suspicion that the bard heard him anyway; he had a smile that Rhoe had often used himself on occasion, and it sent shivers down his spine for reasons he couldn't explain.

Then everything happened at once. Even though Rhoe heard the screams first, the bard reacted far faster. Rhoe saw the short man slide around him protectively, almost shielding him, as Tierra came screaming from their home trailing tears of rage and grief.

"You can't... you won't... do you hear me!" She was wild but firmly in control, and for the first time, Rhoe actually saw her as the fierce fighting warrior that he'd heard about from all of their adventures. Gone was the protecting mother, the stern teacher, even the stoic master. No, this was the very picture of Tierra the deadly warrior.

"Ash'anti fra heath ki." They were strange words, and their utterance stopped her as if she had hit a wall. She stood stock-still, heaving with barely suppressed wrath as her hair continued to swirl as if in a strong wind. Karsis walked calmly towards her with that smile gleaming as if nothing untoward had even happened. Just a minute ago she was ready to tear him apart and he looked like he could care less. Rhoe didn't think he liked the way this was going. Not at all. He opened his mouth to say just that, but before he could, Karsis turned and looked right at him. "Not now Rhoven, let me deal with one problem at a time, would you?"

"Wha—how—" He blinked a couple of times and decided he had better sit down. Heavily.

"Now, Tierra love, why all the anger? I haven't seen you in eighteen-odd years, and this is the reception I get?" His voice was light and his mood forgiving, but something in the way that he said the words told Rhoe that he was put off.

"You know very well that you didn't come here for me, we settled that years ago. No. You came to take away my son, and I would rather die taking you down than let that happen!"

Her voice had risen steadily throughout until at last it was a shriek of defiance. It still didn't faze the legendary bard one bit. Which bothered Rhoe even more. Anymore of this and he would get an ulcer. *And what did she mean they settled that?* That snapped his head around the pole alright.

"Yes, let's hear what the mighty Karsis wants with my family this time--and make sure the answer is the one that won't get your head separated from that pretty little thing called a neck." Gareth was there behind them all, his massive axe cradled in his arms like it was always there. But instead of the usual jovial smile he always wore, he had a scowl that made Rhoe shrink a little bit. And he wasn't even looking at him.

"Well now, Gareth--threaten me once more and she will be a widow. That is a promise know you, not a threat... I detest threats." He was trying not to cause a scene, but Tierra was making that impossible.

"Now you listen Karsis. He hasn't shown anything alright, and put that axe down Gareth please." Tierra's hands were on her hips now, and her composure was back, even as she was held by... whatever had stopped her. Trust his father to steady her even in the worst times. "And another thing..."

Karsis whispered a few quick words—almost a promise, maybe asking for something pleasantly—and the winds whipped the dirt on the road up into a blanket blotting out the three adversaries from each other, and as suddenly as that it was over. But the bard was already behind the female warrior smiling fiercely, hand on the hilt of a finely-crafted sword.

"No." He said as-a-matter-of-fact, "You two listen. I arrived in the village that got hit, and it was one man that did it. Well, not just a *man*; he was something more than that." Karsis shook his head sadly before looking up with silver blazing eyes, "He killed everyone that came at him, like it was fun. It was all I could do to hold him for a bit so we could escape. He will get out and he is coming here." He sighed then, knowing that was the easy part. "And that boy there has awakened. If he doesn't learn what to do with it, he will blindly lose himself one day."

He walked calmly backwards towards Rhoe, his eyes never leaving the two protective parents, "He *sees* things, time seems to slip by him, and most of all when he asked for something to happen... it somehow did."

The last comment was given right to Rhoe, who could only nod dumbly, remembering the tree and the little girl. "I sensed him--or more importantly, his presence--over the village watching the destruction. Friends... this *is* happening."

The big man let out a tremendous sigh, the fight leaving his body. It seemed to Rhoe that he aged just then, but he still held it well on that massive frame. "Let's get inside" Gareth grumbled, as he realized that the hostilities were over. "We'll talk privately."

"But Gareth..."

"No Tierra, we'll talk and hear him out. What he says is true; I've seen it myself. If Rhoe's in trouble, then we have to help him anyway we can. And that includes letting Karsis help him with anything he needs. Now walk into that house 'fore I carry you." His big smile evident, she gave in and shuffled like a kid that's been caught taking cookies from the baker's shelf.

She turned her head and looked her husband right in the eye, craning her neck to see him from her short stature, still held by the strange winds. "You would too, wouldn't you?" she asked.

"Damn right I would. At least I think I can still lift you, you have gained a few pounds."

"Glad you said it!" Karsis said impishly, "She never did listen to me." He made a gesture and the winds died back down, releasing Tierra. Whatever the two of them were going to say next was cut off as they both ran for the house, an angry woman chasing after them faster than they could imagine.

Rhoe could hear furniture breaking from out in the street and wondered what else was going to happen tonight. Absently he looked up in the night sky. *No great gods from on high walking the Heavens? Just as well, mother would've chased them too.* Rhoe quickly strode to his home, wincing whenever a loud crack would echo in the night, then slowed to a snail's pace.

He knew that if he entered that house his world may change, would change. He didn't know why--he couldn't quite put his finger on it, but he just did. He shook his head slowly, let out a breath he didn't even know he was holding, and walked on. It was going to be one of those nights; he could feel it.

3

ALL GROWN UP

She whirled at her opponent, pirouetting on one foot, and brought her sword down in a vicious sideways arc. It was intercepted easily, as expected, and her sword recoiled from the exchange as it had the last time. This time however, she used the momentum from the recoil and spun out of the way as her opponent lunged quickly at her unprotected left side. Still using the momentum, she switched feet and continued the spin into a full rotation, bringing her sword in at her opponent's undefended back. She frowned, tasting the sweat rolling down her face as her opponent, wildly off balance, managed to swing the sword over and behind to block the killing strike and then roll forward to lightly land in a crouch. She feinted a lunge, and a counter spin to throw her opponent off guard once more, and went straight in quickly and efficiently. She smiled slightly as she heard a soft grunt of surprise from the shift of her attack, but they were all deflected nonetheless.

Her arms ached, and she was sweating profusely in this helmet, so she had to end this quickly because her opponent wasn't showing any signs of slowing down. She raised her sword over her head and charged, yelling out her frustration in an ear-piercing wail. Her opponent calmly waited for the charge and raised the sword for the parry that would throw her weapon out wide, exposing her for the killing stroke. Instead, she slammed one foot down hard at the last moment and spun around to one knee, sliding the last few feet to her opponent, who was even now looking down, no doubt in disbelief. Her sword swung low, whistling through the air with the momentum of a speeding arrow, and she was rewarded by the expected jump of her opponent. She let the sword go, grasping her opponent's booted foot in mid-leap and yanked with everything she had.

Her opponent hit the ground hard and stayed there for what seemed like an eternity, indeed. "You were supposed to kill me Allissana, not trip me *and* throw away your only weapon. What could that possibly have gained you, had this been a real fight, hmm? Maybe they would just lay there and you could kick dirt on them?!" Her opponent finally rolled to one side and rose to her feet, sweeping off her helmet and shaking her short hair free of sweat.

"That's not fair Carana. You've said time and time again that if an enemy can't stand, they can't fight. Well, I think that was the 'not standing part,' don't you?" Allissana swept her own helmet free and sent it crashing into the weapons rack, scattering swords, poles, and daggers all over the floor. Both women stood breathing heavily, muscles aching from the long practice session. They glared daggers at each other for long moments, until Carana laughed heartily.

"You've the right of it, at least partly lass. You see, I got back up." With that last word, the High General of the capitol city of Everknight lunged perfectly with her wooden practice sword right for the gut of her shocked trainee. She was met by a drawn wooden dagger from under her practice armor, which, after deflecting the thrust, was held ever so gently near the throat of Carana's pretty neck.

"You were saying that I threw my only weapon?" Allissana smirked through barely suppressed laughter.

The laughter changed into a yelp as she hopped back from Carana's hidden dagger held against her bosom. This dagger was real though, and had almost drawn blood through her practice armor. "That was good lass--really good--but I invented that trick, remember?" The women laughed again, finally picking up their equipment and scattered weapons.

Carana was a mystery to Allissana. She had always envied the older woman for her fierce temper and amazing skill with a blade. But it was more than that. Carana was smart, beautiful, and capable. Why she hadn't wanted to marry into nobility baffled her more than her math tutor (gods curse the man, anyway) did on a regular basis. Carana was easily six feet tall with short, dirty blond hair that looked perfect even after being in a helmet for over a half an hour. It matched well with her sun-darkened skin and brown eyes, but even these features paled in comparison to her physique. The woman was built slender, but had packed that slight frame with every possible ounce of muscle. She had everything-- except a title.

Oh she was the High General of Everknight; Capital of Lythinall, and shining bastion of goodness, blah blah blah. But she was still just a general. Without a title, such as one that nobility carried, she wouldn't ever be anything more. A mystery for sure. Allissana sighed loudly and stopped in front of the huge mirror, stripping off her practice armor. Barely eighteen years old and she could defeat most boys twice her age with a sword. Not necessarily a turn on for most conversations. She studied herself in the mirror, frowning. She was slim, but toned, not as muscled as Carana. Her long golden hair fell over her shoulders, shoulders that were squared from long sessions with weapons training, and her copper eyes reflected the need to do more, to see more of the world. But the king's daughter couldn't do that.

"You're frowning again, *Princess.*" Carana chirped playfully in imitation of the young girl's maids-in-waiting. She walked by and tousled the golden hair into a sweat-drenched rat's nest that had Allissana smiling. For now.

"You're right of course, Carana," she said haughtily, trying not to giggle, "But I've been requested to appear in the council's next session in a little under an hour, and I've *nothing* to wear." She made a mock fan out of her hand and fanned herself like the maids in those 'shirts off' books that most of the castle's women read. That got Carana laughing right along with her, both of them hugging their sides, and sharing this little moment that they usually played out at least twice a week.

Of course, that was when the page opened the door and cleared his throat politely. Then cleared his throat a little louder, to make sure they knew he was here. Then gave up and walked in. After all, the other pages always told stories about Mistress Carana, but she didn't look like she had ever beaten a page bloody before. "Ladies. Mistress Carana, Princess Allissana—" His words choked to a sputtering stop as he faced a drawn sword. The sword on its own wasn't what worried him at the moment, as much as it was the hardened face attached to the strong, unwavering arm that could propel the sword through him if he moved another muscle. Any muscle. Suddenly those stories seemed awfully real.

"Speak boy, and be convincing." She flicked the tip of the sword across to the bench, and motioned with her eyes for him to step away from the doorway. Her voice added to the look of imminent death and the poor fool finally found what little voice he had.

"Well—I —uh..." The page could tell this wasn't what she wanted to hear so he tried again as the over-muscled general rolled her eyes. "I've... been sent to inform you that the king requests your presence in the council chambers as soon as you are decent." The page felt confidence building with every word that came out without stumbling.

By the end he had gained his full composure, albeit his eyes were closed so he could focus on his words instead of the five feet of steel at his throat.

"Wait a minute, did you just say my father *requests* our presence?" Allissana said with dripping sarcasm. Her father never requested anything—demanded, ordered, forbade—but never requested. "Am I dreaming or is the castle under full scale attack by three dragons at once?"

"Calm yourself student. Page Barris--report to the king that we will be there post haste. That is all." Carana had all the authority of the high general in her stance, and voice. She bowed politely to the page and lowered her sword as the young boy walked as fast as his bewildered mind could take him. He'd probably be wondering how she knew his name for at least a fortnight.

"Carana, what's wrong?" The princess's voice was controlled, but strained with the change of her mentor's attitude. What could so ruffle the woman who made jokes about the king and laughed with the queen over tasteless songs of herself?

"The king... your father, never calls me *Mistress* unless it's something horrible. That page named me *Mistress*, a sign from your father that only I would recognize." Carana went to put away her weapons as she spoke, "And no, I wouldn't worry too much youngling, your parents were facing southern barbarians and fell magic well before they had you; they're used to danger. Now gather your gear and let's go. Remember those drills I put you through, the ones where I had you sprinting through the halls. Let's just see if you're going to pass the field test."

Council Chambers, Castle Everknight

"WHERE COULD THEY BE?" Though rhetorical, the question made all in attendance wince involuntarily. Maressa looked around the table at her husband's council and found herself sighing inwardly. As queen she had to be at the king's side, but this nest of vipers had grown too poisoned over the years for her tastes. Council members out for the special interests, merchants looking for a way to cash in, and the occasional lackwit. Bunch of pansies the lot of 'em. With her trained bardic eye, she could tell the king whose words were false--or at least the open falsehoods--without the use of magic, which was forbidden. In fact, her ability to read facial tics and body language had saved her many times. Looking out over all in attendance, her eyes eventually settled on Ralavin Whitestaff, and she had to smile.

Ralavin had been old when she had been dating the would-be king; now the man looked truly ancient. He had his chin resting in the palms of his hands and was busy silently sleeping until the king brought the meeting to order. With his snow-white hair falling down over his wizened eyes, he looked the picture of father time, yet when words were spoken in earnest, there was no sharper wit among the rest of the council. His wisdom had never faltered, being the high Priest of Davalar, god of protectors. Maressa's eyes shifted to the dark bearded visage of her least favorite person in the room.

Frenir Darkshadow was a sorcerer from the southern lands of G'harr, and as such, should never be trusted one tiny bit. He never smiled, and used his position as councilor of foreign relations to try to win little victories for his homeland whenever he could. Oh, he said it was in the interest of peace, but come on, a sorcerer always worked for power first, and power second. One by one the bard let her gaze fall over the others around the great table as her husband fretted over the tardiness of his daughter.

Trost Whaineir, the scribe, was looking bored as usual, peering over his tiny spectacles at whatever documents were important this week. The man was as meek as you could get, and whenever anyone raised their voice he visibly shrank in his seat. He dressed in long robes tied at the waist by a gold cord, yet those robes always seemed a bit too small for his girth. The man loved his food--almost, she reflected--more than he loved his documents.

Then there was Alyssa Baernav, councilor for the Merchants' Guilds. If ever there was a snake in the grass, she was it. She appeared quiet, even docile, but when she wanted something it was her voice that rang out in the quiet room over anyone else. Her long hair was always kept up in a tight bun, held by an ornamental pick, and she dressed in long cut-away gowns that split all the way to her waist. Oh, she was pretty alright, but the cold look in her eyes was enough for anyone of sane mind and soul to walk away while they still could.

Othren Lawkland, the old seneschal, knew everything about the castle that there was to know. He had been appointed to the post when she had married Arian, and he had performed the ceremony as a high-ranking cleric of Ollian, goddess of beauty and songs. He had deep knowing eyes, short close-cropped hair, and a wit that was sharper than Carana's sword. Othren was always Maressa's favorite, next to Ralavin, but lately he had been out of sorts. *Funny*, she thought, *I always mean to look into that but keep forgetting to.* She made a mental note once again, and turned her attention to her love, her soul, the king. Arian Everknight was tall, well over six and-a-half feet tall, and all muscle. His golden locks fell short, brushing his ceremonial armor but lightly, and his piercing blue eyes seemed to hold one's attention involuntarily. Even though he was now in his fifties, Arian could still keep up with all of the day-to-day activities that came with being the King of Lythinall.

Maressa smiled without meaning to—he had that effect on her—and stared at her love for long moments before she realized he had asked her a question. Gods above, he could still make her feel like a farm girl after twenty years of marriage.

"I'm sorry my love you asked me something? I was just looking into your beautiful eyes and got lost in reverie." She smiled again, but this time it was a showy smile, meant to tell him more than how much she loved him. It told him that his daughter was standing in the doorway.

"Where in the great dark pit have you two been!" King Arian whirled in his chair and was on his feet in seconds. Everyone at the table flinched at the same time, except Maressa of course. "I asked for you hours ago! The least you could do was, I don't know, maybe show up on time." His shoulders slumped slightly as he turned, indicating that they should be seated, and quickly. The question he had asked his wife was already forgotten.

Allissana sat quietly, folding her hands in the nervous way she always did, especially when she was in trouble. She tried to keep her breathing under control, but that sprint was one of her best times and she was out of breath. She noticed that Carana had walked quietly to his side, ignoring his gesture to sit, and whispered something into his ear. He grimaced once, then looked over at his daughter and nodded his head; the sign that all was forgiven.

Wait a minute, she thought, *hours?!* Her mind reeled, unable to place the time, but sure that it was only minutes ago that she had raced through the castle to get here. Just ask all the people that got in Carana's way.

The page had shown up and then they left, unless he had stood there for fear of interrupting them? As the king called the meeting to order, Carana sat next to her, placing her feet up on the great table. Nobody said anything--it was Carana after all. "I told him that his message reached us minutes ago, don't worry."

Allissana exhaled quietly. If there was anything she feared in this world, it was father's stern gaze of disappointment. "Thanks."

"As you all know, the two spies that were caught here in Castle Everknight were put to death yesterday." The king's gaze lingered over the table, especially at the councilor of foreign affairs, before he began again. "But what you may not know is that two others were implicated. Unfortunately, those names were lost to us when the lives of the spies were taken by magic right before my very eyes. That in itself lends credence to their veracity." Arian shook his head sadly, "Alas, this can only mean that we have been infiltrated deeper than we expected, and as such I have to suspend all traffic into or out of the castle until we've found these traitors to the land!" Raising his voice at the end to be heard over the instant shouts of upheaval and dismay, Arian sat back in his chair and watched the fireworks blow from one side of the table to the other. He hoped that his wife could pick out the reactions he was looking for, but in this turmoil, she would be lucky to see who was yelling at one another. Carana was up, hand at her sword at a mere nod from the king. No one was allowed weapons in the council hall, but she was the high general. The chaos slowly quieted down to a dull dragon's roar at least.

"This is outrageous! We have business to conduct and if we can't leave, we will never satisfy our contacts so that we can run this very land, your highness!" This from the normally reserved Alyssa. It seems that even she had a breaking point.

"Your eminence, if I do not receive goods for the castle, then you will start running out of essential things... like *food!*" Othren was livid, as his close-cropped hair flew side to side with every syllable.

Carana pulled two inches of steel from its scabbard to remind Othren to keep the sarcasm to a minimum. How she did love putting nobles in their place.

"Your highness?" The quiet voice of Ralavin could almost be missed in the throng of voices, but the king had a good ear, and a soft spot in his heart for the high priest.

"Speak Ralavin. I hear you even if these other lackwits are too busy shouting to grant a little respect." The old priest nodded his thanks to the king and stood slowly, his old bones supporting his frame with ease.

"Your highness, we have even more important business at hand than petty squabbles with spies." He waited for the stunned silence to fall around the table, even watching with interest as Carana's sword slid back into its scabbard as her mouth hung open. Only Allissana was unaffected, not knowing the old man for long enough to know how dire this omen was. Never before had Ralavin put the council's business down before, and most certainly never so light heartedly.

Even the king was too shocked to naysay him; it was Allissana who found her voice first. "Pray, continue your Grace," she said as she leaned back in her chair. After all, anything that ruffled her father couldn't be all that bad.

"Davalar, god of honor, has sent me a vision. In this vision, towns burn and people flee towards Everknight for protection; protection that you won't be able to give them." Ralavin let that last bit sink in well before he continued. "The man, nay, the *thing* that accosts us is powerful beyond imagination; the full power of a god personified." He eyed the councilors one by one ere he continued. "Long and long ago the elves sealed it away with all their power, but now it walks again.

Your highness, the incarnation of Corruption has been loosed upon Lythinall." Ralavin sank into his chair, his energy spent, and waited for the shouting to begin. *One, two, three . . .* He counted to himself.

All around the table shrieks and wails abounded. Only Carana, Ralavin, and of course the king and queen were silent on the matter. Allissana slowly rose to her feet, scanning the rest of the councilors. She could do this the hard way, or the easy way. *Well, when all else fails try diplomacy.*

She grabbed the back of her chair and brought it crashing down over her head to smash into the table, shattering the chair and showering splinters and papers all over the gathering. "I trust I have your attention?" Stunned nods and open mouths looked back at her as she walked around the table to stand at her father's left. "Good. Now, we can all discuss this pleasantly, or the next chair I use might be your own."

"'Bout time Liss." The high general whispered over the stunned silence.

"Thank you Carana. Now Ralavin, are your visions always accurate?" She looked down at her father with knots in her stomach, only to see him grinning like a kid in a sweet shop. It was almost like he was enjoying this.

"Usually no, but this vision wasn't one that was gained from meditation or talismans. This vision came unasked for and had the hand of the divine god stamped on it; trust me when I say that I've felt that hand before."

"But an incarnation, Ralavin? I thought they were only myths." Carana's eyes looked troubled as she asked--more troubled than Allissana had ever seen them.

"They are real enough. One for every god in the Heavens. The five incarnations were created eons ago for the sake of the holy wars when the gods were young; or at least that's what we know." He sipped his glass of water, and Carana waited for him to continue. "In truth, nobody knows except the elves, and we all know how well they share their secrets." Chuckles erupted around the table at the jibe, and Allissana felt her mother squeeze her hand in thanks.

"Well, we've had enough for one day, but this council will meet tomorrow at midsun to discuss this matter again. In the meantime, Ralavin, dig up anything about these incarnations you can find. Send word to every library and sage you know and have them come here. Trost, send word to every hold and let them know trouble might be coming." The king took a deep breath. "Alyssa, tell your contacts that the crown is looking to buy food enough for a siege. And Othren, have all the empty rooms cleared out; we might be looking at refugees. My order to seal the castle is held in abeyance for now. Dismissed." The councilors filed out, each talking to another in whispered tones, and every one of them looking nervous. Arian waited till they had left before clapping his hands. "And you. Liss, that was splendid! We've been waiting for you to finally take charge and show us what you are made of."

She blushed at his praise, but Carana came to the rescue. "Sire, if Ralavin is right, that means we can't stop this thing here." The king nodded solemnly. Knowing where she was going with this, Allissana jumped in. "Well, maybe the vision is right. We can't fight it at the castle, but if we meet it on the Northern Run Bridge, that technically isn't the castle now is it?"

Maressa smiled. "That's my girl, using your head when a sword won't work. You know Carana, we might pay you for these lessons after all." The queen stood, bowed mockingly at her husband and strolled around the table, running her fingers lightly across the finish, skipping the gouges that her daughter made with the chair. "But I also see your fine print. You expect your father to let you go and confront this unspeakable evil-- maybe not all by yourself, but as its leader certainly. Am I right?" At her daughters embarrassed nod, the bardic queen laughed aloud, both at the absurdity of youth and at her husband's shocked face.

"But I can—"

"You can what? Fight this thing? Dear, I know you are good with that blade of yours, but if this thing is ancient, it has spent centuries mastering weaponry and tactics." Her mother's tone, along with the fact that she was right, stoked Allissana's temper so that it was a fire out of control. She hated being babied.

Carana knew her too well. "We better get back to practice, right Allissana? See you when we break our fast in the morn." And with that Carana bowed to them both, grabbed the princess by the arm, and ushered her out of the room before she could make the matter worse.

"Did you have to make her that angry?" Arian asked once the two were gone from the room for the count of three. "I mean, she stood up to the council--with a chair, mind you!" But a look from his wife, and queen silenced him immediately.

"Yes, I did--for just that reason. She thinks she can do anything. Well, she's not sword proof, never mind ancient-evil proof."

"You mean she's not you when you were her age?"

"What was that, my dear husband?"

"Nothing--I only coughed a little dear. So is that a new dress?"

"Shut up, Arian. I'm serious--she really wants to prove herself right now, and this is big enough to pull her in. Truth be told, I'm kind of scared." She sat down suddenly, looking older than Arian had ever seen her. "Ralavin was telling the absolute truth--as he sees it--but it was his eyes." She put her head down for a long while. Just when Arian was about to get up and go to her, she raised her head again, tears streaked down her cheeks, unchecked. "It wasn't him speaking Arian... it was something else, and it was dead sure of itself."

"It will be all right love."

"Will it?"

"It had better be, cause this thing has never seen me angry."

Servants leaped out of the way and mothers pulled their children into doors as the princess swept down the hallways like a vengeful spirit. She knew that Carana was right in dragging her out of there, but damn the world to all the hells, couldn't *she* be right for once? "I had it under control Carana! You didn't have to pull me out of there."

"You couldn't even spell 'control' back there."

"Shut up Carana!" Immediately she regretted that, as her head regretted hitting the stone wall. Even her back had complaints about that particular phrase right now, as it too hit the unyielding surface hard enough to split stone.

Carana held her pinned against the wall sideways as if she weighed next to nothing, and with only one hand. At least all she could see was one, the gods above know she couldn't feel much else except this awful feeling of her spleen trying to escape out of her side. "Listen *Princess*, I don't shut up for anyone. And you know damn well that you're mad because *mommy* knew you were going to say something stupid. Now I'll let you down if you promise to be a good little girl, agreed? I'll take that faint head shake to be a yes, or just a seizure."

Allissana slid down to the floor and watched Carana stomp off down the corridor. She was in a bad mood; she usually didn't slam her that hard at least till the third or fourth time she ran her mouth. Well, she'd show them. She was going to find this thing--and when she did, she would show it what-for. She couldn't explain why she thought she could fight something this powerful, but it was like all the pieces fit when she said it. Like it was supposed to happen that way. She suppressed a shiver that didn't so much as run up her spine as galloped, and she shook her head. Thoughts like that scared her witless. First things first though, she needed to find a few things--like where her feet went, and if they took her legs with them.

The Traitors

"ARE YOU SURE? I mean, do you think they actually did it?" The voice was nervous, as well it should be.

"I'm positive that the creature in Ralavin's vision is the same creature that they unleashed." The man cleared his throat politely to get the other man's attention. "I know you are worried, but no one is going to find us in here. In fact, I've warded the room so that any who do listen will hear only wind."

"Oh, that's right, you're a sorcerer, I almos—" His words died away as rough words were chanted, then all of the air in the room seemed to disappear. He gasped and choked, stumbling towards his assailant with reaching hands. Hands that seemed to the dark figure to be turning into talons they were so curled with fright. "Never forget this lesson. You are here on sufferance, to earn your place, not to speak of things that you haven't been told to speak. Is that clear?"

The room was fading into blackness, but he had enough sense to nod vigorously. Suddenly the air came back in a rush, almost sounding like it was groaning in compliance. He sucked in a great breath and immediately set into a coughing fit. "Sorry... your...eminence. I forgot... " He finally managed to get out, through all the coughing and hacking. He fell to his knees and postulated himself at the feet of his superior.

"Now, there was some reference in the libraries in G'harr as to the nature of the beast that was trapped. Though I admit I never thought it would be an incarnation, let alone the Dark One's own." The man, dressed in long black robes, whispered harshly and made a gesture. The man at his feet slowly rose into the air and settled onto his shaking legs. "I brought those books for you to study; have you gotten anything else out of them?"

The shaking man pulled the book out of his own long robes and cleared his throat nervously, forcing himself not to look around the darkened room for fear of annoying his master again. "The books only say that 'The beast long locked away shall be freed with malice and hate, but can only be stopped by that it despises.' Further, 'No one, be he man, elf, or incarnation, may fight him and live, unless they are touched by the one who is none of these, yet all of them.' What do you think of that?" The man asked nervously.

The man in the black robes chuckled slightly. "I think that they put one hell of a safe guard on this thing, that's what I think." The man cocked his head at his underling, "But there is more you are concerned with?"

The student paused slightly to catch his breath and wipe the sweat off his brow. He adjusted his glasses and continued. "Well, what I can't figure out is how anyone is going to control it. I mean that was what they were attempting to do right?" He sounded hopeful, yet there was something in his voice.

"Yes, we were all hoping to gain a powerful weapon to unleash against Everknight, but it seems to me that we did just that anyway." He laughed at his own little joke, which somehow made him seem all the more frightening, and he knew it.

"But we are in its path! We were going to leave first, but now that everyone knows, it will look suspicious! What do we do when it gets—" His voice rose steadily with every note, and only the back of his master's hand stopped him from screaming the last few words. His pupil lay on the floor rubbing his face with tears welling up, but held them back. Good. He remembered what happened the first time he cried, laid up for over a week with broken arms. The memory made the man in black chuckle again. "Not so old that I can't still dish it out, am I boy?" He lifted the young man up to his feet again with the air in the room, just to show his student the power that he would someday use--if he survived the lesson, that is.

He helped him straighten his glasses and even smoothed his robes. "Now, I want you to go through those books again. Cross reference them with the older books you have here, and find me the means to collar the beast." The man sighed inwardly. This young one was nothing like his main pupil. No, this one may need to be taken care of soon before he caved and let all their plans slip from that nervous little mouth. No one could find out that G'harr was planning on invading Lythinall.

Northern Lythinall

DAR'KRIST WASN'T EVEN ANGRY. Well not livid, at least. That pansy had more magic then any *five* bards could have, and then some. In fact, he was no more a *bard*, then he himself was a *man*. After two days he finally had freed himself from the hardened rock around his buried legs and then had gotten out from under the two buildings that had been dropped on him. Well then. That was a bit offensive. Looking at the destroyed town, upon his own work, the man that was not a man saw it to be good and started walking away.

Carrion birds circled high above, not wanting to get too close until the thing that did this was far away. Dar'Krist chuckled slowly to himself. Only one village and already he had enemies. When *would* they ever learn? Well, he would follow this road; in ages past it used to lead to many towns, but it looked to be taken back completely by the wilderness; who knew in this age what he would find. Still, if this village was way up near the northern forest, there had to be others. He stopped then, dead in his tracks, as a familiar smell rose on the wind. His head swiveled from side to side, taking in the scent that he'd been searching for. Yes, that was the smell of the *bard* alright. It was going the same way, south down the earthen-packed road. *Oh, joy of joys! Something to play with,* he thought to himself.

He resumed his careful procession, taking his time walking along the dirt road. Kicking a dead hand out of his way, he chuckled to himself as he went. *Too bad I always break the toys I play with. I'm coming elfling... soon.*

❧ 4 ❧

FATEFUL CHOICES

"So, what you're telling us is that our son is somehow awakening into a *wizard*?" Tierra blinked again, awestruck at the thought. She knew he had awakened, but didn't know *what* he was becoming. She liked this even less now. "I thought only elves could do that?" They had waited to talk about serious things till Rhoe was sound asleep. It wouldn't do to have him hear the secrets they had shared between them these many years.

"I'll go over it one more time. The boy is exhibiting all of the classic signs of coming into his powers. He even *tranced,* for all of the god's sakes--something that only powerful wizards do, and rarely at that. Or so I've been told." Karsis was resting comfortably, legs crossed and pulled in like butterfly wings, but in mid-air. His longcoat dragged across the ground with the wind coming in the open windows. At least the refugees had stopped filtering in. The poor head priest was all worked up about where to put them all. "As for only elves being wizards, well you're sort of right. But let's not jump into that river just yet." He sighed to himself, knowing that some things were better kept to oneself.

Gareth looked from his wife to the foppish bard sitting in mid-air and back again, feeling out of his depth. He loved his son so much, but it looked like this was out of his hands. "So, what do we do Karsis? Does he just snap into these powers or are they going to take training?" He leaned back in his wooden chair, ignoring the creaks the wood made in protest to his full frame. The chair would hold together, or else.

"How can you be so calm!" Tierra *shispered*, a term Rhoe had come up with to describe how his mother could shout while whispering, a feat he'd not seen anyone else master.

She was pacing back and forth in front of the dying hearth fire, hair whipping around with every military turn. She had busied herself with righting the furniture that she had crashed through to slap the men silly. Not that she'd had to slap Karsis all that hard anyway, the man was as crazy as a purple squirrel. "Just sitting there, when our son could be lost to..."

"*The Darkness Within,* I believe is what you are trying to articulate without understanding. But do go on, I so love a good tirade; especially when it's not directed at me."

"When I want your help—oh forget it! You'd just take it as a compliment anyway."

"I do love compliments."

"Okay!" Gareth stood, flinging the chair that had been tortured by his weight back against the wall with an almost-pleasant crash. "You two can bicker and fight after we've figured out what to do for Rhoe. Now, can we get back to the subject?"

"At least he's calm."

"Shut up, Karsis."

"Actually, I already know what the boy needs, and before you start in with the 'why didn't you say so's', you never let me get that far." Karsis set his feet down on the floor and paced over to Tierra. "Calm yourself old friend, it'll be all right." He put a reassuring hand on her shoulder and smiled warmly at her.

How he missed his friends. Turning so that he could look at both of them, his smile widened. "The boy does need to be trained--you had that much right Gareth--or the power inside him will fester and claim his heart. That is what 'The Darkness Within' means. Now, I can help him along. As a bard, I know something of magic, and we all know that it's high time that he meets me anyway."

Karsis half closed his eyes for what was coming, ready at the first outburst to stop Gareth in his tracks with a spell meant to stop a charging horse. He hoped it would work on a charging Gareth.

"I agree." The words were spoken so softly that Tierra had to turn to face him to see if he was still there. Gareth stood like stone, head bowed, like a man that knows he has no other choice. It helped that he didn't.

"You what!?" Karsis lost all concentration on the magic and sat down heavily on the wooden floor. His auburn curls bouncing slightly as he stared up at the big man with a kind of dumbfounded awe.

"While I'll admit that you're right my love, I won't pretend to even understand where that came from." Tierra gently encircled his waist with her arms and hugged him tight. She knew this must be crushing his heart. "Are you sure?"

"All these years we were afraid this might happen." Gareth smiled weakly. "Well, at least we thought Karsis would come for him and train him as a bard, taking him away from us... but you know." The big man looked like he was up against a foe that he couldn't beat, and that was the right of it. "Well, that day is here, and I don't rightly know that I could do anything for the boy. Oh sure, if someone had to show him how to fight or lift a wagon then I'd be the one, but this is out of my depth." Gareth sighed heavily, sat down on the floor in front of the great bard, and with pleading eyes stared into his shocked face.

"We've never gotten along well Karsis, but in this I trust you implicitly."

"Hey you just...

"I know I said a big word, but try to focus Karsis. I know you won't treat the boy like you treated Tierra. No don't say it; it's in my head that that's what happened and nothing you say is ever going to change that. But Rhoe is another matter."

"Gareth, love why don't we..." Tierra couldn't stand the tension. Her heart was going to burst. Then Gareth turned his head up to give his wife a look of command and the words died on her lips. Turning around so they wouldn't see her tears, she walked over to the hearth and stoked the ashes with the wrought iron poker.

"Like I was saying, the boy needs to be trained and you would never hurt him. Besides, I never bought all that 'bard' stuff. I know you're something more, and if you could help the boy then *everything* will be straight between us. Does that sound reasonable my old friend?"

Karsis, who was only at a loss for words three times in his extremely long life, counted this as number four--if not five and six as well, all rolled into one. Gareth had never warmed to Karsis after the fall out with Tierra, and they had adventured for a great many years together. For him to break down the walls of his disdain like this meant more to the old bard than Gareth could ever know.

If only I could tell them who I really am, he lamented to himself before drawing a breath. Solemnly and without sarcasm, Karsis stood on the wings of air and bowed to the great fighter. "It will be done Gareth, on my life and honor as a Companion of Everknight." He helped the big man up, clasping arms and nodding his thanks to the warrior's deep compassion.

Wiping her tears so they wouldn't know she was this moved, Tierra turned once more and kicked the both of them in the shins. "Are you two done bonding? Can we relax a little now? Gods above, I've been so nervous I don't think I've even eaten anything in hours." Tierra collapsed into a chair, threw her legs over the sides, and let her head fall back. She might still be worried for her son, but she'd be damned if she wasn't going to do it on a full stomach.

The Next Room, Daelyn.

HE WAS LOST. *Flying? No, he was drifting, definitely drifting, but where he couldn't tell. He was surrounded by threads of some kind, weaving a silly pattern around and around him. Rhoe summoned all of his training and discipline and focused it into a single spike. This spike he thrust at the threads as they circled, and with a loud, echoing snap, they dissolved. As they winked out of existence, he found himself tumbling over and over, down...*

Rhoe awoke with a start but bit his lip to avoid crying out. The last thing he remembered was sitting in the chair next to his mother as she threw things at his father and Karsis. After she stopped, they had all settled in to discuss what had happened. Rhoe had talked about what he had seen; the man, or thing, in black destroying the village of Wyndral. Karsis looked even more disturbed, and after having some wine he started whispering. Rhoe remembered that vividly, because it looked like his parents couldn't hear it, but the whispering was intriguing. Then the bard pointed almost lazily at... *Me, he was looking right at me when he pointed.* Rhoe went over it again and again in his mind. That was the last thing he remembered. Now, he heard voices in the next room and knew Karsis had gotten him out of the way.

That overdressed orc's arse put me to sleep! His mind was reeling at being the target of magic, especially since he hadn't really believed in it before today. How his parents, seasoned adventurers, missed it, he couldn't guess. *They must've been in on it,* he thought. *That would explain it.*

"...Try to focus Karsis."

Rhoe crept forward out of the bed and closer to the door. It was tough to hear through a door, but part of his training was to learn just that, and a few other tricks. He cupped his hand and covered his ear to the door with his other to amplify the sound.

". . . The boy needs to be trained and I know you would never hurt him."

Rhoe chuckled at his father's words; he always looking out for his son, even when it was matters of towns being destroyed. But then he caught his father's tone and settled in to listen to the rest of the talk. His eyes went wide at the words coming to him through the door. His parents were Companions of Everknight! This was better than anything he could've hoped for.

"I knew it!" Rhoe barged in through the bedroom door, eyes alight with expectation. He startled his mother so badly she back flipped off of the chair and landed in a crouch, ready to spring, or she tried to. She ended up with her back to the wall a little too early and hung there until the initial surprise went away. Rhoe wasn't that lucky with Karsis.

The bard spun in a full circle, auburn curls swinging with him, and his sword was out and flying at the young warrior with devastating speed. He hadn't expected the boy. He had used heavy air to put him in a thread sleep so deep that he should've been out for a week, so he had launched his sword out of reflex. Just another amazing thing the boy had done in the few days of coming into his powers. Now if only he would live to see those powers honed.

Gareth saw the sword and knew that he was too far away.

He grabbed the nearest chair and flung it with all of his strength. The improvised missile streaked towards the sword, but not fast enough. "No!!"

Rhoe saw a glint briefly flash against the firelight from the hearth. He knew he was in trouble. Then his father picked up his favorite chair and Rhoe thought the bard was going to get it over the head. All of this was happening in the blink of an eye, but Rhoe seemed to have all the time in the world. "Please! Stop." He put all of his feeling into it. He didn't want his father and his old companion to fight. He had heard that they were adventurers together, and how heartfelt their conversation was. Time crashed back to normal as he focused on that one thing-- for them to stop. And the force of air heard and complied, as according to the ancient pact of the wizards, even though he hadn't asked with the words they were used to hearing. The sword and chair both stopped in mid-flight, scant inches from the young warrior's face. They hung there, held by forces that Rhoe couldn't control.

"Yes!" Gareth screamed as he saw the sword and chair stopped, he turned to Karsis and clapped him on the shoulder. "I knew you were good, but that was even fast for you." Then he saw the look on the bard's face and his heart went ice cold.

"You are correct Gareth. That would've been too fast for me," Karsis said with a quiet voice. He concentrated on the flows of air and gently pulled them out of the young one's hands before the boy accidentally created a vortex that could suck them all into another plane. He had to keep reminding himself that that could happen. The boy was untrained, and if the magic was constantly being told what to do without proper instruc- tion... well, the elements were nothing if not mischievous.

Tierra pushed herself away from the wall in a flash as soon as she saw the sword/chair combination start to move away under the guidance of her old friend. She caught Rhoe as he fainted and looked right at Karsis. "What do you mean 'correct'? I saw you, it had to be you. If you didn't... She joined Gareth then in that icy landscape where little demons were throwing snowballs into her heart.

"As I said, 'correct.' I didn't stop them, I had to let you both figure that out on your own though. Now you can actually see that Rhoe needs training." He stepped around the chair and sword, plucking up his sword as he did so, as he settled them on the floor. He calmly wiped the blade clean on his longcoat, completely out of habit, and slid it into his scabbard. "Oh sure, you agreed that he needed to be trained, but you didn't really believe it until now."

"You mean Rhoe stopped both of them--just by being polite?" Gareth was obviously confused. *Nothing new there,* Karsis thought with a chuckle.

"No, he asked the air in the room to do it --politely." He shook his head at the marvel that the boy did without knowing how. "And on top of that, they understood him without invoking them. That just doesn't happen too often."

"Great. Now that we have that mystery cleared up, could someone help me get him on his feet." Tierra smiled awkwardly, not sure if she should be frightened for her son or relieved that he wasn't skewered by a sword. They made him comfortable and talked lightly while they ate and waited for Rhoe to come around on his own. They conversed into the night, greeting the dawn with smiles. The sun shone through the window, alighting on Rhoe's face and he finally began to stir.

"Omens," Karsis whispered to himself, but the other two didn't push this time.

"Well, back from the dead boy?" Gareth's question was innocent, but seeing the look that came over Rhoe's face alarmed him enough to start in his direction.

"Wait." Karsis barred his way with an old charred staff that had appeared out of thin air. With a silent warning nod to his old friend, Karsis turned to look at his new student. "Tell us what you *see*, even if you think it'll upset us." The bard looked at Tierra sharply to cut off any reply she might have had, but she was biting her bottom lip in anticipation. He had seen Rhoe's eyes--they were glazed over. He wasn't Trancing, but he was Drifting. This was a little easier, in that he wasn't leaving his body, but it was still something that only powerful wizards did for fear of the answers that would sometimes come back with them.

"He's coming this way. He's looking for you--and also me, but he doesn't know much about me, just a hint. Gods above he's going to kill everyone here!" At this point, Rhoe got up and stumbled a little, then caught himself. He shook his head as if waking, then looked down at his feet. "Wow, I must've slept like a rock. I didn't even know I was standing." He looked around the quiet room. His mother's face was set in pure terror, and his father looked as if he was about to wring someone's neck. Of them all, only Karsis looked normal, if you could ever consider someone that intense normal.

TIERRA SNAPPED out of it and chided herself for slipping. *I've been out of center for days. This whole thing has me off guard. Pull it together girl.* She took a deep breath, let half of it out and found her center. She could feel her internal balance come back in a second. She let out the second half of her held breath and opened her eyes. *We promised each other last night that we would show him support and not scare him, and what do you do? Frighten him like a thirteen-year-old boy at a barn dance.* It only took maybe all of ten seconds for this, but Karsis was looking at her.

She squared her shoulders and softened her face, "We

thought you had been hurt, little one. Now come here and let me check you out to make sure." She made a fuss over him while giving her husband a kick in the shin to bring him around.

Through it all, Karsis watched and smiled. He could've had something like this a long time ago, but he had settled for the road to adventure. Well, this was some adventure all right. The boy had more potential than any three wizards put together, and was all of eighteen years old. *Hey, if surviving was easy, we'd have a lot less graves now wouldn't we*, he thought. He clamped down on the laugh that was coming and cleared his throat. "We should explain our decisions to the boy so he can get ready to go."

Gareth put his arm around his son. "Karsis is going to take you to Everknight, so you can inform the king about this 'man' you've seen, or *seen*, I guess." He shook his head, like he was reliving a sad memory. "Along the way, Karsis is going to be helping you with your new... *gift*." He looked to Karsis then to see if that was the right way to say it.

Karsis laughed at this little gesture. "Yes Gareth, it is a *gift*, and we're also going to stop in on an old friend at Norhil Hold. We will want to see Lord Tanan and warn him against this black-robed menace, as well as supply up for the long road to Everknight. From there it should only take about a couple of days by horse to reach the capital."

Rhoe couldn't help but feel that if something was easy, then it was wrong. "I'm telling you, an army won't stop this thing, never mind the small force they will send because they think we're overreacting." As usual, they wouldn't listen. He couldn't imagine why the king would send all his men for one man no matter how compelling the story was.

Karsis laughed, but his father seemed preoccupied whenever they mentioned the King of Everknight, though Rhoe couldn't imagine why. "Why don't you come with us father? They would believe me more if you were there."

"He was outvoted, dear." Tierra came to their rescue then. "We have to stay here and help evacuate the people."

Rhoe could tell she was back in control. She helped him pack his bag while comforting him. *Good, maybe now she will stop smashing things with that deadly hair of hers,* he thought. Rhoe couldn't shake that feeling though. *They all know something, I know they do.* He thought about things, things that were drifting around in a fog. Then he remembered the strange conversation he had heard before he had burst out of his room and almost took a sword in the face. "Wait a minute! You were the Companions of Everknight!?" It came out in a burst, bubbling up from the groggy part of Rhoe's mind; what with all the commotion of packing and planning it had been brushed aside. "I heard you all talking, and father said that Karsis hurt mom, and then..." His words died at the serious look that seemed to spring into being on his father's face. *Oh crap.*

"I thought I raised you to be better than an eavesdropper, Rhoven Whiteheart." Gareth stepped closer and laid a hand on Rhoe's shoulder before continuing in a softer tone. "Those things were for us to discuss, not you. If we wanted you to know about them, we would've told you." He seemed to be running out of steam, but Karsis was quick to pick up the torch. Pick up the torch, light the bigger torch with it, then throw both of them into the fire.

"Look, Rhoe, maybe we'll discuss this on our travels." He whipped Rhoe around to face Tierra and pushed him towards her with a flick of focused air. "Can't believe all that you hear when you first wake up anyway." He brushed a piece of lint off his longcoat, then perked up. "And *do* I have some stories about your legendary parents! We fought giants, and tigers, and—"

Gareth's huge hand closed quietly on the bard's shoulder.

"If you don't stop, you're going to see blood, stars, and a lot of bandages." The big man smiled, but Karsis was a little miffed at being interrupted. He was acting after all, and he had to get the boy's mind off the past and onto the road ahead.

"Well, I'm ready." Rhoe grabbed his pack and shouldered it, gripping his father in the tightest hug he could. Then Gareth squeezed back and Rhoe thought he was the one seeing stars.

"Let him breathe Gareth! And let me in there, too." Tierra stepped up to her two brave men and told herself that she wasn't going to cry. She did enough of that last night when they made their plans. They both knew they weren't ever going to see their boy again. "I love you, little one." She stopped herself there for fear of giving away too much and hugged him with all her might.

"Well, I just..." Rhoe wiped a tear away from his cheek and cleared his throat. "I love the both of you. Just be here when I come back. Got it?" He waited for their nods and strode out of the house before he fell down. Why were his legs so wobbly? Karsis had already left the house and was striding down the street, waving at anyone he saw, including two excitable twins bobbing up and down waving their little hands clean off. Their parents were restraining them with everything they had. It was Karsis the bard after all--didn't he eat children? One of the twins broke free and sprinted to Rhoe.

Rythal grabbed the young warrior in a hug, his excited frame bouncing up and down even in the embrace. "We'll miss you--where ever you're going, Rhoe! Come back soon!" Then he was off, and Innal was beating him for being the one that got to say goodbye. Rhoe chuckled and walked on, not knowing why the bad feeling was getting worse.

Tierra watched them walk down the packed earthen road until they were both specks on the glowing horizon. Her body trembled at this, her last vision of her beloved son. Karsis,

Gareth, and herself had talked long into the morning hours about this; it was the reason that they waited for Rhoe to awaken on his own. They had at the most days--possibly hours--before the monster was upon them. Who knew how fast he would get here? That was the real reason that they came up with this trip to Everknight; to get her son away from the bloody mess that was approaching.

"They're gone Tierra. Let's get the rest of the people that want to leave on their way and see what we've got for defenses." Gareth smiled sadly after the empty road, turned to face his love, and laid his rough hand on her shaking shoulder. "He'll be alright, love; we'll see to that when that thing gets here. Karsis was sure it was coming, huh?"

"Yes, he was sure. He's always at least half right, which is why we don't stand a chance." She slipped her arm around the big man, taking comfort in his strength.

"Bah! I don't for one minute believe that this thing is really an incarnation. How does he know? He's been wrong before, you know? Remember that time we faced the dragon and he said that if we just asked..." He was stopped suddenly by the look in his wife's eyes. He had seen that look before. The feeling passed down his spine on what felt like razors, and he shivered in spite of himself.

"Alright, so it *could* be as powerful as he says. But we've fought worse."

"By all the gods above and below, if we *have* I must have been knocked silly, because I can't for the life of me think of any. Can you?"

"Well... not off the top of my head, but give me an hour or so. Now, let's get these people out of here and prepare for the worst. Who knows," he said with a wink, "maybe we'll get lucky." And with that he guided her outside towards the town square. They had to tell the people of their doom and try to save as many as they could. This was not going to be a good day; he could feel it.

Castle Everknight

ALLISSANA HADN'T SLEPT WELL. It could have been the bruises or the slight bump on her head, but what really kept her up were the nightmares. Every one of them was the same; every time she drifted back to sleep it started all over again. Like a warning or... well she didn't rightly know what else it could be. The strange part was the young man in her dream. He was well built but lean at the same time, with long flowing white hair. He didn't so much as walk into her dream as he just was there out of nowhere. *Losing it girl. It was just a dream--a strange one, but a dream. Get a hold of your wits before you start to imagine purple squirrels running up trees.* Allissana shook her head to clear it and got out of bed with a moan. Gods she hurt. Planting her feet squarely on the floor, she struggled to stand, then stretched to work out the pain. Training didn't always go through her head like the wind as Carana always said it did. Even through these exercises though, the image of that boy drifted in her mind.

"Knock knock." The door to her room squeaked open a little under the rough warning, and the voice was one that Allissana had hoped to hear.

"Come in Carana, before you take the door off its hinges." She smiled in spite of herself. She could always count on an apology session first thing in the morning. She would swear that the woman never slept. The door opened the rest of the way and the muscled figure of her very best friend slid quietly into the room and shut the door behind her. Then latched it. This was not good.

No, scratch that. 'Not good' was having a practice sword rammed into your head without a helmet on, or punching a noble between the legs and running like heaven for your father. This was worse than that. Gods she hated that sinking feeling. "What's the matter Carana?" Allissana backed up reflexively and looked quickly to where her sword lay. Just in case. This sinking feeling had better start paying some kind of rent if it was going to visit so often.

"Ssshhh." Carana put her finger to her lips, then motioned for her to follow her to the window. Carana pulled the shades tightly and bound them with the silken cord. Looking around the room she finally let out a breath. "I know that you're serious about going to challenge that monster. No, don't interrupt. I also know that you're going to get yourself killed if you do. So in the interest of keeping you alive, I've assigned an escort for you to the Northern Run Bridge." Carana sat down heavily on the bed, head in her hands.

Gods she's shaking. What could make HER do that! She didn't even finish that thought, instead she sat down next to her companion and held her close. "Alright, you old battle axe. What is going on? And no fancy talk like my father gives me. Give it to me straight."

"I'm going to be your escort if... when we sneak out of here. I can only bring you to the bridge. I can't cross it, but I can make damned sure you get there in one piece." Carana took a deep breath and looked her young charge in the eyes. "You will never know how hard this is going to be for me. And before you say it, no I'm not joking. The acolytes say it's going to rain for the next week, and you'll have to be gone in two days' time." She bit her bottom lip.

She must think I'm daft, but I can't tell her. Not yet, maybe not ever. Carana straightened up and slapped the princess on the back like she was an old war comrade. "So, hurry up and pack. I'll handle the gear for the horses, just don't tell anyone." She got up to leave, then stopped and turned around quickly. "And stay away from your mother for the next two days, she'll know in an instant."

It didn't sink in right away, then it hit her. *She's not only letting me go, she's helping me! But what was all that secrecy about? Does she think my father would banish her for helping me?* She rubbed her eyes and tried to focus, but the morning's revelations were too much. On top of getting no sleep from that damned dream, she had a million things to do. But first she had to finish getting her things together and eat. Gods above she was hungry. She threw clothes into a pack that she had kept hidden away in her closet for just this type of excursion and added a couple of extras; brush, knife, and her father's medallion from around her neck. The clothes she packed were not the frilly things that she was supposed to wear at court, but the clothes that she often wore around her rooms and to practice. Allissana took down her sword—a gift on her eleventh birthday—and carefully wiped the blade with oil as she was taught to, then slid it into her sheath. Throwing it onto the bed, she looked around almost casually and sighed deeply. Her first real adventure and she was going to fight a thing of the gods. *Well, if you're going to do something, do it big.*

She laughed aloud at the memory of her father's words when she had rebelled against her nanny by ambushing her and tying her up before the guards could rescue the poor woman. She slid her pack and sword under her bed and went solemnly to breakfast, with a little bounce in her step.

Arian watched from the corner of the hallway as his daughter walked away from her room. She was in control again.

Good. He tried to guess what Carana had said to her, but for the life of him he couldn't figure it out.

The King of Everknight took a cautious step towards his daughter's room, then stopped. "She's really leaving to fight this thing," he said to himself quietly. He didn't know how he knew, but at that moment it seemed so clear. He shook his head to clear it and continued on into her room, moving with all the grace of the superb fighter that he still was. He closed the door behind him and looked over the room. He spied the covers of the bed slightly off the floor and smiled to himself at the memory. He was about the same age and as reckless as a blind minotaur at a fair. He had vowed that he was running away rather than learn to use a sword just to kill others. Then, as he stashed his gear under the bed, his father's general Cara had come in and told him that she would help him if he wanted her to.

He had beamed at the thought and they had indeed run away, all the way to the first bridge. They had camped out under the stars those first few days of spring, and his father had waited for him at the bridge. He had thought that he was going to be lashed for that, but instead his father, then King of all of Lythinall, had camped out another night with him. It was just the two of them, and that night he had learned of responsibility.

The next day a coach had arrived with his mother and they all went back to the castle to learn together. Because of that, he became one of the best swordsmen of his time, and Cara, Carana's mother, had retired after teaching the young warrior. A few years after that, Carana had come to take her mother's place, but he always had a special place in his heart for Cara. Arian blinked at that memory. How Carana looked like her mother, and now his daughter was going through the same phase. Well, maybe not the *same*, but the principles were there. He gazed off out the window for a moment.

Funny how he never thought about it before, how Carana came so shortly after her mother's retirement. In fact, he couldn't remember ever seeing her growing up at the castle. He supposed that if she were just a commoner that he wouldn't have.

He shrugged his shoulders and went to the bed, pulling out the pack he knew was there. He took off the ring that he always wore and slipped it into the smallest pocket of the pack. It would find its way onto her finger in time, and she wouldn't even notice; at least not right away. Heaving a great sigh, he quietly left the room and shut the door.

Luckily for Allissana, a princess's life at her age was a full one. She was kept busy for the next two days with classes, training, and her duties. The hardest part was keeping away from long talks with her mother. Her father, however, was creeping her out. He was distant and full of smiles; this was not like him whatsoever. He was always in her way, nagging about her duties and for her to take more responsibility. It must've been her outburst in the council chambers. *Good, maybe now they will know I'm not a baby,* she thought. Near the end of the two days, and after many games of hide and seek with her mother, Allissana crept out the back entrance of the castle and headed to the stables.

Carana was there, draped in a heavy black, hooded cloak, and hiding in the shadows. "Are you ready?" She asked, quietly, almost like she was afraid of something.

"Yes. I can't believe we're actually doing this!" The evening sun was setting and clouds were moving in. The spring rains were coming and the river would swell soon. She loved this time of year.

"Well, we are, now get in that saddle and let's go before I have to explain this to some guard that happens our way." The two women rode off without any fanfare, riding towards their destiny, and only one of them didn't have a clue that this was exactly what they were supposed to do.

§❧

THE DOOR WASN'T EVEN LOCKED. The figure crept in slowly, ready to silence any resistance with steel. He slid to the right side of the door and eased it shut just as quietly. He waited a few minutes, letting his eyes adjust to the darkened gloom of the large room.

He could make out the bed, and smiling under his black mask, he crept closer. As he neared the side of it, he pulled his sword in one blinding motion and stabbed downward, impaling... nothing. He swore softly as his sword went clean through the sheet and into the bed of Princess Allissana. His dark heart hammering in his chest, he yanked the sword out from the bed and rushed to the door as he heard footsteps coming down the hall. His master said he could not be discovered, and he didn't want to fail him. Ever. Panicking, he threw open the door and slashed desperately at the figure in the hall, aiming to where a shield would be held if it was a guard. Which, unfortunately, for him it wasn't.

A bent old man shuffling his way to some menial chore was there instead, and the sword came down scoring a wicked hit to the side of his head. His ear tore clean away and the oldster fell screaming to the floor. He regained enough composure to at least yell out a warning. "Assassin!! Assassin in the..." The rest of his message lost to a wet gurgling noise as his throat constricted against the steel piercing it.

Shouts arose all around him and the man ran for the nearest stairwell. *The only luck I seem to have is bad,* he thought sarcastically. He finally regained enough wits to remember where his master's room was and headed down the last corridor, cutting through two more victims, though they would probably live if tended to quickly enough. If he could only reach his master's room, he could hide. No one would search that room; his master was too important. As he rounded the last corner the air seemed to thicken considerably. Stumbling, he threw his hand out to the wall to steady himself. He choked and tried to heave air into his lungs by sheer brute force, but the air seemed to grow solid in his throat. He tried to hold his breath, but stars were crowding his vision already. The last thing he saw was that empty bed, signaling his failure. Then, with a slow slide to the stone floor, he finally closed his eyes. Everything was darkness.

Council Chambers, Castle Everknight

"WELL FRENIR, he was outside of your quarters, how do you expect us to sound?" Othren leaned slowly over the council table to look the councilor of foreign relations square in the eye. He rested his chin in his hands, as if to strike an innocent pose, but only came off like some malicious angel.

"If anyone cares, the other two victims shall live, by the grace of Davalar." Old Ralavin bristled with annoyance at the bickering councilors. "My King," he started, turning to look at the grave-faced warrior, but his question was stuck in his throat at the look his king wore. Arian had taken the assassination attempt upon his daughter to heart and wanted all who were responsible to hang slowly with salted steel wire.

"Ralavin, you are right. Glad I am to hear that you saved those innocent people, but the fact remains that someone tried to kill my daughter!" His voice had risen so loudly that many at the table flinched from his force of personality alone. "Now.

Does anyone wish to tell me who this cur was, or am I going to have to replace my Councilors?"

"You can't just replace us... your Majesty."

The pause was barely noticeable, but Arian caught it just the same. Alyssa tried to seem confident, but even her unshakable demeanor paled next to his anger. How he missed his wife at these damned meetings, but she was out riding the countryside searching for their daughter. Arian knew that she would not find her until the princess wanted to be found. *Damned if I was the one going to tell her that. A black eye looks bad on a king,* he thought.

He couldn't even smile at his own thoughts. "Do not misunderstand me Councilor Alyssa; I do not presume to *replace* you. What I meant is that after you are all dead, we would need new councilors." He swept his gaze over them all, watching their nervous chuckles, until it was apparent to them that he was far from kidding. Even Alyssa had no retort to that. Good.

"His name was Gremin, my lord, and it seems that he was under Councilor Othren's supervision as Seneschal of Everknight Castle." Frenir spoke quietly, but assertively, his eyes never leaving Othren's. The Councilor of Foreign Relations smiled then, and Othren looked away first.

"Alright, now we are getting somewhere. Othren, find out where he is from, and how he stole one of the knight's swords." Arian looked around the table, his eyes searching for the right person, then settled on Trost.

"Councilor Trost, I want you to figure out how a healthy man who just sprinted away from castle guards happened to fall over dead. Look in the archives for something. I want to make sure this wasn't a magical attack, though I suspect it was." The king finally sat back in his seat and surveyed the room. "Now the worst news. I know where my daughter went; where she must have gone." He took a deep breath and silently envied his wife riding through the rain and mud. "My daughter has gone to face the beast that walks towards this very castle. She has gone to fight the incarnation." That was the signal for the room to explode with cries of outrage and general unpleasantness. Arian looked over at Ralavin, one of his oldest and closest friends, and shrugged helplessly. Some days you just couldn't win.

DECISIONS

He stopped about a half mile outside of the village and cocked his head to one side, listening. They were organizing some sort of defense--that much was open to him--but something was wrong. There weren't any guards riding his way to stop him. That was odd. He had taken his time getting here, hoping that the bard, or whatever he was, would've warned them. He so loved the fear that came with his approach. Dar'Krist shrugged and started walking once more. It wouldn't matter. They were all going to die when he arrived, so let them try and muster their courage. The inhuman thing that was the incarnation of death and corruption didn't care. When he reached the village gates, he slowed enough to lay his hands upon the wooden palisades and felt them start to decay. The wood groaned, then fell apart with rot and ruin. He strode through the opening, pushing his *sight* ahead of himself and saw the line of refugees lining the earthen road to the south.

Run little beings, run while you still can. You will tire before long, while my thirst is endless. The thought pleased him more than he thought it would. He would have to follow them, adding to their fear the entire way. This worked out better than slaughtering them all in their homes.

Dar'Krist snapped his hand out in a blur to slap aside a humming quarrel that zipped at him from somewhere off to the left. He turned and *saw* the figure behind the wagon and lazily turned in that direction, chuckling to himself. He slowed near the wagon however; something wasn't quite right. The wagon tipped toward him suddenly, and he leapt back, catching sight of the behemoth behind it. The bear of a man was growling with the supreme effort needed to lift such a weight, and when it reached the pinnacle of its height, he pushed it over with a yell of defiance. Dar'Krist rolled up to his feet in a crouch, then spun in a tight circle to avoid the foot that came sweeping out at his head. This was well-planned and thought out with his arrogance in mind.

"A challenge at last?" he asked, his wintery voice sounding like the grave itself. The big man was coming in at him in a rush, while the owner of that deadly foot—a woman no less—looked like she was turning to flee. Dar'Krist stood slowly to face the oncoming man, and his *sight* never even registered the steel balls that slammed into his neck. Even as he tried to turn the blow into a roll that would lessen the shock and attempt to cushion the impact, the man hit him in a ferocious charge that picked the black-robed warrior off of his feet. *Well then, this could actually hurt a bit,* he thought as the man pummeled him.

Blow after blow rained down upon him in seconds, and he couldn't help but laugh out loud as the huge fists impacted his bones again and again. The incarnation hit the ground and sent forth his mind in a circular wave of death that had even the discarded wagon crumbling. The big man was flung off of him by the sheer power of it and rolled to a stop several feet away. Dar'Krist stood slowly as the dust cleared, feeling his ribs crack into place as they slowly began the healing process. He grabbed his head with both hands and cracked his neck, stretching almost in mock pain. He crouched suddenly as the woman went flying high over him in a kick that would've finished the fight if he were mortal, and was shocked by the resilience of the female warrior.

No, not just any warrior, he thought to himself as he turned towards her, silently applauding her skill. It was a pity that she would soon begin to feel the effects of the rotting disease that afflicted all who came into contact with him.

Dar'Krist received yet another surprise, as he cocked his head to one side, and moved one foot in front of the other, more for balance than attack. This shift allowed him to spin in a turn that brought him face to face with that powerful man bearing down on him with a huge axe. "You people are hardier than most, aren't you?" And with powerful arms of his own, he caught the axe blade in his bare hands and twisted.

Nothing human could've moved that quickly, Tierra thought to herself as she flew over the man's head. She ducked into a roll of her own and came up perfectly balanced, ready to defend against the monster's next attack. Instead, she saw him spin completely around and catch Gareth's axe in his bare hands. "Oh crap." With a resigned sigh, she threw herself at him in a forward roll and kicked out at the thing's feet, hoping to catch it off guard. That went over like a jester at a funeral. The man in black simply leaped up as he twisted the axe free from Gareth's powerful grip. She had seen bigger men try to overpower her husband and fail; maybe Karsis wasn't embellishing this time. This guy was going to be the death of them both. She crouched and spun again, gaining momentum for her steel ball, and lashed out at the thing as she pivoted away from its reach. Her leg shot up and hit squarely in the center of its back. It didn't even seem to notice.

Tierra shook her head and assessed the situation. She could

feel herself slowing down, not a whole lot, but something was eating at her bit by bit. The female warrior tried to stand, but that made her head spin. Throwing both hands out to block the backwards swing that the man launched at her, Tierra flipped out of the range of his vicious strike only to find herself lying on the ground instead of her feet. Struggling to her knees, the last thing that she saw was that swirling black cape, tattered and ripped, twisting about the strange thing that seemed a man, right before his foot caught her and sent her a dozen feet into the air to crash through a shattered door.

"Tierra!" Gareth's breath caught in his throat as he saw his beloved wife go crashing through the door to the old bakery. This thing had stripped him of his axe, then spun and knocked her around like a rag doll. He had tried to get a swing in, but his own axe was keeping him at bay for the moment. Sweat broke out along his brow, and he was going to lose soon if he didn't finish this quickly. He charged ahead, screaming his fury at the evil standing between him and his love, and ducked the swing of the axe. Coming in low, Gareth saw it coming back around just as low, aiming at his neck. With no time, he did the only thing he could think of. He punched straight out at the haft with all of his might. He was awarded with the sound of splintering wood, and then he hit the thing in the swirling black cape with his powerful shoulder.

They rolled around the earthen road, and Gareth fought to get a grip around the thing's neck but his breath came short now, and suddenly the whole village seemed to spin. He felt something pick him readily off the ground and hold him, then he was sailing through the air. Gareth hit the wall to the bakery hard enough to take out most of it with him. After a few seconds of supports groaning, the rest of the building crashed down on top of him.

Dar'Krist sniffed loudly and stretched his arms out wide. *That was a good workout. I think I actually broke a sweat--and quite possibly a couple of ribs,* he thought smugly to himself as he surveyed the village. A frown appeared on his rough face as he finally caught on to the ruse. They had distracted him so that the rest of the town could escape. Fools. He was still mildly irritated at not having sensed that ball that the warrior had tied to her hair, but it had worked out in the end. He thought about sifting through the wreckage just to see their bodies fester with his disease and rot before his eyes, but he sensed an urgency from the south. Events were moving fast; he could feel them entwining around him.

"Not even you Fate, will be able to stop me this time," he called out to the heavens. He gathered up his cloak, and started walking through the town, headed south. *No one can stop me this time.* And that was when the large rock hit him right between the eyes.

His head snapped back and he cried out in shock more than pain. His eyes blurred and he spun out of reflex, throwing his *sight* out around him. *Stupid... letting my guard down.* Dar'Krist *saw* his attacker and almost fell with the shock of it. It wasn't a brave knight, nor was it an elven lord. No. It was a pair of human children! The two looked like twins, and they seemed scared out of their minds. Three quick strides brought him to them, and he grabbed them up and smiled.

"You killed them!" one of them screamed, crying hysterically. The other one was sobbing, the festering rot already taking him. He threw them both into the blacksmiths yard, watching them roll like rag dolls into the forge and knock embers into the hay. *Well, that was definitely strange,* he thought as he left the empty and burning village of Daelyn behind.

Northern Run Road

THEY HAD WALKED for almost two days, and Rhoe was trying very hard not to notice the line of smoke in the sky where Daelyn should be. "Are you sure we're—" he started before Karsis cut him off.

"Yes, for the fifth time young one--we need to be doing this." He never lost the spring in his step, even though he was thinking about his old friends as well. They usually came out the better in a fight, but only because usually they had him there. "So please stop asking, and try to focus on what you're going to say to Tanan."

The gates of Norhil Hold came into view then, with lookouts calling down for them to identify themselves. Once Karsis did his usual flourish and pulled out his flute they opened the gates wide. Rhoe shuffled in after him, concern tiring him out more than anything.

"Rhoe! As I live and breathe. I haven't seen you in... well, I don't even know how long." The lord came striding out to meet them, his slender form gliding through the inner courtyard, dismissing the guards out of hand. Rhoe smiled despite his worry. 'Uncle' Tanan was his favorite. Lord Tanan Norhil was dressed in a black silk tunic with black breeches, sporting a long, dark blue cape. Broaches and pins adorned his clothes and his high black boots clicked when he walked. His steps were light and graceful, and his thin wiry frame was in perfect form despite years of easy living.

"Hello Tanan—uh—I mean Lord." Rhoe stammered over his words, forgetting that this was the Lord of Norhil.

"It's fine Rhoe; you need not get courtly with me. I've known you for all of your life. Now come tell me what's brought you."

He turned to Karsis and moved his fingers quickly, signing something, while guiding Rhoe towards the main keep. Karsis signed back discreetly, letting Tanan know that it was urgent they talk in private. Lord Tanan was talking like a sprite now, telling stories about young Rhoe and weaving through the maze-like hallways. Soon they were in a quiet room and Tanan turned to lock the door once they were in. Rhoe realized that there were no windows or other means of egress from this room, and for no reason he could understand, that made him nervous.

"Okay, now that we're alone and away from prying eyes . . . what happened?" His demeanor had changed considerably in a heartbeat, and his brow showed the storm clouds of worry like Rhoe had been feeling.

"Daelyn probably has fallen, and refugees will be a day behind us so we need to prepare for them." Karsis was speaking as if he was talking about the weather. Rhoe couldn't imagine what he had seen that made this seem so trivial. "It's the Dark One's incarnation. He's on his way south; I'm not sure why or where he's headed, but he's coming."

Tanan's face fell, though Rhoe could still see his mind working. "My parents stayed behind to face him, but the smoke..." Rhoe couldn't keep it in anymore and turned away from the two great heroes to let the tears leak down his face. His shoulders shook with his quiet sobs.

"Easy Rhoe," Karsis said from behind him, placing his dainty hand on the young warrior's shoulder. He stroked his white hair and Rhoe could feel soothing warmth flow into him. "It will be alright. Let's get some sleep and we can set out in the morning." He turned to Tanan and his eyes seemed to gleam. "May we grab some provisions from you before we leave, lord? We have to get to Everknight to warn the king."

Tanan's mind was spinning but he kept his cool. "Of course, my old friend, and I will get you rooms far from prying eyes as well. I'll be busy for the rest of the night I'm afraid. I have to get the guard ready to hold against this thing." He stepped up and embraced Rhoe in a tight hug. "Your parents are the bravest people I know, if anyone can make it through this, they can." He secretly placed his ring in the folds of Rhoe's robes, hooking it into the rope he used for his belt. The ring had tiny hooks and he clasped them tight. He may need this in the days to come. *The gods know we all will,* he thought. Then he bowed low and led them to their rooms.

Rhoe said he wasn't going to sleep right away, but soon he was out cold and snoring loudly. Karsis laughed quietly, then went about making sure they had the provisions they needed and read for a while. *So far so good,* he thought to himself, *now we just have to make it to the bridge in time.*

They rode out of Norhil Hold the next morning on horses given to them by Lord Tanan. The early spring air was crisp and clean, and the sun had just broken over the horizon. They both felt much better when they saw the line of refugees coming down the road in the distance towards the keep.

They still didn't know if his parents were with them, but somehow the fact that they saved all those people made both of them put it aside for the moment. They rode south down the Northern Run Road, and after a half day of silence, Karsis started to explain what Rhoe was, and how he could control his new powers.

"Rhoe, the main reason you need training is that if the power inside you can't be released with control, it will turn to rot and fester, corrupting your heart." He sounded serious for the first time. "The stories of black-hearted wizards were never far from the truth and they have absolutely no remorse." Karsis shook his head slowly. "But enough tales of wicked deeds, we must teach you how to use these great gifts." He pulled his horse over on the side of the road and tied him to a tree.

"So, what will I have to learn?" Rhoe asked, a little daunted but ready for the challenge. He pulled his horse over as well, tying it around a tree away from Karsis's horse. He wondered if it was going to be anything like training with his mother, 'cause those years toughened him up. "Wait, before we start: what exactly is an incarnation? I found stories in some of the old religious books in the temple in Daelyn, and they said incarnations were the voices of the gods or some such."

Karsis sat floating in mid-air, his coat swaying in the spring breeze and his hair bouncing in time with the leaves on the tree. "Rhoe, incarnations *are* the gods. At least a part of them." He took out a small harp from the inside of his enchanted coat, tuned it with deft fingers, and started to play softly. "I'll tell you what I know."

"Long and long ago, the gods fought over the land you see here. Not these particular mountains and forests, but land that was here in the distant past. Their wars spilled out of the Heavens and rained down on the land like a plague, soon destroying all that they were fighting over. They vowed then and there that they would never fight amongst themselves again. Instead Syll, goddess of magic and nature, thought of a plan to invest some of their power in a mortal.

"These mortal champions would be their voice and hands among the people. It was decided that they would all find worthy champions. Among them were Norar, god of thieves; Davalar the Protector, god of honor; Ollian the Fair, goddess of song; Syll, goddess of magic; and even Krist the Dark One, god of plague and death. So it was that the first incarnations were born to the earth. Over the centuries, some of the incarnations were killed; they didn't age, but they could still be slain by mortal hands. They were replaced by the gods when they did fall, but only one has never changed."

"Kris . . ." Rhoe's mouth was full of something gagging him, almost stopping his breathing, then it was gone. He coughed and spit, but a firm hand grabbed his shoulder and straightened him up. Karsis's silver eyes were boring into him, as if he could *see* the depths of his soul. Gods, they were intense.

"Never speak that name without music playing. Ever." Karsis had a slight quiver to his voice. It actually scared Rhoe more than anything else.

"But you were pla—"

"Ever! I was playing the harp, you were not. I don't even want to describe to you what would've happened to you had the Dark One taken you into himself. Don't look at me like that; *those* stories are true, trust me." Those last words were spoken in a whisper, almost as if to himself. Rhoe let it drop and waved him to continue with his story. "The Dark One's incarnation proved the most resilient over the centuries. His given name was known as Dar'Krist, and it was he that started many of the world's deadliest plagues. The first time, his fellow incarnations imprisoned him in the sea. That lasted for centuries, but the second coming of the incarnation of corruption saw a great war. The time of the great elven forest, as it is called, saw humans enslaved by the elves. They did this arrogantly at first, to show them the ways of nature and turn their eyes to things of beauty instead of conquest." Karsis paused, gripped by a sadness that seemed to pass over his face in a blink, then was gone again.

"It was during this age that the incarnation was set free. The elves opposed him, since the other incarnations had scattered to the far corners of the realm. The elven lords threw their slaves at him in waves that were appalling. Hundreds died, many rotting away at the slightest touch of the powerful being's hands. Elven archmages hurled spells from on high. Great knights led their forces against the incarnation once the human slaves failed and eventually the elves magic encased him deep within the earth.

They wove a mighty spell of Sealing over the earth that locked him away, and there he has been ever since. Untill now."

Rhoe was struck speechless. The detailed account of the story almost made him feel like he was a part of it somehow. Like he was actually there, calling down the mighty spells and leading the people in their victory over the darkness. *It's like he was there. The look in his eyes, the tone of reverence...* Rhoe's thoughts whirled. He stood up suddenly, almost pitching head first into the fire pit, and stared at the bard with eyes of astonishment. *I didn't even know I was sitting... and when did he start a fire?!*

"Before you say anything young one, no I was not there. I hear that so many times when I tell this story that soon I might even start to think that I was." Karsis cleared the ground that was underneath him, rose a little higher in the air, and set his feet down gently. He brushed off his burgundy longcoat and smoothed the ruffles with a care that would seem to most people that he was nobility. "You see, I am a bard. What that means is that I am responsible for passing down humanity's history, so we can learn from our mistakes and grow from them. Bards have a power to make the stories real to the listeners, not completely, but for those that love them it seems that they were there. Am I right?"

"But... you. It seemed that you really were there, and the fire... what time is it?"

"Rhoe, breathe. It was a story, that is all." Karsis moved his hand slowly in front of Rhoe, almost like he was a noble king dismissing a page. "I could not have been there, that was over two hundred years ago. As you can see, I'm only in my early thirties." He walked in a slow circle around Rhoe and the mystery camp fire.

"As for this fire, I started it when I was telling you the story. The time? Well, my young student, it's almost late evening. You see, that is another thing that untrained wizards have happen here and there, and that is losing time." He stopped again and threw a stick into the fire that was laying on the ground. "Even though time passes normally, you tend to forget that you are anchored in it, so you forget some of the things you were doing."

"But you didn't lose any time?" Rhoe was confused; he was missing something, he knew it. He remembered the times over the last few days that this had happened. *But I was always alone,* he thought furiously to himself.

"Rhoe, you have come into immense power recently; it's a lot to take in one sitting. Never mind having the incarnation of death awaken and to have seen him." Karsis used his words like magic, not actually casting anything on the young warrior, but he knew how to misdirect someone with a hint here and a lure there. "So why don't we sit, and I can start telling you all about the magic within you."

Rhoe sat next to the fire, mentally putting all his questions in a back room in his mind for later. He listened for hours as Karsis spoke of elves and the powers they could wield. He was supposed to ask the elements around him to do things, nicely. He fell asleep going over some of the things he could ask for, drifting off trying to pronounce some of the words.

Karsis was truly amazed. The boy took in so much so easily. Now he was asleep, and Karsis sat down next to a tree and went over a book he kept in his pack just to pass the time. He wasn't worried about attack; the warning stick he placed in the fire would alert him to anyone coming close enough to harm them. A couple more days and they would be at the Northern Run Bridge.

RHOE AWOKE, half-choking back a primal scream of despair. He coughed and spit, trying desperately to get his bearings. He rolled out of his bed... only to find himself on bare ground. He was on his feet instantly, frantic eyes darting this way and that, until settling on the smoking fire pit that had kept him warm throughout the night. *That's right--I'm not at home. It's been days and I'm on the road.*

Still shaken, but at least coherent, he looked around for his companion. Karsis lay against a tree just out of the firelight, auburn curls covering his smooth face. He was apparently asleep. *How he could've slept through that is a wonder,* Rhoe thought to himself as he settled back down and stoked the fire. What had scared him so badly? He hadn't had a nightmare in gods only knew how long, but this felt somehow different. They had traveled for another day, after their long talk, and had passed the Havenar split. In another day and a half they would be at the Castle of Everknight. Things were going well, so what lay on his mind so heavily?

"Trouble sleeping my young pupil?" Karsis hadn't moved, not one inch, but it was his voice light. Perky and insolent.

"Nightmare, that's all." Rhoe was shocked to see the famous bard sit straight up in alarm and stare at him with those silver eyes. A shudder ran through Rhoe's body as he remembered how deep those eyes had seemed when they first set out on the road. Karsis looked at him, staring intently for over a minute. Just staring, until finally he raised his eye brows and made a "Humph," turned around and started walking around the camp site.

"Young wizards don't have *nightmares* Rhoe, they have *premonitions*, or flashes of the future if that big word is too much for you." The bard bent over and picked up a stick out of the fire, then drew his sword with a flourish, "Now, did you see trouble coming here, or far away?" Not that Karsis was too worried, but he liked to be prepared for trouble.

"I... I don't know, it just.." Rhoe was confused. He'd been

training on their trip to use the powers inside of him, but it was still hard to believe he was a wizard. Noticing the impatient look on his mentor's face, he regrouped his thoughts, just like his mother taught him, and froze. "Tanan," he said in a diminutive voice, a voice that quivered with fear.

"Oh, well little one I'm sure it is nothing, probably fell and twisted his ankle or some such while chasing a wench or three." Karsis slid his slender sword back into his scabbard, turned a complete circle and sunk down again crossing his legs as he went. Rhoe knew he was hiding something from him.

"You know what it is, don't you?" It was a statement more than a question, but there was enough fear in it to make the bard wince.

Karsis tossed his stick back into the fire. "Rhoe, sometimes it's better not to know."

"Tell me, now." Rhoe was on his feet. Funny, he didn't even remember standing. He clenched and unclenched his fists to the beating of his heart. A heart that felt heavy with loss that he couldn't even name.

"Rhoe, let's get one thing perfectly clear." The bard stood, slowly, methodically, turning in a reverse circle of how he just sat down. His sword was out before he was facing the shaking warrior. "You don't demand anything of me. *Ever.* You didn't know that till now, so I'm going to let that one slip. Now, sit down before you force me to teach you a lesson."

Rhoe calmed his breathing, found his center, and sat. He stared at the bard, and for the first time noticed that the man looked truly dangerous; it was not just your run of the mill 'I'm going to kill you' dangerous, but more like the 'Your soul will be fed to howling demons' dangerous. *Don't think I'll do that again anytime soon,* he thought to himself. Karsis winked at him then and Rhoe almost thought that he had heard that particular thought. He shook his head as if to banish it, flicked the long hair out of his face, and gave his mentor his full attention.

"Your Uncle has stood against some of the most dangerous creatures on this earth. I used to adventure with him, remember? But not to worry; there is an old prophesy about this thing, and we're a part of it. If he fights like I know he will, then he'll be fine, as well as the people he is sworn to protect."

Rhoe did feel somewhat better, but there was still something off. "I felt as though I had looked into the eyes of... I don't even know how to explain it. It was just an evil, creeping all over me." Rhoe started drawing circles in the dirt near the fire pit, its fading light making his creations glow slightly as the embers danced above it.

"Like maggots on rotten meat." Karsis knew that feeling well.

"Yeah, that's it," he said as he shot to his feet. He had to do something to get his mind off of this feeling. "As long as I'm up, can we train some more before dawn?" Rhoe felt dizzy, probably from standing up too quickly. That had to be it.

Karsis smiled quietly to himself in the dancing shadows of firelight. "Sure. Now first clear your mind and focus on what you want the air to do." The bard shook his head and marveled at this boy. *That was a close one; he can see better than I thought. Better start giving him challenges to see what he can do.* Even deep in thought, he could *feel* Rhoe start to form the question in his mind. He was going to try to wrap him in air.

Rhoe opened his eyes and whispered to the winds. "Please winds, hold that man there." But the man wasn't there. The winds picked up, then dissipated before they could find him. He heard chanting above him and his instincts kicked in. He dove forwards into a roll and came up facing the other direction. He looked up in time to see Karsis smile and feel the branches of the tree he was next to wrap quickly around him.

"We have to start you on more of the elven language soon; it flows quicker than common. Now did you think your enemies were going to stand around and wait for you to ensnare them?" He floated down gently, coattails blowing in the slight breeze. "Now you start training." He released the young warrior, and danced away quickly as Rhoe, dirty but determined, started again.

This is going to be fun, they both thought at the same time.

Northern Lythinall, Norhil Keep

HE SAW the keep ahead of him and slowed, wanting its inhabitants to know he was coming. Let them sound their horns--it simply heralded his arival. But after a couple of minutes there was still no movement. He sent his *sight* out into the keep and saw the decoys left behind to fool him. Clever. And the trap was impressive. If he walked in and attacked those decoys, it seemed that the floor would give and drop him into a pit of fire. He could see the smoke leaking out of the trap door, and even could spot the trip wire. Without his *sight*, he would've been slowed down for days regenerating that damage. Oh, he would've killed them all anyway, but he didn't want that kind of delay.

Lord Tanan saw him standing there and thought that Rhoe was dead-on about how dangerous this *thing* was. He knew dangerous, and this was it and then some. His cloak hid him for the time being, even from the power this thing had, mainly because he wasn't being looked at.

He moved quickly and quietly, like the master thief he was. If this thing didn't move on soon, he would have to distract it. Gods above, he didn't want to do that.

Dar'Krist let his *sight* out before him once more, looking for the signs of the refugees fleeing before him. Wait. He focused on a point some seventy miles distant and *pulled* it closer to his eyes. A campfire still smoldered, and one, no two people had left just recently. Dar'Krist was fascinated by this, mainly because he could feel the power radiating from not just one, but both of the travelers. This was unheard of even in his age, never mind in this feeble time of knights and laws. Well, he would just have to—

His musings were interrupted as the point of a slender sword burst through his chest and blood sprayed from his mouth and nose. The impact drove Dar'Krist to one knee. The sword was yanked free, slicing his insides as it went. *Dark One's blood, this was one hell of an enchanted blade!* he thought. He was sick of getting caught unawares. Why was he losing focus? The boy?

As Tanan pulled the sword free he rolled to the left and slashed again, but the blow was deflected by the thing's bare hand. "Damn, I was hoping you would stay down... No?" He rolled again as the black-robed man launched himself up and came down with a stomping foot, then a scything back hand.

Insolent fools, he thought to himself, as he focused inward and started to heal the damage done to him. He had no time for this. He gathered his power and draped it around himself like a comforting cloak of death, and smiled. This hero would die, and then he would follow these two individuals that had perplexed him so.

Tanan felt it, and knew it was his time at last. He couldn't flee and give up his ruse, and he couldn't beat this thing. His plan of disabling it and hiding didn't work so ... wait. "Hey, you done fighting? Am I tiring the big bad guy out?" He rolled again, this time right at him, and ducked under his punch, and took his kick. He knew that was coming and used both attacks to move into position. His arms were weak and his skin was tingling. *Now or never,* he thought.

Dar'Krist had him at his feet. He heard at least four ribs break, and the man's clothes were starting to decay with the field of death around them both. Then the man looked up and smiled, taking his sword and ramming it straight down into the earth... through Dar'Krist's foot! The incarnation screamed, more from anger than pain, and launched a kick with his other foot sending the man flying into a ditch forty feet away; the man didn't move.

This was the second time he had been hurt: first that big guy and the little warrior, and now this sneaky man. He focused his power into a needle, and sent it into the sword. It resisted at first, but after a minute the enchanted blade crumbled to dust. Free again, Dar'Krist spent most of his power in a rush, healing his wounds and closing them up. Angered beyond words with the setbacks he was having, he walked around the empty keep and continued after the two strange people. He would find this bard and his friend and make them pay. *And then I will use your skin to make another living cloak,* he thought, as he left Norhil Keep behind.

An hour later, Dren and Stard decided it was safe to move. The straw stuffed into their armor was itchy, but it was worth the price of living. They helped out the other guards in the keep's outer ward, taking the straw out of their armor and finally opening up the trap door. No fire greeted them, but instead a huddled mass of refugees and residents of the keep lay hidden with burning brands. After everyone was accounted for, they went out to find Lord Tanan, but no trace of him remained, just his cloak in a ditch.

"First the two missing kids, now this?" Dren said ominously, He wasn't superstitious, but with talk of things walking the earth again, it never hurt to wonder. "What next, dragons?"

"Let's just get back in and see to the people. The chancellor will know what to do." Stard shrugged and walked back to the keep, leaving Dren to stare at the horizon and wonder what was happening to all his heroes.

North of Everknight

QUEEN MARESSA HAD BEEN RIDING for what seemed an eternity. Heavy rain that fell like boulders tossed out of the Heavens pounded her like she was a gladiator. She was so caked with mud that she was sure that if she was stopped, she would be taken for a monster. The queen smiled then, thinking of the many roads she had traveled just like this one. That is until she remembered why she was riding this road in the first place. Her smile faded, replaced with lines of worry, though no one would have seen them on that dirty face. *Where are you little one?* she thought to herself, surprised that she could hear herself think with all the rain. It had been a long day and not one person in the two villages that she had stopped in had seen any riders. Her daughter was smart not to stay in the villages. It was what she would've done.

Carana is with her; I've got to stop worrying. She would know I would be coming after her. Maressa brought the horse to a halt, right in the middle of the small lake that passed for a road. She looked to the northeast and thought suddenly of the small hunting lodge that Arian used to use in his youth when he wanted to escape. "That sneaky little bitch," she whispered to no one but the rain. With those words, the smile came back. This smile wasn't one of fond remembrances, however. This one was a mother's answer to a daughter's challenge. The mirthless grin shone brightly out from under the mud-caked face as the queen left the road and headed across the puddle-strewn fields towards the light woods.

ALLISSANA DRAGGED the body of her closest friend and mentor through the heavy door, slammed it shut, and slid down to her sore arse. "We made it, Carana. I told you... I could... carry you." She was struggling for breath, but she so loved to gloat. The hunting lodge was just as she remembered it from when she was a girl. The warm room had a small lamp glowing to show her the fire-stoked hearth glowing restlessly. Something was out of place, but her mind was trying desperately to think of what had brought her friend down so decisively. It seemed impossible but it had happened.

"Make it stop... Please, brothers... make it stop." Carana was huddled in a ball near the door where Allissana dragged her. She was whimpering softly, like she had lost her mind, and the sheltered princess had not a clue of how to help her.

"What happened to you Carana?" Again, something was nagging at her mind, but she had to stay focused on her friend. She tried to remember when it had happened, the exact moment.

Her mother had always taught her to 'think from the beginning' as she called it, so Allissana sat back and tried to recall the events as they unfolded. She remembered that Carana had been jumpy the whole day when they left, mostly about the rain. The first day it had only drizzled, making the trip dreary, but passable. Carana had bundled herself up tight, saying that the rain would make her miserable. They avoided the villages so as not to draw attention and camped out in the wilderness. They talked about life on the road, as the princess had never been on her own like this.

That night it had started to pour. They had no need of a tent, as Carana knew how to make a shelter between two trees with some rope and a tarp she had brought. The rain sounded melodic amongst the leaves of the trees, and it lulled her to sleep.

She had awakened out of a dream of that boy with the grey robes again, and when she realized that the melodic noise that had awakened her was only the rain pounding the trees, and not some mythical elf come to steal her soul, she started to drift off to sleep again. That's when Carana started screaming. Her first thought was that someone was attacking, but a quick scan showed no man or beast were near her companion. No arrows protruded from her leather jerkin. She remembered thinking of magic, but why that thought had popped into her head she couldn't remember. After trying to calm her down and find out what was happening, Carana had yelled for her to leave her behind. The thought of her friend's voice at that moment was still with her, and she shuddered in spite of the warm room. She had never heard Carana, or anyone she ever knew, sound so utterly afraid before. It was despair--just pure and utter despair.

Anything that could do that to the battle-hardened woman next to her would cause her to do the sensible thing and run so fast that her arse would have to catch up later. She shuddered again, and it had nothing to do with the rain-soaked clothes she still had on. Nothing was near them except the rain. That was the only thing, except perhaps magic, but she had only ever heard stories from her mother and some of her tutors at the castle about it.

"Well, at least we're safe for now. Come on Carana, let's get you out of those wet clothes and let the heat soak into your bones..." Her hands froze at the thought. Dread seeped through her consciousness, finally grabbing her mind and giving it a good shake. The room shouldn't be warm. The room shouldn't be warm and a lamp shouldn't be burning.

She did a quick count in her head. She had only been here about three, maybe four minutes, so that meant that no one was lying in wait. Or so she hoped. She stood slowly, letting her hand drift next to her sword, but not touching it. Gods above she was shaking.

She scanned the room and finally saw what she should've seen upon entering. A dirty cloak was bunched up in the corner of the hearth--close to the fire, but far enough to prevent it catching--and a small backpack was leaning on the chair that her father used when he would tell his hunting stories. Carana whimpered to herself behind her, and Allissana caught movement out of the corner of her eye. She turned with the instinct that came with years of training and pulled the sword out with a downward stroke to deflect any thrown weapon. In her inexperience, she threw herself off balance and almost went head over heels as she met no resistance. Instead, she managed to scare the wits out of the poor man trying to wedge himself into the corner of the room. He was so frightened that he was shivering more than seemed humanly possible.

"Oh please, don't kill me! I didn't mean to be here. It's just warm, and outside is so cold. Please mistress, don't kill me!" The poor man was dressed in ragged leather armor that seemed too big, and his hair was a tangled mess of dirt and grime. He appeared small, but it was hard to tell since he was huddled in the corner. The faint odor of filth that she thought was the lodge instead seemed to be coming from him.

"Step out so I can see you, stranger. You won't be harmed, unless you intend violence towards my friend or myself." Allissana was both proud and shocked to hear herself sound so commanding. Father had always said it would come naturally.

The man crawled towards her hesitantly, on all fours and keeping his head down as if in supplication. She sheathed her sword, but hesitated letting it go. Keeping her hand on the hilt of her weapon, she took two cautious steps towards the man.

Just jumpy from the fright he gave me. He's just tired and cold. Her thoughts didn't comfort her at all. He stopped about five feet from her. "What's your name...?" The question died on her lips as he lifted his head and looked at her with eyes that were clearly anything but human.

She took a step back, but he was impossibly quick. He wasn't shivering, he had been tensing his muscles for this attack, and his leap at her throat was perfect. His hands found her and his legs wrapped around her waist. His putrid breath filled her nostrils as she fought to stay on her feet. If she went down, she was as good as dead. They both knew that. He wrenched her around and pinned her arms as well. He had her helpless.

His voice was grating in her ears like scraping a sword on iron, and he talked calmly to her, like they were strolling through the garden. "Give me what I want little one and it will be painless." He tightened his grip on her throat, choking the life out of her.

Even though she had been trained to hold what little breath she had left for a chance to fight back when he thought it was over, she could feel the darkness closing in around her quickly. Feeling his bony ribs pushing against her chest, she was horrified to see his face start to resemble her own! Her own voice, much distorted and a little deeper, came out of the thing's festering mouth, "That's it, almost there sweetling. Let me finish you like a good gir—!"

His sentence was ended prematurely, and she felt a sharp pain in the center of her chest, then a flooding wetness covered her as his fingers lost their strength altogether. She collapsed onto the floor, rolling from instinct to give herself some room if he came at her again. Allissana had no idea what had happened, but she wasn't falling for anymore tricks until after she had at least gotten some air in her heaving lungs.

"Attack *my* daughter will you!" came the hardened voice from near the door.

Allissana barely registered that welcome voice as she started slipping into unconsciousness. She couldn't get enough air into her lungs fast enough. She would have a good nap first, then figure out why Carana had called her daughter . . . yeah, a nap sounded good. *Maybe I'll dream of that handsome boy with the grey robes and white hair again.* With that last thought, Allissana gave in to the darkness.

A little while later, after getting her daughter into a chair and throwing the dead body out into the rain, Maressa focused on the other living person in the room. She needed answers.

"Tell me again why you disobeyed me!" Maressa was livid, her face so red that she could've been mistaken for a demon.

The Queen of Everknight paced back and forth in the lodge, every so often steeling a glance at her daughter sleeping in one of the chairs. "Well?"

Carana rubbed her sore neck again and tried to think of an answer that wouldn't involve beating this poor woman to a bloody mess. "Look, she was leaving anyway. You couldn't talk her out of it; I couldn't talk her out of it. Deepest hells woman, Davalar himself couldn't have done it. I went with her to protect her!" Her head hurt and this questioning wasn't helping any. She stole a glance at the girl she had trained from a very young age and quietly berated herself for not seeing this coming.

"Carana, listen. I know you're angry for not..." Maressa, anger flooding out of her, looked at the floor. She didn't mean for that to be said, but she was exhausted. She had ridden hard, through the rain and mud, only to find her daughter in the grip of a gnome. This was not her best day ever.

"Say it! Go on, say that I wasn't able to protect the princess. I know that!" She was on her feet now, the rage flooding her veins, the strength that she had honed over all of the decades flowing into her fists. But she wasn't angry with the queen. "Say it! Because I failed, she could've died." She was angry with herself.

"Carana, stop. You got her here safely and I thank you for that. There are worse dangers in the wilds of this kingdom than gnomes, and you watched out for her when she probably would've walked right into the first village she came across and announced to the world who she was." The queen took three quick steps to stand in front of the big woman and put her arms around her.

This was a huge risk. The odds that Carana was going to throw her into the wall, then possibly kick her spine out through her skull increased greatly with how she had been yelling at her. But sometimes you had to take those risks for your friends. Being this close to the woman that had trained all the men at the castle and her daughter she finally realized how big she really was. Her arms had a hard time encircling the muscular beauty, and she only came up to her chest in height.

"She saved me." Carana's voice was barely a whisper.

"What did you say?" Maressa held her out at arm's length and studied her face. Her talents for reading people had never worked on Carana. There was always something a little off about her anyway, but this time it felt like things had changed.

"She. Saved. Me. Plain as that. We were staying the night out in the rain when something came over me." She fumbled for the right kind of lie to tell a full-fledged bard that would work. "Must've been magic of some sort; I was in agony. Allissana dragged me and the horses all the way here, all by herself. Getting here with both horses and me in this weather in a whole day is a feat I don't think many could accomplish. I only remember bits and pieces of the trip, that's why I was out when the gnome attacked. Happy?"

"She dragged the horses?"

"No, she... you know what I meant!" The queen had a way of diffusing most situations, she had to admit. "If you hadn't come and ran your fancy sword through that..."

"Its name is Deathsong."

"Fine. If you hadn't come and ran Deathsong through the back of that gnome, then it would've drained us both." She smiled softly down at the princess pretending to sleep. It was these years that Carana missed the most out of the many centuries that she had spent walking this earth. The playful years. "I'm still impressed that you only nicked her; I never knew that you were that good."

"You know well how good I am with this sword Carana! I was in the Companions of Everknight. !e had to be the best, or at least better than those who tried to kill us." They both shared a laugh at that, then Maressa noticed that her daughter was stirring, or at least pretending to stir. *When did she learn that little trick? Well, I guess she's heard about enough.* Maressa glided close to Allissana and pulled out her hand harp. She started to play soft music, then added the words to a little spell that she always kept memorized for situations just like this one.

When she had heard voices, Allissana remained motionless. She had trained herself from as early as she could remember to lay quiet, as if sleeping. She did this, at first, to hide the fact that she liked to stay up late at night. But as she grew, it became useful to find out information about people. People liked to say things about you when they thought you were sleeping. She could clearly hear her mother's voice, and she was livid. *Thank the gods of grace that they think I'm sleeping,* she thought to herself. She had been the target of that temper a time or three, and it was something she didn't relish facing the way she felt right now.

". . . Say it. Because I failed, she could've died." Allissana wasn't playing hero anymore. The deep regret in her friend's voice was enough for two lectures--hell, maybe three. For the first time, she had come close to death. Not simply being disarmed on the training mat, but drained of all life by something... not human. Gnome. They had just called it a gnome. In the back of her mind, they were still talking. She couldn't believe her mother had come, never mind saved her like that. What the hell was a gnome anyway?

"Its name is Deathsong." Her mother was talking about her sword. Funny, she had never even known that her mother knew how to lift one, let alone fight with one. Then Allissana heard something she would never forget. Ever. "I was in the Companions of Everknight..." Oh my gods. She twitched slightly in shock and surprise, but covered with a stretch and some quick repositioning. The Companions of Everknight! No way in all of the heavens would she have ever thought that. Her father, sure, she knew he must have been. The stories of King Arian the Brave were in every book, but she had always assumed that father had met her mother after that time. Apparently not. It was then that she heard her mother's harp start to play, so soothing and peaceful. She had better get up and face the music, so to speak. *Just a little nap 'efore I dew . . .* and that was the last she saw of her mother for a long time.

The queen stood slowly, putting her harp aside on the table. "Now that she's asleep, we can talk business."

The seriousness in Maressa's voice gave Carana gooseflesh. *No good can come from this,* she thought to herself, fighting to keep that thought off of her face. Bards could read people like books, and over the years she had kept her secret from all who could possibly figure it out on their own... or so she thought. "So talk my Queen. What else do you want to scream at me about? Or would you rather tell me how disappointed you are of me?" Carana was a master at baiting people into letting their emotions get the better of them. Probably wouldn't work on a full bard, but what the hell.

"I know who--or more precisely, *what*--you are Carana."

That simple proclamation hung in the dank air of the lodge like fog over a fetid swamp. Maressa could see warring emotions cross Carana's face as she digested the words. She could only hope that rage wouldn't be one of them. She knew if the woman wanted her dead that her fancy sword work would be less than adequate against someone who had trained for centuries.

"You mean that you know that I'm a longtime friend of you and the king himself, right?"

The sound of her barely constrained voice worried Maressa more than a little. It meant that she was trying to give her a way out. A way out of whatever she was going to have to do to her. This wasn't going at all like she thought it might, and she thought the worst. "Carana, give me just a minute to explain. I found the lost books last month. I'm sure you know which books I'm referring to?" Carana nodded her head woodenly once and waited for the queen to continue. Maressa cleared her throat and tried her best not to look worried. "Well, I finally figured out what some of them say. You see, I've been studying the old tongues, and had started translating some of them, when I found one book set aside from the others..."

"Dost Frein en Krist." Carana's voice had, if humanly possible, an even harder edge to it than before. But then again, the woman wasn't really human.

"Yes, it means..."

"The Fall of Evil."

"Yes, well--since you know the book, you know what I found. It states fixed events in future history. Prophesy. I read as much as I could translate, and at first I didn't know what half of it meant; that is, until our daughter's outburst at the council meeting." She looked at Carana carefully, seeing her visage soften considerably. If rock could soften.

"So..."

"It says: 'And on the day the child decides to stop this evil, the incarnation shall pledge herself to her, and protect her always through fire, earth, and air. Water, however, will set the child on the path to freedom, leading her to the One who is All and None. The two will bond and journey to find the means to give what the Evil despises.' That's as far as I got, but you can see that after your leaving with the princess on something so foolhardy... well, I knew there had to be a reason." Maressa stopped and leaned on the hearth for support. This was all catching up to her. Finally seeming real. Real enough to lose her little girl to some foolish book. She took a deep breath to steady her voice and continued. "After finding you here, obviously put down 'by magic'--which I didn't buy for a second mind you--I finally pieced it all together. You are an incarnation. Which one I'm not sure of, but there it is." She let out a deep sigh, and started walking towards her longtime friend, knowing that she might kill her to keep her secret. It didn't matter; she was her friend and she would put her faith in her or no one at all.

"All those book smarts and I can't believe you missed something." Carana was smiling now. That same old mischievous smile that she gave others who thought that because she was a woman, she was weaker than they were. Carana paced the distance to Maressa quickly and grabbed her by her shoulders. Her grip was painful, but the queen tried to keep the terror off her face. Incarnations could probably read people like books.

"What did I miss? I... well..."

"I'm the incarnation of protection. 'The incarnation shall pledge herself to her, and *protect* her always,' I mean, come on

Maressa." She was laughing now, a deep hearty laugh, that seemed to spread through the lodge and brighten the room's dull glow to a roaring inferno of peace and tranquility. Or maybe it seemed that way because she wasn't being slaughtered by a gnome. Win, win.

"So you're not going to kill me to keep your secret?"

"No, my queen; we don't do that to friends. Friends that can *keep* secrets, that is." Carana pushed her away, holding her at arm's length, smiling at her. "It's going to be a long night, if you're interested in learning about us. Will the princess over there sleep till morning?"

"Yes. I used a full strength Sleepsong on her just in case you took it the wrong way." Maressa met her friend's smile and went to pull a chair closer to the hearth.

"Always thinking ahead. Alright then young one--we'll talk, but answer me this. How in all of the god's names did you learn to read Auld Tongue?"

"It took me a while, but I pieced together what I could from a book called, 'Translations from the Auld Tongue' by Caralann." Her face fell as if struck by a lightning bolt sent from the Heavens.

"Just figured out that was me too, huh? Well, not so high and mighty now, are you? So where shall we begin? Oh, I know. We'll start with what you should know." Carana sat and stretched out pulling her feet under her as she readied herself.

"You're a bard, so you've memorized the beginning a long time ago. I'll make that part short. The gods wanted a way to solve their quarrels without wrecking the whole of the earth, so they choose mortal champions. Over the years some of us have been replaced; only Dar'Krist has never been replaced. Yes, I know I'm not allowed to say his name or he could find me. Very well and good for mortals, but I'm an incarnation, he's my brother--or as close to it as anyone's going to get. Anyway, the part that the bards don't know is this; the incarnations *can* die. Oh, we heal rapidly and are resistant to all sorts of poisons and such, but we can be killed by mortals and immortals alike." She took a drink from her water skin and continued.

"We never age, and some of us have lived for so long that we're skilled at a lot of things, especially things like fighting, weapons, tactics, et cetera... Unfortunately, we incarnations also have a weakness. We each have one element of nature that's anathema to us. Mine, as you could've guessed, is water. Not just any water, but large quantities, like the rain storm or rivers.

"But you shower, I've seen you."

"Again, large quantities--washing quickly isn't enough to harm me, but it isn't just the pain. We're petrified of that element as well, we can't help it. I've conquered my fear of a bath over the centuries, but when I was in that shelter, I wanted to die. Your daughter saved my life for real your highness. Just like you're going to by never telling anyone about this conversation?"

It was a question, but Maressa never had a second thought about it, not even a lingering doubt. It took a lot to tell this to her, and she would never let her friend down. "Of course, Carana, you know I wouldn't tell anyb—"

"Not even Arian."

"No. Not even my husband; you have my word on it." Maressa drew her hand up to her chin in contemplative thought. "What are the others'-- their weaknesses--if it's alright to ask?"

"No one knows, 'even we mighty gods,' to quote scripture. Every incarnation has one, there is Water, Earth, Air, Fire, and Ether."

"Surely an incarnation isn't afraid of Air!"

"Again Maressa, large quantities. Whomever it is, they like the indoors... a lot. They might even live outside but be petrified of high winds. We don't know how it's going to affect us when we're told."

"Told? I thought you didn't know...

"The incarnations of old picked their weaknesses, but they stay so that when one dies—as did my predecessor—that weakness travels to the next." Carana held up her hand to forestall any other questions the queen had, nay, the bard sitting where the queen was. *The stories were all true, bards can talk someone to death.* Pushing that thought aside, Carana closed her eyes and began again. "It has been passed down to us that the incarnations all picked what elements they would be vulnerable to. Syll, Norar, Davalar, and Ollian chose, but The Dark One refused to pick until all others had picked. It is rumored that the others didn't want him having the upper hand, but as the last choice he automatically had his element chosen for him. Since this wasn't part of the agreement, he argued about the fairness, and was reprimanded for his outburst. We all think that this was the last straw for The Dark One, as what little temper he had left was thrown out the proverbial window and onto the sharp rocks below. At full velocity. Twice."

"Wait a minute--ether? That pretty much sums up a hell of a lot of different things Carana? What could their weakness be?"

"It could be anything; that's what I'm trying to tell you. Even mine could've been something simple like being submerged under water, but it isn't." She paused, sensing the girl stir in her magic-induced sleep. "We've been talking for a while now. What are you going to do about your daughter?" Carana held her breath; this was the defining moment. If Maressa decided to keep her here, or even to go with her, it could ruin everything.

"I'll let her go. We don't have much choice, do we?"

Can I stop my queen from ruining the world? Maybe we

could . . . Carana came out of her thoughts with a stupid look on her chiseled face. "What did you just say?"

"I said I'll let her go. Now wipe that look off of your face and help me with this chair, it has to look real if we're going to do this without a certain someone suspecting anything." She winked at the powerful being sitting there on the floor opposite her and realized that the castle had one powerful defender, and true friend.

❧ 6 ❧

PATHS FOUND

"Again, young one." The bard walked his horse along the packed earthen road as rain poured down steadily. Riding in a downpour like this could be dangerous, plus he wanted to take this time to have Rhoe practice more. The rain wasn't bothering him as he was deflecting most of it with magic. He couldn't get all of it, so he was still wet, but it helped. He watched the boy with an eye trained to spot imperfections, but also with one that had waited for this chance for what seemed an eternity.

The young boy tossed his long white hair out of his eyes, spraying water at the flippant bard just for spite, and concentrated once more. "Ashanti, water, part." He waved his arms out from himself in supplication. Nothing happened. Again. The boy was soaked through and getting aggravated.

"You are asking wrong. Ashanti means 'pleased.' the word you need to say is Ash'anti, 'Please.' Now try it again, unless you think that you have had enough?" Karsis flipped his own hair in Rhoe's direction and laughed at the face the young boy made at the statement. The boy was doing well despite the failures. Most wizards had years to get to this point, yet here the boy was in his first week and already practicing in the field. It helped that he had no choice. He would never be allowed in any school of the elves anyway.

For hours they had been traveling, and every time Rhoe had said that he'd had enough, Karsis had launched into a mock battle. If Rhoe wanted to get anywhere, anytime soon, he would have to keep walking his horse and practicing, no matter how exhausting it was. They couldn't afford to keep stopping and having these fights, especially in the pouring rain. At least he wasn't bitter about Karsis not being soaked.

"No Karsis. I'll try again and again and again if I have to. I know how important control is; my mother taught me all about control." He thought pleasant thoughts about his mother and father. They had to be alive, they just had to. His anger at the whole situation lent him strength. "Ash'anti water, part for me!" He screamed this last in anger and defiance to the heavens, willing the rain to do what he wanted. The rain moved away from him at an alarming rate, then swirled and funneled upwards in a raging torrent.

"Ash'anti wan, Ash'anti urbis dwoen." Karsis waved an arm skyward and brought the water under control. Once that was done, he turned a serious eye to the young boy, nay wizard, who looked at him with fear in his eyes. "That was *not* the work of a wizard. That, my young friend was almost the work of a sorcerer." He carefully let the water go, letting it fall back into a rain column across the road as he turned away from the young boy.

"I'm going to regret this--but what is the difference?" Rhoe knew what was coming, but his curiosity was always a hungry creature. At least he thought he knew what was coming. He wasn't prepared for the great bard to stop his horse dead in its tracks like they'd hit a wall.

His auburn curls bounced as he turned his head so sharply that the rain sluiced off of him in an angry scythe, slapping Rhoe in the face like a spurned woman. "What's the difference?" He shook himself slowly, as if trying to come out of some bad dream, "The difference my young *student* is that where wizards ask nature for their help, sorcerers demand it." Karsis led his horse to a huge tree on the side of the road. He looked up, whispered a few words that Rhoe couldn't make out, and suddenly the tree grew its branches out over the bard and his horse like a solemn roof.

"Now get that horse tied up over here, there is plenty of room and maybe you can get dry." Karsis took out a stick from his pouch, gathered up some dead wood, and touched the stick to the wet pile. He waited with patience—that some would say he didn't have—for the boy to come into his shelter. Within minutes the kindling was burning steadily, even growing so that the warmth covered them both. "Sit down and listen to me carefully." The bard sat cross legged, floating into the air on nothingness. He watched Rhoe sit comfortably, then, gathering his memories about him like a warm cloak, he began.

"In the history of this land, the elves ruled supreme. They commanded the forces of nature as friends and allies, and when the humans came from the far south, they had bitter war. The elves prevailed, and soon after the humans were their slaves." He paused, almost reflecting on something, then took a deep breath and stared at the young boy, with silver eyes intent on his very soul. "But compassion won out in the end. After the war against the Dark One's incarnation, there were some who marveled at the strength of some of the humans. There were then pairings of human and elf, if one would believe such a thing. But I digress. In the end, there was one who taught humans elven magic. For this they were banished." He was still for a long time before collecting himself once more. "These elves traveled to the southern reaches of their great forest to make a community for themselves. They had brought their human slaves, and the ones who now commanded magic began teaching them as well. However, their magic was different. They were too hasty, and demanding. They never grasped the concept of *asking*. They had been slaves for so long that their despair flowed into their magic. When they used their magic, they ripped apart the very nature they were using, forcing the elements to obey them. Thus started the second great war between the humans and the elves."

The young warrior couldn't help but stare as the story unfolded, as caught up in the story as if he were there. "That's not anywhere close to how I've heard the story... but somehow it seems more real to me." Rhoe scratched his head in confusion. Lost for a moment, he shook his head and bade Karsis to continue with a silent nod.

"Sorcerers don't ask for anything. They rip it out of the ground, or air, as they wish, more often than not destroying the surroundings at the same time. Wizards, however, ask kindly to have nature help them in various ways, such as asking for branches to hurl spears at their enemies. The trees do this if asked, never sacrificing too much, but what they can spare. Sorcerers would take down the entire tree and send it hurtling through the woods to strike their enemies, possibly breaking it in two to cause the most devastation." He looked at the rapt gaze of his young student and was pleased by what he saw in his sorrowful eyes. Regret. "But enough of this, it's getting dark, and we have hours before we arrive at the bridge to the Kingdom of Everknight. We'll stay here tonight. I sense that the rain is going to get worse before it stops."

"I . . . I didn't mean to do that Karsis. You know that right?"

"I know. You are young yet; mistakes are the path to enlightenment. I've made so many I should be ascending to the heavens any day now." He laughed, but suddenly the rain began to pour out of the sky like an avenging angel hell-bent on justice.

He could *sense* something, or a lot of somethings coming out of the high grass to their right. The fire crackled, and his stick glowed red and exploded in a harmless shower of sparks.

Right, that's it. Trouble. He had spent the entire trip instructing Rhoe how to use his powers to yield specific effects, but hardly even brought up a wizard's other senses. "Something is coming Rhoe, get up and be ready."

Rhoe saw Karsis levitate up some more and set his feet a mere inch from the ground. The sight never got old for the young warrior. He too could feel something; more than that, he could actually *feel* them. He peered out into the pouring rain and felt his *sight* grow focused, sharp. Karsis had explained that he could use the power within him to *see* things far away, rather than just what he was limited in his nearby surroundings. His *sight* slowly went forward, peering through the rain, then he noticed them. Huge shapes trudging through the grass towards their camp. Then large eyes found his and bored holes into his soul. The intrusion into his mind by another was painful, enough to drop him to his knees, screaming.

"Hells Rhoe!" He couldn't believe that the young boy had tried that. If you weren't grounded in your *sight*, whomever you were looking at could actually *sense* you as well. "Your *sight* isn't trained yet. They noticed you through your own power--now they know we're here." As Rhoe tried to stand, he grabbed and balanced him. Having someone penetrate your senses was about as painful as letting a mountain hit you in the small of the back, except you lived through this. He steadied the boy then slapped the horses to send them out into the night; he could call them back in the morning. "Sit tight young one. I'll go out and stop them, you rest here. Besides, I've been taking it easy on you; it'll feel good to let loose on someone for a change." With a swirl of his burgundy longcoat, Karsis dashed off into the torrential downpour, his auburn curls bouncing in time to the sword on his hip.

Rhoe couldn't see or hear anything in this rain, so he slid his back to the tree and gathered his knees in close. He could deal with the pain. It had caught him off guard is all, and he used the meditation his mother had taught him to ease the pain out of his body and spread it back into the night air. After a couple of minutes, he heard a sound on the edge of his dampened hearing and chuckled to himself. *Must have had a bit of fun, now he's coming back to gloat about how easy it was.* These thoughts had barely formed when a huge shape came into view from the heavy downpour.

It was about eight feet tall, and thankfully the rain diffused most of the rotting smell that hung about this thing like some foul perfume. Leaping to his feet and gathering his balance, he watched it come into the light of the fire. Rhoe saw that it was an ogrann.

Oh, this is going to hurt, he thought as he realized that Karsis had made his little roof big enough for it to fit under as well. The beasts were from the hills and made sport of hunting humans. They were grotesque and ruthless, never mind packed with more muscles than an elephant. This one had about five teeth left, and bits of hair hanging out of his fanged mouth. It lunged quickly with a huge spiked club, but Rhoe rolled towards it, out of the way as it smashed the area where he was sitting, the fire and his traveling pack taking the brutal hit. Rhoe came up in a crouch and side kicked the beast's great knee with all of his strength. It felt like he hit a brick wall.

"Hold still littles, I'm hungry and I doesn't want to work for me supper." This thing was obviously the leader of his pack, just because they rarely learned to speak the common tongue. Not well mind you, but this one actually sounded educated. Rhoe thought furiously as the thing swung a meaty backhand as it turned to get its bearing on the young warrior. Rhoe stood and flexed his leg muscles, propelling him straight up into the air to grab a low-hanging branch that made up the overhanging roof. He swung his legs up just as the club came around where his head was moments before. He swung his feet onto the large club, startling the big brute. The thing pulled the club hard and when the young boy jumped back, the monster was thrown off balance and hit the trunk of the tree so hard that the whole thing shuddered.

Well, when in doubt . . . He thought to himself, as he could see no way to hurt this beast with the direct approach. Cornered and caught off guard, he was out of time. He wished he could have readied himself and been on the offensive from the get-go, but that wasn't the case. He gathered his will and closed his eyes, focusing on the ogrann. "Ash'anti roots, up and attack!"

Rhoe wasn't sure it would work the same, not knowing for sure that the roots weren't a separate part of the tree. He had always used 'tree,' but the thought had just come to him. He rolled to the far side of the ogrann, and watched in fascination as the ground trembled slightly. The beast spun around in bewilderment and looked down with a stupid look on his brutish face. The ground rumbled louder, then burst out in a shower of dirt that sprayed the ogrann in the face, momentarily blinding him. The club swung out wildly, clipping Rhoe's arm and tearing skin. Blood sprayed out over the small camp as Rhoe screamed, more from surprise than anything else, then brought his pain into focus. He spun quickly back, now out of range completely, and watched as the thick roots began tunneling up out of the deep earth.

The great beast roared when the first root lashed around his thick ankle, neatly snapping the huge bones like they were dried twigs. He took a step towards Rhoe, but another grabbed his upper thigh and lashed itself tighter than the first one. The beast was screaming in pain now; he was almost out of his tiny mind with it, as root after root struck out and brought the huge ogrann down. By the time he was down on the ground covered in roots, he was far from alive. "What have I done?" Rhoe whispered in horror. Tears streaked down his face, uncalled for. He had never been the instrument of such a gruesome act before, and he felt it in the pit of his stomach.

Karsis was enjoying himself. He hadn't fought ogrann warriors in... well, at least ten years. Not in these numbers that is. There had to be at least ten or twelve beasts out here, swinging their spiked clubs at the famous bard, but never hitting the mark. The curtain of rain hid their bellows slightly. "My, but are we slow tonight gentlemen. Here I am, and you can't even give me a bruise. And you," Karsis pointed at one great beast as he climbed over a dead companion to get at the elusive bard, "tripping over your own compatriots? How shameful."

The brute looked confused for a second, even looking down at the dead ogrann he was stepping over, and so never saw the silver sword flash out and slice high into his leg. The cut was deep, and the leg wouldn't support his great weight anymore. Down the beast came, crashing on top of his buddy. "See, I even warned him." One more quick slice at the thing's neck, as he leaped over it in the pouring rain, and he was away. The others came on, and one by one they fell to Karsis's wit and steel; a few were also taken by the powerful magic that coursed through him. Blades of grass slashed about, almost as deadly as his own sword, and large fists of water knocked them about, keeping them off balance. As the last few ran howling into the wind-driven rains to seek escape, the great bard heard something on the winds.

He sent his *sight* out over to the encampment, and saw the massive ogrann's bound form twitch once, then move no more. "That can't be good." He went bounding back in the driving rain, running by *sight* alone—which was dangerous, even for one such as he—and skidded to a halt when he saw that his charge was indeed alive and well. Sort of.

"Stay here he says, I'll be back in a minute he says." Rhoe leaned against the tree, holding his wounded arm close to him and wore an angry look on his tear-streaked face. "Didn't see this one coming, did you?" He sounded morose, and looked even worse.

"Well, young one you did very—"

"*Not* right now, thank you. Instead, can you tell me why, when I asked for the roots to help me, they killed him?" The young man sighed heavily, grimacing from the pain he must be focusing away.

Karsis quickly studied the scene and the young man, taking only a couple of seconds, then it came to him. *He looks distraught, almost guilty for killing... He's never killed before!* Karsis almost laughed aloud at the realization, but held control and put his serious face back on. "Look Rhoe, you did not do anything like a sorcerer this time. When one asks for things from nature, one has to realize that nature doesn't comprehend these complex emotions that we guide ourselves by. For instance, if you asked the roots to hold the ogrann, they would've held him."

In a small voice, the young warrior interrupted his mentor. "What if I asked them to attack?" The boy hung his head even as he finished the sentence, like he knew the answer. He felt like a killer, even though his life was in danger, his mother had always told him to think his way out of a problem, not strangle it with a great tree's roots while he watched every bone in the thing snap horribly.

"Then my student, they would've interpreted that you needed it slain by the urgency in your voice. If you were under attack, and hard pressed, they would've attacked the Ogrann with all their strength." He was truly amazed at the boy, right out of the gate. "Which is not a bad thing here; I mean look at the size of this thing. The ones I fought were half and again this size." Karsis added a wink to make sure the boy knew it was a bit of an exaggeration. Sometimes a swelled head could be good for getting over things. Rhoe smiled and winced as he moved his arm again.

"Let me look at that scratch." The bard lifted the arm gently and whispered words into the wind. The pain was gone and the skin fused together, not much, but enough to stop the bleeding. "That'll be sore for a couple of days. You put it in a sling for the rest of the trip, okay?"

"What did you do?" The boy's face had a look on it that said to all viewing it that he had seen the sky open up and rain whips and daggers.

If he only knew the truth, thought Karsis. "I used magic, dear student. What did you think I was teaching you all of these days, elven khoss?" Now that was a thought; he hadn't played that game in decades. Loved the game really. Should teach the boy to play it someday. Maybe make a decent player out of him.

"But how in nature did you... who would you ask... I'm confused."

"Now that is the first thing you've said in days that I can whole heartily agree with." He covered the Ogrann's body with dirt with a flick of his wrist, finishing Rhoe's magic by prodding the roots a little more (lazy thing, roots) and watched as the roots pulled the body into the earth, closing it up after them.

He pulled his legs under himself to float in mid-air once more, and smiled, ready to amaze his student once more. "There are elements, like I've stated before: air, water, fire, earth. Then there is one more element that only wizards know how to use. Ether. This element is a big one, and from it wizards can pull all sorts of power. But even the others have more uses than most could comprehend. Air contains wind, and can affect breathing, or even weight." Karsis points to the air under his floating form, and watches the boy nod in fascination. "Water, for instance, can be used to form lightning when combined with air; and fire can be used to create the absence of heat, to freeze, et cetera. Ether is the force that holds most of the world together. It is responsible for health, life--to a degree--light, even what we perceive as real."

Karsis wove his hands in front of his face, and suddenly he looked like a woman. "This dearest Rhoe, is a glamour, and the elves taught me how to do this a long time ago. Ether can be used for all sorts of things... it even contains the most powerful aspect out of all of the elements. Love."

"You've got to be kidding me." Rhoe screwed up his face at the absurd idea. He didn't want to laugh, but right now, seeing Karsis as a woman was just too much. He saw the bard move his fingers and had about enough time to wonder what in the world his teacher was going to do this time, when he couldn't laugh at the woman in front of him anymore. She was gorgeous. Those auburn curls, those curves... well, he might have to take that wet jacket from her, she might catch her death out here. Rhoe moved closer with a hunger in his eyes that made even Karsis fall back a step.

Boy must have some repressed tension in there somewhere. Seems his mother had that when I met her too. The bard murmured once again, just as Rhoe was reaching for their shirt. *Heh, I'll bet my horse that the young one is still chaste... that would explain a bit.* Karsis laughed at the boy's face.

"What?" Rhoe jerked his hand back, appalled at his behavior. "Karsis, I'm sorry, I..."

"See?" The bard held one finger up to silence his pupil. "A glamour of love--or in your case lust--is powerful magic and has kept me alive more times than I can count. And I can count pretty high. It affects the very emotions around us all and can be a useful tool. But. You are. Never. To use this for your own gain. *That* is the sorcerer's way."

"How did you learn to do that?"

"I thought I already covered that. The elves trained me. They were patient with me, but if they find out I trained you... Well, we'll blow up that bridge when the enemy's on it huh?" The boy was tricky; he could *Sense* Karsis wasn't being completely honest, and he was *seeing* through things he shouldn't be able to. This wasn't a good sign.

"Will I get to meet a real elf, you know, like you did?" Rhoe was exhausted. Maybe it was using the magic, or the stress form the guilt. He almost couldn't keep his eyes open.

"How did I know that was coming? Listen, you sound light headed from all of the excitement and I'm sure you could use--" Rhoe was already out cold. Karsis pulled a blanket out of his magical coat's pocket, and a fluffed pillow for himself out of another other pocket and got comfortable. He threw another warning stick onto the damaged fire and from his inner pocket he produced a copy of his favorite book. *Dost Frein En Krist.*

Royal Hunting Lodge

ALLISSANA CRACKED AN EYE, ever so slightly, and peered at the room in the dim lantern light. She was in a soft chair, sideways, and her boots and cloak were off. She heard Carana snoring slightly in the corner by the door and could see a shape sitting in the chair across from her. The shape was cradling a harp like it was her life; her mother alright. Allissana crept out of her chair and stretched soundlessly. *How did I sleep so soundly? Gods above I feel like my old self again.* She kept her thoughts under control though; her mother was a bard after all, and apparently she was a legendary member of the Companions of Everknight. She'd never get over that little tidbit of news. She walked quietly over and saw her things, her pack and cloak, right next to her mother's leather armor. They were about the same size, and even though it was stylized to match her mother's personality, Allissana had always thought that it was for show. *Humph, I'll never think of her like that again,* she thought.

She reached out reverently and picked up the neatly folded armor and carried it under her arm while slinging the pack over her shoulder. She would need armor for what she was going to do, and her mother might not rush after her without armor. Just then a slight melodic hum came from the side of the chair where her mother was sleeping. Allissana started. *Oh gods, what now?* Her thoughts were in a tumble, then she spotted it, her mother's sword. Deathsong. She had never thought much about the sword, except as any child wonders where their parents get such dangerous and exciting things. She assumed it was ornamental, something to show the courtiers, but after experiencing what she had these past couple of days she looked upon the sword like she did with her mother: with new eyes. The sword was expertly crafted, bearing etchings of an ancient language, and set with dark gems in its hilt. *Deathsong.* Its name was rumored to be of an old bardic tale of love and war, but as far as she knew no one but her mother and father knew the truth.

She couldn't take it. She couldn't. Allissana turned towards the door with her pack over one shoulder, and the armor under the other arm when the sword chimed softly once more. Allissana cringed in quiet annoyance. *Fine, you win sword.* It was half a day's walk to the bridge. She didn't dare bring the horse in case they tried to follow her, and she may need a good weapon all on her own. She wouldn't admit it to herself that the gnome had frightened her.

She tiptoed over, and holding her pack strap with her teeth, grabbed the sword off the ground and placed it under her arm with the armor. She could feel the warmth cascade over her body and almost dropped everything right there. Shaking her head in wonder, she finally made it to the door. She paused in the doorway and looked back once more. She had to do this alone. Carana was in enough trouble, and was probably still weak from her magic attack in the pouring rain. Her mother would only try to stop her, but without her armor and her weapon maybe she would think twice about running after her right away.

I must be crazy, she thought as she stood there, trying to gather up her courage. Even though she would agree whole heartedly that it was a suicide attempt, something deep inside her urged her to go on anyway. With a tear falling down her cheek, she said her silent final goodbyes to her mother and best friend, then headed out into the dawn to find her destiny. If the end did come, well, she'd jump that burning bridge when she came to it.

Northern Run Road

DAR'KRIST WALKED SLOWLY past their camp site, sniffing the wind and trying to get a *sense* of them. One was connected to that woman with the braid, he was sure of it. The other could be elven, but even the smell of that was off. No matter, he was almost on them. They were probably headed to the same place he was; for what passed as a king in this land. Not that the king would help them. Everyone was powerless to stop him this time, but if they got word to the elves it would cut short his playtime with these human lands--and he was having *so* much fun. Suddenly he felt them, but at the same time *saw* them ahead traveling towards a large bridge. His head swam with possibilities and he shook his head to clear his thoughts. He could catch them upon the bridge and slay them there. The wood looked thick enough to hold out against his powers for a little while at least before it started rotting away, as long as he kept his anger in check.

You are mine little ones, Dar'Krist thought to himself as he gathered his strength and ran for the bridge. Oh yes, he would slay them here and throw their bodies into the rain-swollen river and march on to the castle anyway. This was going to be fun. And if his mind hadn't been clouded, he might have noticed the two hiding in the grass next to him, or even seen the lone female on the bridge waiting to fulfill her destiny.

KARSIS AND RHOE had ridden for miles; now they were walking the packed earthen road. Even his training did not prepare him for sore muscles that he'd never used like this. They hadn't called the horses back after the night of torrential rain, instead they walked the rest of the way for reasons Karsis didn't want to discuss.

Twice they had spotted refugees from the north, coming down in wagons to seek the king's shelter, but Karsis led them away to hide in the high grass, always in the name of stealth. Rhoe knew they couldn't help them anyway; he wanted to see if his parents were among them, even though he knew the answer to that already. *Focus, put the grief aside until you have time,* he thought to himself, words from his mother years ago. For the last four hours the great bard had been preoccupied and had actually given Rhoe a little slack on his lessons. That's when the young warrior knew something was wrong. He had thought that maybe it was all the rain they had gotten, but could now feel that wasn't it.

The morning sun was reflecting off of all the wet leaves from the night before, and the crisp air had the feel of change carried on it. Rhoe's curiosity finally got the better of him. "Okay, Karsis you want to tell mmpphh--" Suddenly Rhoe had a hand over his mouth in mid-sentence, and saw a look of determination, perseverance, or fear flash across the bard's face, which made him swallow his words.

"Shh, little one," Karsis whispered into his ear. He pulled him off of the road and into the bushes, or rather some high grass that had grown near the muddy stream that ran off of the river. It was enough to conceal them from any passerby. "Watch and be silent for once. Concentrate on being one with the grass and everything will be fine. Nod if you understand."

Rhoe nodded while flat against the damp ground. He felt the urgency in the bard's voice and didn't even think of ignoring his orders this time. His scalp itched from the high grass, but his concentration was strong and he ignored it with practiced ease. Beside him lay the bard, eyes closed in deeper concentration than he and sweating from the exertion. It was then that his eyes were drawn to the road, and he saw it.

The black-robed figure passed by, walking with determined purpose. Rhoe watched that black cape flutter the wrong way in the breeze, and he thought he may pass out. *How could anyone stand up to that!* He thought as the sheer power radiating off of the thing hit him as it passed their concealed location. He regretted that thought immediately as the reminder of his parents hit him again. Did that monster out there even care about anyone, did he have special friends that were killed somewhere, did anyone love him at all? *Where did that come from?* And that's when Rhoe realized that this was the reason that people would stand against this thing--so that he didn't take loved ones away anymore.

"Something is happening," whispered Karsis from his position next to the young warrior. Rhoe noticed that a clouded look had come to the man in black, and suddenly he took off at a great pace, legs pumping incredibly fast after something Rhoe couldn't see.

"Wha... mmpphh." Rhoe tried to say but Karsis put his hand over his mouth before he could get much out.

"Shh! He's still close enough to hear you, just not hear me if I whisper." The bard carefully let go of the young warrior's mouth and rolled over onto his back to stare at the clouds. It took Rhoe a minute to figure out that he was counting. When he reached one-hundred, he sat bolt upright and tugged at Rhoe, dragging him out of the grass. "Let's go. He can't get too far ahead of us for this to happen the way it should." And with that cryptic message they were speeding after the most fearful thing Rhoe had ever seen.

"But what did you do?" Rhoe asked, his breathing regulated to his footfalls on the packed earthen road.

"I projected an image of us far ahead of where he thought we were. It shouldn't have worked as well as it did, but someone else clouded his mind somehow. No, don't ask me--I'm just as lost as you on this." Karsis ran like the wind, burgundy longcoat flapping behind him like some dark banner, and his auburn curls bouncing like a small bird in a wind storm. It came to Rhoe then what the bard was doing and he almost laughed at the simpleness of it.

He controlled his breathing even more, slowing it to the point where he could let it out without missing any words due to his quick movement. Measuring his steps perfectly, he closed his eyes as he ran and opened his mouth. "Ash'anti, wind speed me along." He said the words perfectly, careful not to shout but to say them with urgency nonetheless; he was rewarded with a fleet feeling under his feet as the wind came beneath him and blew at his back. He released Karsis's hand so as not to drag him along, and ran with all the strength he had. Soon he was outdistancing even the fleet bard, and with his warrior's grace moving faster than any human or even elf had ever gone.

Karsis was thinking. It wasn't something he liked to do while running often, not since his youthful days of outrunning the authorities, but he needed to do it now. Rhoe needed to face the incarnation with the chosen girl alone; he couldn't be there to interfere. How he was going to get him there without bringing him he didn't know. He knew the kid could run fast—his movement was almost breathtaking—but he was moving incredibly fast now with the wind guiding him. And then in mid-thought, he heard Rhoe's voice rise above the footfalls and the howling wind in his ears. "Ash'anti, wind speed me along." Karsis nearly stumbled right then and there. The implications were staggering. Not only had the boy figured out the right spell to use, and how to apply it to the situation in a matter of seconds, but to cast it while moving!

Not many wizards--and they were almost exclusively elven and quick on their feet--had ever been able to cast while moving *that* fast. He could do it, but he had been doing it for a lifetime, possibly two. This young warrior, who was barely able to grow facial hair—though elves had no facial hair either, but that's neither here nor there—had been able to not only cast his spell perfectly while moving at the speed of a full-grown horse with a dragon behind it, but was able to think about the consequences of the spell taking effect on those around him as well. He had let go of his hand before the wind hit him full blast.

The great bard Karsis slowed his charge and cancelled the help of the wind. Walking now, he dusted himself off and made sure that his jacket wasn't wrinkled, then began to whistle a merry tune as he walked towards fate. The tune was an old one, and if it happened to be about a certain bard, well that was just a coincidence now, wasn't it? He hoped the girl was alone and that Rhoe could swim, otherwise the book of prophesy he had been reading would be good only for kindling in his next campfire. If there was a next campfire.

Rhoe felt the wind behind him, and had never felt so alive. He felt he could take on the gods themselves, and little did his mind know, that he was about to. Rhoe squinted his eyes, to see the bridge ahead, but his eyes were watering with the whooshing air. He focused his mind, but he remembered the headache that had visited him when he used it against the ogrann, so he grounded his *sight* and closed his eyes. He *saw* the black-robed man take his first step upon the wide heavy wooden bridge, and the warrior standing on the far side obviously making a stand against this powerful foe. He narrowed his *sight* a little more and the image of the warrior became clear: it was a woman, nay a girl! So this was how the *sight* worked when you used it right. He could make out such details even this far away, but he was starting to get dizzy, so, just in case, he pulled it back little by little until he cancelled it altogether.

He refocused his energies into getting there as quick as he could and as he came upon the last bend, the bridge came into focus for his own watery eyes to behold. He knew that the man-- or thing that looked like a man--would *sense* him coming from behind. He even guessed that the thing would stop him forcefully if he even came close to him. So he had to improvise. As he raced in behind the man in black, Rhoe saw the thing turn quickly and sweep his foot around low to force the young warrior into the air. Rhoe expected something like this and instead leapt sideways to the rail of the bridge, landed with both feet against it, pushed up into a spiral flip that threw him sideways in the opposite direction with all of his momentum, and landed right next to the girl; who by now had her mouth firmly on the bridge next to her feet.

"Hi, I'm Rhoe. By the way, this is going to hurt a bit--you know that right?" He nudged her a little to jog her mind back to the present since their doom was coming at them like a runaway carriage. She still hadn't moved much, so Rhoe slid her behind himself protectively in a small hug of reassurance, and only then realized that this was going to *really* hurt. Not just *fall down a small cliff* hurt, but *fall down a cliff and land on a jagged outcropping of rock covered in salt* hurt. He had no more time to think, only to dodge and block as the thing attacked first with its fists in a one-two strike that Rhoe parried with his forearms, then with two vicious kicks aimed at both his side and midsection. He blocked both of these with his legs, bringing them up and over in quick succession, but was violently pushed back by the attack. Rhoe kept backing up, staying in front of the woman. Now that he'd seen her up close, he realized she looked about his age. At least this thing wasn't casting magic; as if it needed to.

Allissana's world had turned upside down. Everything had gone well: she had snuck out and away from her mother and Carana and made it to the bridge in time to see that thing step onto the ancient structure, and she felt it tremble! Then, as she wrestled with the fact that her legs wouldn't listen to any reason until she had a signed note from the common-sense department of her brain, *he* showed up. Just like in her dream: one minute she was facing this thing alone, then out of nowhere he simply appeared by her side. Years later, when asked about this, Allissana would never quite know what pulled her out of that shock and back into the fight; but suddenly she drew Deathsong with a ring of steel and spun around the young boy in front of her, lunging straight at the unprotected midsection of the man as she did so. This move would've caught any normal fighter completely off balance, as they would be wholly intent on the first foe, but this thing wasn't human. Not by a long shot. It deflected the blade with a bare hand without even looking at her and went right back after the boy. Not good. As she backed to the side and around, trying to flank the thing, she looked around for a strategy that wouldn't entail her getting horribly beaten by an evil god-like being.

She noticed then that the bridge beneath them was quivering. She didn't know at first what was happening, but the 'how' didn't matter, just the 'what do we do when it does' seemed to matter. The planks of deep wood that were easily six to seven inches thick were starting to decay, and she could hear them start to protest under their combined weight. On any other bridge, any other place in this land, this would be a common occurrence. However, as she had seen a squad of war horses and their riders parked on this bridge with three carriages and it never so much as squeaked, it seemed a bit worrisome.

So, the bridge was going to let go and they would all plunge into the swollen Northern Run River after a spring rain. Fantastic. *Great, and I can't swim,* she sighed in her mind, realizing that she wouldn't probably live to hit the water anyway. Well, she would have to make sure that this thing was in no condition to swim when it got there. She backed farther away from the thing in black tattered clothes and took deep breaths as she headed to the castle side of the bridge once more. It would think she was retreating, she hoped. The boy was right about one thing, this was going to hurt.

Pain shot through Rhoe's body. The sad part was that he had blocked almost everything that this creature had thrown at him. He couldn't imagine what he would've felt like if most of these had landed. The surge of adrenaline was starting to wear off and the pain was beginning to seep past his blocks little by little, just as this thing's strikes were doing. Then suddenly the girl spun around him and lunged. Rhoe hadn't even sensed her begin the move before it was completed, and when he saw that the thing casually deflected it with his bare hand, it made his worst fears bloom like a bad flower. The thing was toying with him. The thing must've seen the understanding dawn on the young boy's face for he chuckled slightly and nodded in confirmation. Rhoe heard the girl backing down the way she had come silently and he breathed a little easier. She would be safe for a little while at least.

"Yes, youngling, I'm simply testing you. Not even using my power on you," he chuckled ominously. "You're quite good. You fight almost like her, you know." The black, tattered cloak swept forwards impossibly fast and hit Rhoe square in the chest, flinging him backwards about ten feet and down to one knee. "She had to be your mother, no?"

Rhoe's pain was gone. It wasn't just the pain blocks that his mother had taught him, but something deeper. In the calmest voice he ever has used he spoke to the water all around them. The swollen water was raging under them, and even though it was at least twenty feet under the bridge, he could feel it hear his words. "Ash'anti, water, sistren dwoen dosit krist." The look he gave the murderous being was enough to give the powerful creature the slightest pause; then Rhoe smiled as tendrils of water curled up from the river and started towards the creature like the coming of the tide. Sadly, they never made it.

She was a good thirty feet from them when she saw him take the hit that sent him back and forced him to a knee. It had to be now. Allissana gathered what courage she had and took a deep breath. She ran full-out at the man in black with her sword held above her head, and started screaming her lungs out to draw its attention. She rushed past the young boy who could only stare in open-mouthed shock, and when she was only ten paces from the deadly thing in black, she stomped down hard with her left foot and spun down to her knees, sliding across the weakening wood. The tendrils of water collapsed then as she brought her sword around in a vicious arc that would take the man's knees off clean if it would've connected, but he calmly jumped the swing like he knew it was coming. Allissana wanted him to do just that.

She let go of Deathsong in mid swing and grabbed the booted foot of the man as he hung in mid-air for that split second. No matter how powerful the opponent, their weight always comes from their footing--as does their balance. She slammed him down face first with everything she had and was satisfied to hear his muffled shout of alarm and pain as his face bounced off of the weakening boards. It was in this moment of triumph that she noticed how bad the bridge looked right where he was standing.

Knowing what was coming, she scrambled to grab Death-song and threw herself towards Rhoe as the man leapt to his feet.

"Hold on to me! Please!" she screamed in fear as the bridge shook wildly, suddenly coming apart under the powerful man's weight. The minute they touched, she felt strength flood into her as if she didn't know she was tired--but then they fell and the cold waters washed over them both, and her fear-laced mind went dark before she could scream.

He saw the girl-child coming for him and took pity on her. *One last desperate act in the face of oblivion,* he thought and calmly awaited the predictable overhead chop that most warriors would deliver when overmatched and scared. But then she surprised him. *Twice in as many weeks, this is getting out of hand.* He watched her spin around and slide on her knees, bringing the sword around in a deadly arc. If he had been a lesser fighter, that might've finished him right there; thankfully his reflexes were faster than hers, and he casually leaped her swing. Alarm bells rang in his head the minute he jumped as her thoughts were laid bare. *No!* Too late he saw his doom as she threw her sword away completely and grabbed his foot in mid-air. Curse the wench! But at least he saw her start to lose strength as she connected with him; the disease was spreading quickly. Then he hit the bridge, and as he jumped up onto his feet he felt the weakened wood give way under his weight as the anger fueled his power to decay the thick wood at an alarming rate.

He clawed at the support beams as he flailed away towards the rushing water, but couldn't grasp them with enough force to stop himself. Dar'Krist fell the twenty feet and hit the water with a mighty splash and sunk quickly out of sight as pieces of bridge hit him and the currents took him away, his cloak fluttering like an angry child, until that too sunk from view.

DAR'KRIST NEVER SAW the two people, one on each end of the ruined bridge, stare with mixed emotions at the cold rushing waters below. One, almost afraid of the sight, and the other, silently applauding the brave stand taken today. Karsis wove a quick spell and walked over the gap to comfort the woman, but before his feet could touch the other side, she grabbed him and sobbed uncontrollably into his shoulder. "There, there." He reached up and patted her on the head for loss of anything better to do, it was rare that someone caught him off his guard.

"Oh. I'm sorry." Carana sniffed and wiped her eyes as she let go of the bard. She hadn't lost her composure in over fifty years, but here she was weeping like a lovesick elf. Something about the man in front of her, seemed familiar, but she couldn't quite place it. No matter, she'd figure it out later. "We have to get back to the castle and let the king know what happened here," she said finally. She knew that Allissana had been touched, or had touched, the incarnation of Corruption, but if that boy was the One and he had embraced her before they hit the water, then maybe she had made it, only to drown. *Get it together Caran; they'll be fine, you were told that part at least.* She put her thoughts to rest and walked back to her exhausted horse. This was going to be a long trip.

Karsis watched her walk away towards the horse, which looked like it had run from all the way from the Snow Peak Mountains to here, and couldn't get past the sensation that he knew this woman. His mind was nagging him about it, so he shut it out and concentrated on the water instead. His *sight* couldn't see them and the way the current was moving they were a good deal down river by now.

He turned in a quick spin so that his jacket flowed out around him and bowed to the woman. "Gracious lady, may I ride with you, I seem to have mislaid my horse." He came up from his bow to find the angry face of the woman almost parallel with his. He hadn't even heard her move. Gone was the grief, and the tears, and her composure was rock steady.

"If you call me 'lady' one more time, prissy boy, they are going to be putting pieces of you back together for the next two decades." She pushed one stiff finger into his chest and instead of the soft flesh she expected, she found hardened muscle, but she didn't let it phase her. "Just who do you think you are in that getup anyway, Karsis the bard?"

He straightened his shoulders and flexed his arms a little to relax the jacket in case he had to teach this whelp a lesson. "In point of fact, tramp, I *am* Karsis the bard. Now, we can either ride to see my old friend the king, or I can spend the next few minutes leaving pieces of you all over this lovely ruined bridge. Well?" He waited for her to look him up and down, which everyone did when he made grandiose threats like that, and when she did, he had his sword already in hand. Unfortunately, so did she. They stared at each other for a couple of awkward silence before she spoke.

"Alright--you're good. You might even be who you claim to be, but that doesn't matter. We have to get to the castle. So, you don't call me lady, and I will entertain the notion that you're the great bard, okay?" She spun away and started tightening the straps on the saddle, putting away her sword in a blink of an eye.

He was impressed. "Okay, tramp. I can agree to that."

"Carana."

"What now?"

"My name is Carana. Now get on, or by Davalar, I'll leave you here."

He jumped up and slowly floated down onto the horse behind her, slowly sliding his arms around her waist as a lover might. "So, do I hold on to you... here?"

"Have you ever tried playing the harp without fingers?

"Can't say that I have, although there was this one time in Alrin when I only had one hand so...

"Oh, gods above what have I got myself into?" She clicked the reins to start the horse into a canter, and let the wind block out the voice. She was hiding it well, but she still couldn't believe that this was *The* Karsis the bard. *Get a grip girl, he could be a fake. Alright even I didn't believe that.* She laughed out loud, and it must've coincided with a witty remark because Karsis went right on with his story. This was going to be a very long ride indeed.

Karsis looked out over the countryside and tried to remember the last time he was here. It had been so many years ago, but then again that was the story of his life, wasn't it? He continued his asinine story, just trying to keep her off balance, and enjoyed the wind through his hair. Yes, sir, this was going to be one great trip indeed.

❧ 7 ❧

MEETINGS

H e was supposed to be in council, but no one was dumb enough to tell him that when he looked like this. The king stood at the open gates of Everknight Castle, staring down at the bustling city below. It was only a village in the time of his grandfather, and started to grow year by year. He watched the wagons navigate the narrow streets and shook his head.

"They'll make it, dear. Carana stayed behind to watch her back." Maressa placed a comforting hand upon the shoulders of her husband, her love, the man she couldn't tell her secret to. It would only upset him anyway.

"I've got one of those feelings, that's all." He turned and looked at his beautiful wife and smiled. It was genuine; she always made him smile when he looked into her eyes. He turned once again to watch the traffic below, and that's when he saw the horse and riders.

"Ho, the riders!" He called out, his heart lifting when he saw that someone was with Carana on her massive steed. But his voice died on the wind at his wife's shocked gasp next to him. He peered closer, allowing his eyes to see what his heart wouldn't. It wasn't his daughter behind the High General of Everknight. He started running then, great strides that took him closer to the news he dared not hear for fear of his soul breaking. *No, gods please not my daughter!* he thought, trying to run with tears building up in his eyes. Carana saw him and held her fist up to the sky--a sign that all was well. He stumbled, great heaving sobs of relief wracking him as he collapsed to the ground in mid-stride.

"The king is down!" came the call from the walls, and within seconds knights ran from the open gates with weapons drawn to cover their monarch. His wife beat them to it.

"Stand down! It's all right men!" The queen shouted to be heard over the clanking of armor and rattling of blades. Everyone was on edge lately. They had kept most of the troubles a secret, but rumors were as common in a castle as deceit, and they were all whispering about something coming to the castle from the north. "Arian, Love, stand so they can see that you're not dead... or I may kill you myself," she whispered to him, guiding him up to his feet.

"By Davalar--you would, wouldn't you?" He asked, finally gaining his feet in his great armor. The songs always left out how hard it was to stand back up in this heavy stuff. The knights saluted and started to surround the king and queen anyway; it was in their job description to be suffocating and overprotective.

Carana reigned in her horse and slid off, revealing the dandy behind her and Arian just about fell down again. "My King, the menace has been stopped." She hesitated for a second, trying not to choke up again. "The princess somehow collapsed the bridge, spilling him into the rampaging waters, but fell in after him."

"No!" The queen screamed and lost all composure, falling on the shoulders of her husband. "She can't swim!" Her tears came freely now. She had lost her baby girl, and it was all her fault.

Carana's stance faltered a bit, slight bend in one knee, but she recovered. Tears welled up in her eyes despite her bravado. "We need to speak privately my lord. Karsis has more to tell." She bowed and moved to the queen's side, hugging her and letting the woman bury her shoulder in her chest.

"Karsis, you come on the wind of grave tidings indeed." The king bowed his head slightly to the bard and then held out his hand eliciting gasps from most of his knights. The king gave them reproachful looks as he clasped the arm of one of his oldest friends. *They should know better. Could it be that they truly don't know who this is?* His thoughts were mired in grief knowing that his daughter fell this day, yet a pride swelled in him from somewhere.

A warming feeling, spreading out from his chest to cover his whole being, gave him strength and rooted his calm for all to see. She had saved the kingdom this day, and they needed to hear that. "Know this, knights; your princess has given her life for all of you this day, and she has made her father, her king, proud." He smiled at Karsis, who was biting back some awful retort if he knew the man at all. "Davalar be praised."

"Yes well, all very well and good but if we could follow the girls to a more private room your highness." Karsis swept by him, clapping him on the armor then spinning around two of the guards that tried to block his way. "You there, fine job but you may want to check the other horse coming up the road." He ducked one more knight with a grace they had never seen, and he was off skipping after the queen and the high general of Everknight like a child at a village dance.

Arian smiled, despite the grave news of the day. His god had given him strength--he knew that--and that was good enough for him until he talked to Karsis. Something more was going on here if that man was involved, and he only hoped some of it was good for once. "Men, no--come back there is no other horse..."

Maressa was lost inside of her own head. She was drowning herself in grief and there was no edge to grab a hold of. Then she felt strong arms encircle her, and whisper words to her. She couldn't hear them well though; they were like wisps of smoke in a field at night--hard to see and almost impossible to catch. One word came through her fog though. "Alive."

"Wait, what?!" The queen snapped out of it instantly. They were walking through the open gate, leaving her husband with the knights and Karsis. She stopped Carana and spun her around. "She's alive?"

"I said there is a *chance*, my Queen. She fell with a remarkable young man that seems to be related to your old friends in the north. He is a warrior and she yelled for him to grab her." Carana guided her once more, trying to get out from under any watching eyes.

"That must be Rhoven." Relief flooded her being, if he was as good as his mother, he could save her from drowning. "We've never met him, but of course we heard all about him from Tierra's letters." Oh, how she wished they were here right now; she missed her old friends so much. She longed to go back to the days of riding the countryside and fighting evil, carefree and wild.

"Okay, well now that you're better and I don't have to slap you silly, let's go before that bard starts singing again." Carana sighed as she saw him weaving through the knights to come after them. "Gods he wouldn't shut up the whole way home!"

"You don't know the half of it; you should see Karsis when he drinks." They turned and went in, and Maressa silently thanked all of the gods that Karsis was here. She knew he would know things about all of this, and with his attitude, he would also probably knock some sense into the council as well. *And gods if he doesn't look the same as he did all those years ago.* She shook her head as if to clear it. She'll think about that later.

From his vantage point high on the walls, the figure whispered to the wind and focused in on what the queen was saying. The wind groaned in response, obeying despite not wanting to leave the high skies. "Hmm, Karsis... Well, that makes this whole thing interesting." He turned away, not bothering to hear more, especially if the legendary bard was there. He was rumored to have learned magic from the elves themselves. He let the wind go, and felt it soar upwards in protest. He thought about how this may change things, and realized that it might work to his advantage after all. "Time to play the great game then. Your move Karsis." He passed into the castle, his cloak swirling into a hidden pocket and went to his room to think.

An hour later, the four of them were sitting in the king's personal chambers, out of their armor and sipping drinks like old friends. It seemed funny to Arian to see Carana look out of place. "So--what you're saying is that this book you have predicted Rhoven and Allissana would have to be at the bridge to stop the incarnation of corruption?" He just couldn't wrap his head around this. He missed the days when he didn't have this much responsibility, back when he was a small boy.

"In a nutshell, yes." Karsis was pacing with a drink in his hand, and he kept throwing Carana looks every couple of minutes. Why did she draw him so? "However, unless you are someone trained in prophesy, reading it--even hearing it--can be dangerous. He caught Carana shoot the queen a subtle look, and filed it away for later.

"And you're sure that the northern villages are gone?" Maressa felt a little better, once she had heard an actual account of the battle on the bridge. She was so proud of her little fighter.

"Yes, my Queen." Karsis stopped and leaned on a table. "Norhil Hold should be intact, as Tanan has an ingenious plan if I know his devious mind, and we saw the wagons heading here before the fight, I believe they stopped in the outer villages first.

"We've just had reports of the refugees. We're putting them up outside of the city in tents for now." Arian was calm again, and collected; his natural leadership skills shone through the gloom of the day. Even without his armor, he seemed a knight in shining armor. "Without Gareth and Tierra's sacrifice we would've lost a lot more people."

"Ah, well about that your majesty." Karsis finally sat in one of the comfy chairs and threw his legs over the side, swirling his drink. "You see there is a good chance that they are alive as well. Maybe not in one piece, but alive." Karsis was saving that little tidbit until everyone had started to come down from their 'she's alive' high.

"How?" Carana and Maressa exclaimed at once, the former jumping out of her chair almost in excitement.

Funny--Maressa seems confused, but Carana seems like she's just going along with it, he thought. This woman was perplexing him more and more every second. This is what others must feel like when dealing with him. "To put it simply, Rhoe touched them, or more importantly, he embraced them. This will cancel out the rotting effect of his touch and lessen the draining power that his mere presence induces." He watched the confused looks around the room, all except one.

"And Tanan? He could've made it too?" The king asked with an anxious crack to his voice. Arian sounded hopeful, which was funny because those two had never seen eye to eye. Funny how they remained friends but the king and Gareth fell out. *Ah yes, I've always meant to find out what drove them apart, but so many evils, so little time.* Karsis's thoughts were quick though because his favorite mystery was about to speak.

"I've studied some prophesy before Karsis, and have even

read the book you're talking about. If he embraced Lord Tanan, then yes, he should be fine. However, that doesn't stop the thing from killing them with force." She wasn't going to speak up, but she saw the way the legendary bard was watching her. He knew something, and she had played this game for way too many years to fall into this trap. Carana stood up and walked to the window, looking high out over the city below. She had watched that city grow and now it could all tumble away. "I know you know the stories Karsis--you all do--but this thing wouldn't die from water; it would only slow him down." She was still worried about Allissana deeply.

"Slow him down? You mean my daughter almost drowned for nothing?!" Arian was getting angry. He was a man of action and the frustration was setting back in.

Well, that didn't take long at all, he thought. "Actually, it will slow him down considerably, and if you've figured out from that book where they are headed Carana, you would know that." He laughed then, knowing where they were going and what would be meeting them. *May the gods have mercy on your sanity young one.*

"Well, I for one am thankful that we all have a chance at least." The queen felt better, without knowing why exactly. The gods must be watching over them. *Well technically they were,* she thought, stealing a glance at Carana. "Let's get you settled in a room Karsis. I assume you'll be staying for a bit?"

"Why thank you your grace. And yes, I'll stay on for a little bit, but I have to get to the Misty Woods in about five or six days. At least I hope to." He watched Carana for a reaction, not buying her cover up on reading the book one bit. "Then I will return."

"And I will send a patrol up north to search for our friends. They have to know we haven't given up on them." He hung his head, his shoulders heavy with the responsibility of remaining at the castle. *They need me. I should be the one to go, but I can't leave the traitors here in my absence.* His thoughts were turning dark, so it was time for him to retire from this happy reunion before he spoiled it. "Karsis, if you need anything—" he began, then caught himself. "Oh, who am I kidding? You'll just take it without asking." He laughed and rose, setting his drink down. He stretched and then bent down to kiss his wife. "Good eve lovely, I'm off to do some paper work. Please entertain our guest in my absence?"

Her eyes were troubled; she knew his thoughts too well. "Of course, my dear. Then I will retire and entertain you as well, so hurry up with those reports, lest you find them thrown to the floor by my own hand." With a wink to Karsis, she smiled and Arian laughed on his way out.

Carana watched the two legendary lovers and felt a pang in her own chest. She had always wanted something like that, but could never even try. The solitude of immortality is disconsolate thing. That was when she caught Karsis looking at her again. This time he wasn't so much scrutinizing her, but the look he had was one of... pity? *That's right, he's supposed to be a lot older than he looks, and the queen said he looked the same as when they last met, over two decades ago.* Her thoughts were spinning. Could he have the same problems, albeit on a smaller scale?

Just then Karsis seemed to come to a stunning conclusion, for he jumped up and shouted for joy at the window. "Thank the gods! I had forgotten all about that!" He frantically downed his drink, then the king's as well, grabbing the two ladies' hands and pulling them to their feet, subtly whispering some ether into the queen's direction to make her forget her troubles for a time. He had to be cautious, as she was a master bard as well.

"What, Karsis? Is there some other evil coming? Are we besieged?" Carana was ready for battle, if only he would tell her what was coming.

The queen was laughing, all the stress falling off of her like so many cobwebs in a flame. "No, Carana. I think he just realized that our favorite tavern would still be here. Am I right old friend?" His laugh was infectious, and she could use the time away from the castle, though that felt weird.

"Why yes my dear, forgot all about it till just now. That's when you know evil is afoot--when I forget about The Laughing Sprite." He twirled around, sending his longcoat flowing out and hitting the girls as he spun round and round. He produced a lute out of his magical inner pocket and started to play as he danced around the room and out into the hall, singing the entire time:

The drinks are cheap and the food is stale,
but the girls are pretty, healthy, and hale.
The barkeep's nice, but really can't smile,
'cause he sees me coming from at least a mile!
Now let's away 'afore the rush
and take our fun from the drunken lush.
Here it is, we're almost there.
I'm ready to find a wench so fair
to wash away all sorts of fears
and drink and dance all through the night.
I'll make my way down by the pier
and find my home in the Laughing Sprite!

KARSIS'S VOICE echoed down the hall as he finished the chorus and broke into another refrain of inanity.

"Gods, that was horrid." Carana had been around for ages and had never heard that particular song, and she thanked

Davalar for that small miracle. "Will he be doing that all night?"

"Oh, my dear Carana, are you in for a treat. Yes, he will be doing that most of the night. I can't believe he remembered that song." The queen was almost blushing, that song had brought back so many memories that she was dizzy. "We wrote that together during one drunken night when we closed the place. We lost a bet and had to write a song about the tavern that no bard would want to sing."

"Well, you succeeded--I've never heard that one." Carana sighed. She hated to admit it, but she needed this too. "Let's go. I can regret this in the morning."

"Oh, you will." The queen was skipping now, following the hallway where Karsis was still singing in the distance. "It wouldn't be fun if you didn't!" She didn't plan on staying too late, she really wanted to find Arian later, but she had a devious plan of setting these two up for the night. They needed it.

Ruins of Daelyn

IT HAD TAKEN days to search the ruins of the town for any survivors. Everyone should've evacuated, but sometimes frontier people were stubborn. Gareth was still a mess--his ribs almost all broken by her guess. She wasn't a priest, but she knew the signs from seeing them on him in the past. She wasn't much better.

Her arm was broken in at least three places, and she was pretty sure her hip was so thrown out of place she could rest her chin on it. *That was one of the worst fights I've ever been in,* she thought, *and I've been in some doozies.* They had found the twins, or at least they had found Rythal. His brother was a decaying mess that made even Gareth wretch when he saw it. She had taken the little one aside to check him out and he had as many broken bones as they did, but most of them weren't crippling. Mostly his collar bone, arms and his right leg. But he would heal--physically at least.

"What the hell were those two doing up here?" Gareth asked, as he came back from burying Innal. He wasn't supposed to be doing anything but resting, but he never listened anyway. He winced as he sat down next to her to catch his breath, as deep breaths hurt like hell.

"I'm not sure." Tierra was just as confused by that. Everyone had gotten away, only Old Fannie had stayed that they knew of. She was rotted just like Innal, but they found her sitting in her favorite chair on her porch. Just being near that thing was enough she guessed. "The only thing I could get out of Rythal was that a voice told him to come back and *save us*." She shook her head, still amazed that they were even alive.

"Think Rhoe is okay?" Her husband asked. He clearly was still worried, but after fighting that thing, they had every right to be, Karsis or no Karsis.

"Yeah, you heard the bard--he had to be at that bridge to face this thing." Tierra shuddered again, and it had nothing to do with the afternoon chill in the air. "He was supposed to stop it there, and then go on a trip with some girl." She looked down at her shattered arm. "And the last thing we did was lie to him."

"Hey now, it's alright. You taught him all sorts of control, and Karsis says that's what takes the longest when you're training wizards." He didn't know anything about that, but for once he was listening to that dandy. Then something made his skin tingle, and he got that feeling down his spine that he only got when someone was watching him.

"Gareth?" She saw him tense without turning around and reach for his axe that was no longer there. She scanned the road without moving her head and saw it: a figure just in the shadows of the forge, slinking towards them. She stretched her arm behind her and started to undo the steel ball from the braid in her hair.

"You know what I need honey? I need a kiss." Gareth leaned forward, seeing that she was doing something behind her back. He figured if she needed cover, his bulk would do fine.

Just then, something rolled into the street and rushed them before she could bring her arm around. A small hand grabbed her wrist and flipped over her so he was out of the reach of Gareth.

"Wait, don't hit me!" The Lord of Norhil Hold landed softly and winced, feeling his sprained ankle give a little more.

"Tanan!" Gareth roared, surging to his feet and instantly regretting it. His ribs grated and he sat back down hard, breathing through the pain.

Tierra twisted Tanan's arm to free her own, and sent him sprawling before she heard her husband's exclamation. He hit the dirt and rolled with it, crying out as his bruised back landed on rocks. "Gods Tanan, don't you know better than to sneak up on us?"

"Wasn't... sure... you were... you. " He was trying to breathe as well, and he finally sat up and they saw that he was just as badly beaten as they were. "Let me guess--tall fellow, black cloak, powerful as hell and massive temper to go along with it?"

"Tell us that Norhil Hold didn't fall. Did Rhoe make it through?" Tierra was worried now. She assumed that between them and Tanan's forces they could've stopped it, even though Karsis said they had no chance.

"Well, that thing didn't get inside, but that's only because I fooled him. Bastard destroyed Morlan though." He stretched his good arm--well his less-hurt arm--and bowed his head for his fallen sword. "That damn blade saw me through a lot of fights."

He stood up finally, and looked around at the broken buildings and smoldering blacksmith's shop.

"He beat me good, even though I should've had him. Threw me in a ditch and left me for dead." He kicked a rock, just because it was looking at him funny, and looked at his friends with solemn eyes. "I'm glad you're alive. When I realized I wasn't dead, I rolled out of the ditch and took off up here, hoping against hope that I could find you." He saw the expectation in Tierra's eyes, and realized he forgot all about the most important detail.

"Yes, Tierra--Rhoe did make it through and left on horseback with Karsis before that thing arrived. If it weren't for them, the entire hold would've been slaughtered." He had missed his old friends, and he couldn't believe how much Rhoe had grown.

"He told me to save you." The voice behind them made them all jump, not one of the trained adventurers even hearing the boy approach, dragging a broken leg at that. His eyes were distant, and his voice was scratchy. His whole demeanor was that of a wild rat that had been drowned, brought back to life, then thrown off of a cliff.

"Rythal? What's wrong?" Gareth was worried about the boy; his mind must've been shattered as bad as his leg was at seeing his twin brother die like that. He shook his head sadly, feeling helpless.

"He told me to save you." The boy was like an empty shell at the moment, no intelligence darted behind those vacant eyes.

The healers are going to have their hands full with this one, Tierra thought as she led him back to his blanket. She laid him down and made sure he had something under his head. She didn't know if he had a concussion, but there was nothing for it now. Rest was what he needed, that and to stay off that leg. She checked the splint she had made and tightened it just in case. "Now no more getting up little one." She kissed his forehead and hobbled back to her companions. It seemed they were in the middle of something.

"Yes, he would send someone Gareth, don't worry. You two still not speaking?" Tanan wasn't upset, but she knew when he was trying not to sound angry, and this was one of those times. She sighed to herself. The years had stretched on and the king and Gareth hadn't spoken more than two words in all that time.

"If he thinks we're even alive Tanan--and we shouldn't be." He made a fist, because he was unable to kick something with his ribs the way they were. Gods above he wanted to hit something! "The refugees have made it by now, and all he cares about is the people. They're safe, end of discussion."

"Boys, boys." Tierra limped over and put a hand on her husband. "Arian will most certainly send someone up here, if only to assess the damage." She winked at Tanan, to show him she was placating the big man. "But don't you think for one second that the king wouldn't want to recover the bodies of his old companions." Her visage grew serious, and she moved directly in front of her husband.

"And if you don't trust him, then trust me." Her eyes softened, and she bowed her head. "We were all so close--like family--and I've never pried into what happened between you and Arian, but I beg you. Think past your anger and remember what a good friend he was."

Tanan felt out of place. Watching these two have this moment was truly heartening; however, since he didn't have a special someone, he may vomit what was left in his stomach any moment. "Can we get all mushy on the road guys?" He kicked a rock around the street, trying not to look at the lovebirds. "I mean, we can bunker down at the Hold until someone arrives, and it would be better for the whelp than this street."

Gareth threw his hands up in mock surrender. "Okay, okay.

I'll admit that Arian wouldn't leave us to rot--does that make you happy?" He grabbed her shoulders, gently staring into her eyes.

"As happy as a one-armed warrior can be my love." She bent her head and raised up on her tiptoes to kiss him gently, then turned to Tanan. "And you're right, let's build a stretcher and get that boy to the Hold. In our condition it should take about what... five days?"

"By all the lonely gods I wish you were kidding." Tanan tried not to laugh, because it hurt something awful to do that, but they did all share a smile. They made a stretcher and started their feet shuffling towards Norhil Hold to wait for help to arrive.

The Rushing River

THE WATER WAS MERELY an annoyance to Dar'Krist, but the rocks were more of a deterrent to him. He could hold his breath for an incredible amount of time, and his powerful limbs could navigate almost any current. He could propel himself up to get air when he needed it, and he didn't care about getting wet. Bashing into large rocks at the speed he was going, however, put a damper on regulating his air.

He threw his *sight* ahead of him in the raging, spring-swollen waters, and tried to keep himself straight. If he started spinning again, *sight* wouldn't help him all that much. His arms went out wide and he pushed up to break the surface again, to grab a good lung-busting amount of air, and to peek at his surroundings. He crashed back into the river and cursed under his held breath. There was no way he could get to the edge because sheer cliffs bordered the river on both sides and rose more than fifty feet above the water. He could only guess that he was being carried through the 'End of the World' mountain range, but only because they have been here as long as he had been alive.

He had been close to unconscious for most of the trip, as the bridge landed around him and pinned him under for a while, and even his great strength couldn't lift all of it and hold his breath this long. *Curse those two children!* He thought, and immediately paid for his lapse in concentration as he started to spin around with the current. His sight honed in again and it seemed like the water was rock free for the moment. He sent it up and out and saw that there was a break in the rock wall coming up. *Finally,* he thought, *I can get out of this damned river.*

He drew power from the water around him and shot out sideways, swimming powerfully against the rapid current. He broke the surface and let his *sight* go, swimming and using that could be disorienting, at best. He used his eyes as his guide and then he saw the green trees and the pristine beach that lay ahead. His eyes widened then, as he saw that young warrior staring right at him and pointing. All but helpless in the water, Dar'Krist cursed under his breath and put his head down and swam for all he was worth. He knew what the boy was going to do, curse all the gods, and there wasn't anything he could do about it.

❧

RHOE WAS RUNNING out of options. He held a piece of bridge with one arm and an unconscious girl with the other. The weight of their wet clothes was dragging against the current, threatening to pull him under, and her wet cloak was tangled around his waist. They had fallen together, spinning downward after the rotted bridge, but he at least had the satisfaction of seeing that damned man hit the water and the main part of the bridge slam into him. He had tried a wind spell during the rapid fall, but with her and the air rushing by it didn't work; he could've sworn he didn't hit the water as hard as he could've.

She had screamed and blacked out, either from fear of heights or water. He only managed not to drown right away because of the large piece of bridge he hit when the rain-gorged waters swept him up and threw him around like a ragdoll. Out of reflex he grabbed what he hit so it wouldn't keep pummeling him, and it kept him afloat. He dragged her over it and had managed to not black out. The current was so fast that he couldn't even track the landmarks as they swept down river. He knew they were going fast, and it was everything he could do to stay on this makeshift float. He saw a forest at one point--they must've traveled miles in a matter of minutes--but then he noticed the mountains coming.

They had been bashed against rocks and spun around so much that the only way he knew where he was going was the way the river was dragging them. At one point he lost his grip and was under for a long time before pulling himself up; then he had hit a rock so hard that he was almost torn away from the float. Only his mother's training at control kept him alive. He didn't know how badly she was injured, but at least one of his legs was either broken, or a muscle was badly torn, and maybe three or four ribs were cracked. One of his eyes was swollen shut because of a rock that almost broke apart the bridge float, and the fingers on the hand holding her were mangled from a rock that they had smashed into.

Now he was losing strength and the walls of this mountain valley they were hurtling through seemed endless. His thoughts oddly weren't for himself, but for the poor girl that would drown if he succumbed to the current. He closed his eyes and searched deep within himself for more strength, more endurance, but the bard's tales were just that. There was nothing there that he hadn't already used up twice. The only thing that he did have inside him... *Gods above I'm fool,* he berated himself. He had tried to summon the winds to break his fall, but had tried nothing with the water. "Ash'anti, water, hadar ea ubel." He sputtered through the lapping waters going up and over them. He prayed that it worked the way he asked. He had tried to have the water hold him up, but he had only just started learning the elven tongue, and he wasn't sure. Then he felt it. The water swirled around him, buoying him, and carrying him in a field of calm.

He breathed a deep sigh. Just then a break in the mountain wall drew his eye. It seemed that there was a beach near a forest. However, past that, the mountain wall seemed to keep going into the horizon. Sobbing with hope, he started kicking as hard as he could to the side; with the calm water swirling around him, it was almost easy, the water seeming to understand what he needed. Within moments he was panting on the sands, pulling the girl up and kicking their way out of the water. He was exhausted, but when he looked back at the river that they had narrowly escaped, he saw a form swimming at the same shore and coming quite fast.

"Oh no you don't. This time you're going to stay down." He pushed to his feet, standing on his ruined leg, and pointed at the figure just to make sure the water knew what he was targeting. "Ash'anti water Sistren dwoen dosit krist!" he yelled, conveying the urgency that, this time, he needed. Then, for reasons he didn't fully understand, and was too tired to even notice, he said it again without the elven words. "Please water, take down this evil!" This was what he tried to do on the bridge, until she shocked the linens right off of him, and he lost concentration.

The thing must've seen what he was going to do, because he

was swimming even harder now. He almost made it too. Almost. Tendrils of water, as thick as tree trucks bashed into the figure, as smaller ones wrapped around his waist, pulling him back into the center of the raging waters.

The figure screamed once, then disappeared under the white caps as the larger tendrils collapsed down upon him, sweeping past the beach and on into the horizon. Rhoe looked upon this and smiled, then promptly gave in to the blackness and pain that had been waiting like a jealous lover at midnight to pounce. The last thing he saw was the girl's face, smiling contently next to him in the clean sand. *Funny, she doesn't even look hurt...* and then he thought no more for a time.

How strange. Liana had never seen people like this before. They weren't sprites, or dryads; they didn't have wild hair like a korred, or even wings like some of the other faeries. She had heard the one with the white hair speak elven, yet he didn't seem to be an elf. Oh, sure he had the hair of an elf, but not the ears, and didn't elves dress better than robes?

"Breathe," she told herself. She was getting all worked up and Avaryn always told her to breathe when she got carried away. She wished he were here. Then she remembered that she could call him with her whistle! Wait, they were sleeping, then she wondered briefly why they were napping on the beach, and her curiosity overwhelmed her, like it did every hour or so, and she flitted out to take a peek at them. She was only about four-teen inches tall, with gossamer wings and curly hair, and she flew quickly over them, for fear of waking them and then they would see her. Heavens they were big, and that one was female! "Oh a girl thing!" She got carried away and blurted it out, then flew quickly back into the trees, lest they awake and eat her. She hid behind a tree and peeked out, and saw that they were still sleeping.

What are you doing little one? Avaryn's voice sounded in her tiny head. He had sensed a presence here and his queen had sent him to investigate. Why was he not surprised that Liana was here?

"Oh Avaryn! LookIdon'tknowwhattheyarebuttheyaresleeping!" She ran on with her words so fast that if he didn't have telepathy he would have been lost. She was an excitable little faerie, and that was what he liked about her.

Calm down little one. Breathe. He snorted once, knowing that when she got this excited it was nigh impossible to calm her down. To his utter astonishment, she took a deep breath and blew it out.

"Okay. I saw these two come out of the water, and he spoke-someelvenwords–" She stopped herself and took another steadying breath. "He spoke some elven words and he asked the water to do tricks. Then he fell asleep next to her. And itsa-girlthingAvaryn!" Another breath. Then a deeper breath.

Okay, let me go and see them. They look like humans, though if you say that the one with the white hair asked the water to help him, he may be elven. He calmly walked out onto the beach, his hooves digging in deep with his great weight. The sand was loose and warm, and he could smell blood. He shook his mane out once, then saw that the male was indeed hurt, and horribly so. She was fine however, not a scratch on her. *Funny that,* he thought, then he heard tiny wings and sighed to himself with practiced ease. He knew she wouldn't be able to stay away. He needed to let the queen know about this, mainly because this wasn't the dark presence he had felt. He closed his eyes and sent out his *sense*. There it was. Far away down the river, but heading this way. That was when Avaryn *sensed* just what it was. It was an incarnation. Great. They were in very deep trouble.

"Are they alright? Do we need to fix them? Oh, my Trees is that *blood*?!" She flew down and hovered over the man's leg, poking it with her tiny sword.

She saw that Avaryn was gazing out at the river, and his eyes were all cloudy. She had the sudden fear that he was under a spell! Quickly she flew into his face and started to shake his head back and forth. "Avaryn! Are you okay? Ohmygodtheygo-tyouwhatamIgoingtodo?" She was in a panic, and she just about had an episode when the woman on the sand stirred and made a weird noise.

"Ahh!" Liana screamed and flew straight up, gathering her courage.

Stop little one, I'm fine. The girl is coming awake, do try and calm down. Avaryn nudged the woman and tried to help her come back to the conscious world. He would need some answers, and soon. He gauged that the thing would be here in about three days, and then... well, things would get interesting.

Liana hovered in the air, then slowly fluttered down to the girl as she tried to sit up. "Hi, I'm Liana, I'm sorry that I thought you tried to control my friend." She flittered around the woman's head as she tried to find the source of the tiny voice. "But it has been an eventful day so far, and I'm kind of excitable."

Kind of?

"HEY!"

Just saying.

She was lost in a strange place. She felt safe, yet knew that she was in danger. Pulled in two different directions, Allissana chose to stand her ground in the middle and not budge. She looked one way and saw the bridge collapse, the young warrior flying to her rescue and grabbing her just like she had asked--nay, begged him to.

The other way she saw a comfortable room with everything she needed. It was a warm, safe, place. A place where she wouldn't have to deal with the threats of the realm. *That was never me,* she thought, and walked towards the bridge. She saw it then, what had happened before she passed out. She had seen the water down below, and her inability to swim and how high up they were had caused her to scream and blackout.

That was the last thing she remembered. Her eyes opened slowly as sounds started to come to her. She was lying down, on something not rock or grass, and there was a horse snorting, and some sort of other sound. Rushing water? She tried to sit up, and immediately got a formal letter from her head to never do that again. Then she heard the tiny voice and she swung her head slowly around searching for where it was coming from. She saw the tiny faerie and her eyes went wide.

"Did you say your name was Liana?" Allissana asked, not sure if she had hit her head that hard or if she was still dreaming. She saw Rhoe next to her with her peripheral vision and she relaxed a bit knowing that he was still with her. *Now why is that?* she thought, but decided to ask herself later.

"I did, I did! That'smynamewhatsyours?" Liana had landed in front of the girl thing, now that it seemed that she wasn't going to try and eat her, at least right away. She noticed Avaryn lowering his horn to the man's leg, channeling his energy through it to heal the man's wounds a bit. This frightened the girl thing a bit and Liana flew up and tried to calm her. Blind leading the deaf. "No, No. It's okay, breathe." She made an exaggerated motion of breathing, proud that she could help someone else for once with this mantra. She heard Avaryn snort through his healing and shot him a scowl just to keep him honest.

"Oh Rhoe! Is he okay? What is your horse—" Allissana

stopped suddenly when she saw what Avaryn really was. He was defiantly not a horse. There, healing her would-be rescuer with his horn, was a unicorn! The magnificent beast was at least fifteen hands high—thank the gods she worked in the stables as a child—and had a beautiful gleaming white coat. His mane was a silver shimmer and his horn protruded at least a foot and a half out from his head. "Oh, I see. I must be mad then. I've lost it. Great." She laughed to herself a little, and seeing the confused tiny face looking at her she laughed even more.

"You are kind of a crazy girl thing, you know that?" Liana put her tiny hands on her hips and gave the girl her best 'what do you think you're doing?' face. Trees know that she had seen others give it to her enough.

"I'm sorry, it's just been a bad couple of days." She composed herself, slightly, and finally stood up in the soft sand. She couldn't give her real name, unsure of where she was or if she had enemies here. Her mother had taught her that. "My name is Liss, and it is a pleasure to meet you."

If you would be so kind as to place this boy on my back, we can bring you both to where our queen waits. Avaryn wasn't going to talk with her, but if he had Liana translate they would be here for at least three hours. He nudged the boy over towards her to show her what he wanted, then watched her face as she looked around for the source of this new voice. It dawned on her then that the unicorn in front of her was talking in her head. If he could have, he would have laughed.

"Is that you in my head?" She had thought there was another faerie around her, but then she saw the unicorn nudge the body of Rhoe and everything clicked. *Well, they were supposed to be magical. Also supposed to not exist either, but hey.* Her thoughts were in a tumble. She needed to think, but had no time. What was it that her mother always tried to teach her? 'Footprints in the sand aren't made by sitting' or something like that. *No idea what that means but let's just go with instinct.* She grabbed Rhoe and gently tried to lift him up. His dead weight made it hard to lift him the way she wanted to. She stumbled in the sand and he landed face down. This was not the way things were supposed to go. In all the stories she heard, things like this didn't happen to the heroes. Lying bards.

"I'll help! I may be little but I've got a strong heart!" Liana flew down and grabbed a handful of wet robe and beat her wings furiously, her little face turning deep red with the effort. To her surprise, the body moved! "I'm doing it! I'm doing it!" Then the body sat up faster than she was pulling and she flew off across the sand, tumbling head over wings.

Rhoe became aware of his surroundings all at once, like snapping out of a bad dream in a thunderstorm. He was on the sand and evil was coming. He moved his arm a little, then the thought of the girl laying helpless next to him had him sitting, then rolling to his feet quickly. His astonishment at seeing what seemed to be a unicorn only slightly outweighed the sight of the girl he had saved. She was standing, soaking wet, but apparently unharmed. Not a scratch. He looked down at his own leg, expecting to see how bad it was, and felt his mouth open even further when he saw most of his wounds closed and starting to heal.

How long was I out? Rhoe thought as he looked around, trying not to notice the obviously mythical creature standing next to him. He sighed mentally, and turned to the girl first. "Are you okay?" he asked her, moving cautiously to her side, not knowing what was going on. "By the way, what's your name? We were a bit busy when I introduced myself."

Allissana smiled, not knowing why she liked the boy so much. "My name is Liss, and I haven't thanked you for saving me back there." She looked around then, noticing the beautiful forest behind them.

Rhoe looked around too, and it was then that he saw the little winged form fly up covered in sand. He blinked a couple of times, then shook his head to clear it.

"Youthrewmeacrossthebeachyousillyman!" Liana wasn't excitable, she was so far into the realm of hysterics that there wasn't a word for it yet. She hated sand in her wings, it made her itch terribly.

"Liana, it's okay--he didn't mean to." Liss was starting to like this little hyper thing. She had always loved the old faerie stories and dreamed of becoming one when she was a little girl. Now that one was right in front of her, her childhood came rushing back.

"Okay--faeries and unicorns." Rhoe was sure he may still be dreaming. "Where in the heavens are we?"

Unicorn. Singular. Something about this young boy was nagging at Avaryn's thoughts.

"What now?" Rhoe looked around for the source of the voice.

You said unicorns, as in many, but I am only one. In fact, I am the last one of my kind. The boy had no pointed ears, but his hair was plainly elven, not the sickly white of age. He stood as a warrior might, and even moved to shield his friend when he awoke out of instinct. The queen needed to meet this one.

"Oh, that makes sense--it's only the unicorn speaking in my head." Rhoe chuckled to himself. "Karsis would love this right now, probably have something witty to say."

"You. Know. Karsis?!" Liana fluttered right up to his face, her eyes dancing with delight and her voice getting higher with each word. She had completely forgotten how much sand was stuck to her gossamer wings. In fact, they beat so quickly that most of the tiny flecks flew right off.

Avaryn, closed his eyes and snorted. This was taking too long. *Can we please at least talk on the way to the queen? We don't have long before that thing you washed away comes back. Maybe two or three days.*

"What?" Rhoe and Liss both exclaimed at once, scaring poor Liana into hiding behind Avaryn. Rhoe couldn't believe that the thing was alive, never mind on his way back. Somehow though he could *sense* the truth from this mythical creature. "Okay, it... I'm sorry, he is right. I think the unicorn is a he, I mean it sounds like a boy in my head, right?" Rhoe's thoughts were spinning, it was coming back.

My name is Avaryn young one. Gods above these humans were almost as bad as some faeries. *It's about a day's walk to the Court of Trees, and we can talk along the way.*

"Sounds perfect. Avaryn, my name is Rhoven, or Rhoe for short, and with the rest we seem to have gotten, I think we can walk till dusk, then find a place to sleep." He was still confused on how long he had been out, and what had healed him? The faerie? The unicorn? He never thought he would miss Karsis after their long trip, but...

"Letsgoletsgoletsgo!" Liana had given up with calm--this boy thing knew Karsis! She hadn't seen him in over ten years but still remembered the time he stayed with them for a while. "The faster we go, the quicker I can hear how you know Karsis the Faerie King!!"

They walked off of the beach and into the forest. There were no plain trails like the humans would have, only animal trails, but it was still better than nothing. Allissana--or Liss as she was to these people for the moment--was astonished. Rhoe claimed to know the famous bard Karsis, and then these faeries seem to think that he would be their king? This was a world that only had existed in stories for her, and it felt like a waking dream.

And then there was this boy.

She kept saying "boy," but he had to be at least eighteen like she was. Yet he was so carefree that it seemed he was young. As she walked behind them she stared at his back, the wet robe clinging to his muscled frame. She hadn't noticed during the fight, but he was truly a warrior. The way he walked, with perfect balance, reminded her of how Carana danced with her sword. Liana and Rhoe were deep in conversation about Karsis and she had the feeling they didn't know she was still there.

She wasn't used to being ignored, being the princess and all, but for the time being, it was a blessing. It gave her a couple of hours to think some of these things through, and sort her mind. *Like why he was in my dreams, and why, oh why, do I feel this attraction to him, like we were meant to find each other.* She shook her head and tried to get the sand out of her wits.

Rhoe never thought that he would find someone to out-talk the great bard. Yet here she was. He liked the little faerie, but he was starting with a headache. She was almost as bad as the twins. "So he was named an official king because he had married the old queen accidentally?"

"Yupyup, and he has the seal of the Trees and everything." She flittered around trees and branches effortlessly, drifting on the breeze, all the while never faltering in her babbling.

"The trees?" He was missing something here, he could hear it in her voice. The dense forest all around him felt like it was studying him, like it knew him. He saw the huge trees soar into the canopy, and knew that these woods were ancient.

"No silly--Trees!" She flew down and around, grabbing his belt and pulling to the left. "Look, elves have their gods, but here, the Trees protect us."

"Ah, I see, or at least I think I see." He glanced all around one more time and tried to *see*. The trees were so old here, older than any other tree. That much he got from his *sight*. They had roots that traveled down so far that depth was inconceivable to even this form of vision. He was taken aback. "This is the root of magic isn't it? Trees this old, the elements this primal?" he asked without knowing how he would know that, like it was instinctual. He saw Avaryn stop in mid-stride with one hoof in the air and stay that way for a couple of seconds. It was then that he forgot that his *sight* was still on. He saw Avaryn through and through, the very heart of magic coursing through his blood, focused all the way up into his horn. He was somehow ashamed at what he saw, almost like it was a private moment he had intruded upon.

It's okay young wizard. If you truly know Karsis, then I trust you knowing what you saw. Not many know the truth of what unicorns actually are. He was shocked that this young one knew how to use *sight*, not very well mind you, but still it was truly astonishing. Maybe Liana wasn't embellishing when she said he had asked the water for help. *Just try not to use that on any other being until you are out of the forest. Some are not as forgiving, especially of humans.*

Liss saw Rhoe staring at Avaryn, after he had talked about the Trees, then he bowed. Not just any bow, but one of clear reverence. She would give anything to know what they had talked about in his head.

"Comeoncomeon!" Liana yelled from up ahead, "I found a spot they can snoozeforabit!" She was getting worked up again, and couldn't wait to talk around a campfire for a while. She hadn't done that in forever!

They passed through the tall oaks and pines, never seeing the little eyes watching them. So intent were they on each other, that he never had to hide that well. He knew trouble when he saw it, and these newcomers were that and a bag of berries.

ᘚ 8 ᘞ

FRIENDS ALONG THE WAY

Waves of pain shot through Karsis' head. He had been awake for over an hour, and he still hadn't stood up. He had closed the little tavern last night with Carana, and had tried to keep up with her drink for drink. That was a bad idea--worse than when he had kicked that dragon in the shin. He had even tried to take her to bed, but had been thwarted, which rarely happened.

"Good morning Karsis." Carana's voice pierced through the haze. She was already up and cheerful. *That woman was truly born of evil*, he thought.

"Did you ever find someone to warm your bed last night?" Carana asked. She was actually quite fond of the bard and was wholeheartedly impressed with his performance last night—both on stage and on her—but the last thing she needed was another complication.

He finally rose, spun around, and whispered to the ether under his breath to relieve his mind of the pain. "Dear Carana, I did not. None in this fine establishment could hold a candle to you. So, alas, I slept alone in the dark." He wondered briefly where the queen got to last night; it wasn't like him to miss things like that. She still had it after all these years.

"Well let's up and to the castle. There is a council meeting that you may want to sit in on, and it would make me smile to see you thrash those pompous asses verbally." She rarely spoke so much, but this flippant bard seemed to put her completely at ease.

"Lead the way, high general." He bowed at her and immediately regretted it. The rush of blood to his head erased the slight fix he had put on it, and he felt dizzy on top of that. The last thing he wanted to do was listen to pompous windbags. They sauntered up to the castle proper, passing the early morning merchants and workers in the streets.

The crowds stared at him as he walked by with his confident gait, and he saw in their visage the rumors that were flying around town. By now everyone knew that Allissana had 'fallen,' and everyone looked heartbroken about the princess. She was well-liked. That would be good for her return. They passed the gates without delay, mainly because the high general said so. Within the hour they were outside the king's chambers and wondering if they should bother him.

"The door is usually open this time of day," Carana mentioned, worry in her voice. Her hand was on her sword out of habit, and she was scanning the hallway for danger. "I don't hear any sounds of trouble but—" She never finished the comment, because her mouth fell open when Karsis opened the door and danced in.

"Knock knock, hope you have clothes on!" Karsis said as he barged in. He had heard the worry in her voice and decided against propriety. Besides, they were his friends and would forgive him. Maybe. "Ready to greet the day folks?" He looked around and noticed that there was no one there.

She was on his heels as he spun through the door, and she

cursed under her breath when she saw that the bed wasn't slept in. "Right, that's it. General alarm it is." She turned, ready to shout, when he caught her arm.

"Wait, great lady--I have a better idea." He went back out into the hallway and whistled for a page. He wasn't sure how they knew that the whistle was always for them, but every castle was the same. A page ran right up from around the corner and bowed deeply, starring at his feet. "I have a question for you, young sir. Have you seen the king this morn?"

Carana knew that the page wouldn't speak, out of fear more than obedience. "It's okay Fenton. Just answer the good bard. She reveled in the shocked expression on the poor page's face at knowing that she knew his name. She knew them all.

"Well, he was writing in his study last night, and hasn't come out." He kept his eyes down, but he peeked a little at the end. "May I go now lady?"

Karsis held out his hand and lifted the chin of the boy gently. "You are a perceptive lad Fenton. I may call upon you again, so keep your eyes open for anything out of the ordinary... from anyone, even the councilors." He knew the boy was going to wince, but held onto his face and narrowed his eyes, boring into the boy. "Don't worry, I will back you up if anyone says anything about you. You have my word as a bard." He let go of the boy and was comforted when he saw the young one straighten his back in pride and nod once, spinning on his heel and sprinting away. "That will help us with things that we can't see or hear."

"You are more sensitive then you let on dear Karsis; that almost seemed sincere." She wasn't trying to be sarcastic for once, but it still seemed to come out that way. "Now let's check out the study, I have a bad feeling about this." She drew her sword and tensed to sprint when he laid his hand on her shoulder again.

"I think they are okay, Carana. If you remember, the queen was going to surprise the king in his study last night; I fear they never got to the bedroom." He chuckled and started walking towards the study at a slow pace. *That* was where she disappeared to last night, he should've known.

Carana followed behind, a little overwhelmed. She hadn't felt this awkward in, well, since before she had been claimed by the god Davalar as an incarnation. She should've seen that the bed was made, and remembered what the queen had said. This bard was creating a fog in her head, and she wasn't sure she hated it.

MARESSA BLINKED her eyes at the bright sun coming in the windows. It took her a second to figure out where she was, but then she felt her husband's strong arms around her and remembered. She had surprised the king in his study, and they had stayed the night in here, on the table—as promised—and on the couch, even against the windows.

She wasn't sure what had gotten into her. *That deviant Karsis probably cast something on me.* She would've never had a wild night like that when her daughter was missing and possibly dead, but somehow the dark thoughts were gone; and she knew that Allissana would be okay. Her husband—Arian, The King of Everknight—lay next to her, and when she turned her head to look at his beautifully rugged face, she saw a shadow cross the window. She barely had time to draw in a breath to shout when all the air in the room whooshed out the window as it blew off its moldings. She ducked her head as the papers flew towards the open window, then she saw her husband go on the attack.

Arian threw the closest thing he could get his hand around at the figure in the now-open window. The hard leather boot spiraled end over end, grabbed by the wind, and struck the figure in the shoulder. The huge knight dropped back down, desperately fighting for air that wasn't there. His great lungs heaved with the effort, and his vision started to dim.

Maressa grabbed his face and turned his head, kissing him full on the mouth and blowing the air she had held in her when the windows burst. It was a last ditch effort, praying that her husband (whom she thought was still sleeping, the sneak) would be able to thwart the assassin before she died. She slid down sideways as she finished and tried to get out of the way.

The king surged to his feet, holding the precious gift his wife had bestowed. By Davalar and all the other gods, he was going to make it count! He pretended to stumble and fall to his knees near the window, then when he thought the assassin would be gloating, he lunged and grabbed for a shirt or cloak. His big hand grasped a fistfull of cloth and he pulled with everything he had. He dragged the man into the room, and was heartened by a thud as the man's head hit the floor with enough force to split a skull--but the wind didn't stop leaving the room.

Well, that's the end of that ploy. What else can I do before I die? The king's thoughts were dim, but then the door to the hallway crashed open and flooded the room with air, if only for a couple of seconds. In came Karsis and Carana, weapons drawn and ready to take on five dragons it seemed, or at least two. Gods above he was going to owe this man again, and sometimes that was worse than the danger you were in.

Karsis had gotten to the door of the study and noticed that his longcoat was being sucked underneath it. Alarm bells going off in his head, he shouted to Carana to draw her sword and slammed the door with his shoulder, then promptly bounced right back from the solid oaken slab.

Carana laughed heartily, then brought her foot up and slammed it into the center of the door. She was rewarded with a splintering crash and rushed into the room, dragged along by the sudden rush of air. Karsis joined her, his sword dancing before him. "Arian!" she called when she saw her king on the floor, then the air rushed by her and her voice was lost in the roar.

Karsis saw the man on the floor before he saw anything else. This man had asked, nay, commanded the air to leave the room and nothing short of magic was going to stop it, even his death. The bard whispered quickly, asking for the wind to stay and comfort him, and felt the air start to slow. Then he saw the man look right at him.

"You!" the man screamed over the calming winds as he surged to his feet. Blood flowed from a cut on his scalp. He said something under his breath while pointing to Karsis, but wasn't able to finish.

Carana stabbed her sword into the man's ribs, piercing clean through to the other side. The words he may have uttered came out with a whimper and a gurgle of blood. "Die traitor!" she yelled as her anger flowed into her blade. She spun as she pulled on the blade, nearly slicing him in half as she ripped it from his body.

Karsis ran to the queen's side even as Arian was trying to crawl to her. Before the king could see or hear, Karsis asked the wind to help her breathe again and saw wisps of air rush into her lungs. The air in the room was gradually returning to normal, but this would help her immediately. "Easy Maressa, everything is okay. Just breathe." He saw her eyes open wide and as he turned he cancelled the request, lest he burst her lungs.

"Karsis . . . we owe . . ." The king was trying to sound formal, but he was too weak, and struggled simply to get air into his chest.

"Yes yes, I know. Your life, the kingdom, blah blah." Karsis stood and walked over to the king and offered his hand. "You're my friend, and the king, I will always be here for you." He was serious; this assassin thing wasn't good. Moreover, it was a trained sorcerer from G'harr.

Carana wiped her blade off on the dead man's cloak, then looked around. "So, I turn my back for one night and you guys sneak away and almost get yourselves killed?" She was smiling. Killing always did that to her.

"Carana." Maressa said the name quietly, she stood with help from the chair that was on its side. "You have been spending entirely too much time with this bard."

"It did sound a little like me," Karsis quipped, then ducked as Carana threw a vase at him. Arian tried laughing, then gave up and tried coughing instead. Carana grabbed another vase and stopped as Maressa got in the way, stumbling.

"Wait! Those were expensive." The queen was getting stronger, but couldn't stop the woman if she wanted to. "Besides, we all have a council meeting in a couple of hours, and with this man as proof, we could make some progress."

"I don't think he will be able to testify, Maressa." The king said with a bit of an edge to his voice. This was yet another attempt in just the last tenday. He was going to find who was leading them and make an example of them, in a real, violent way.

"Don't worry dear, leave that up to me. You go clean up and get ready." She had a wicked smile on her face, and couldn't wait to see the councilor's faces. "And Karsis, I want you to see if you could get some eyes and ears in the castle that I don't have."

"Oh, don't worry--I already have." In fact, he was worried about the poor little page; G'harran sorcerers usually had more than one assassin. If they hadn't changed their tactics in the last fifty years, then there were at least five in the castle. "You know I think I will go check on them right now." He bowed and excused himself, but not before whispering a thanks to the wind for saving his friends.

Word was out all over the castle. An attempt on the king's life never could be hushed, and servants would always talk. She couldn't do this anymore. Killing that snot-nosed brat was one thing, but the king? He was what held this kingdom together; even though she always fought his decisions, she respected him. She walked to the door and knocked quietly.

"It's open Alyssa, do come in."

She opened the door cautiously and saw the man sitting at a table with a small meal. *Must've had it delivered,* she thought, *that's why I never see him at dinner.* She walked in and stood there, realizing that she really didn't know what she was going to say.

"Let me guess, and I'm throwing rocks in the night here: you're unhappy that we tried to kill your king?" He smiled deeply, amused at himself. He was growing tired of this wench and her mouth.

"The deal was to kill the princess, and you failed at that. I did what I could to discredit the king's plans and even tried to make her look bad, but I won't be a part of this little conspiracy anymore." She was ready for him to draw a weapon; she wasn't a helpless little councilor. She was the leader of the merchant's guild and had been trained by some of the finest fighters her father could afford.

"I agree." He said it calmly, as if they were discussing the clouds over the city, not treason.

"You do?" She had her reservations about his sanity then. She honestly didn't know what he was going to say, or want for her silence, but this wasn't anywhere close.

"I do. If you want out, then I can hardly argue with you. You won't ever have to worry about your part in this ever again." Then he looked over at the mantle and smiled. When he turned back to her, he spread his hands wide. "Obren, air leave this woman now."

Her eyes widened, and she went for her dagger under her cloak. Too late. Her hands closed on the hilt as she fought for air, and the three steps to his table seemed like miles. She couldn't even scream.

"You see, you are of no use to us anymore my dear council-woman, and we tend not to keep things that have no use." He stood and walked to her as she sunk down to both knees, the dagger clanging helplessly on the stone floor as her hands clawed at her throat. "Pity, I was going to keep you around if you wanted to help, but since you want out... well, have my blessing." Once she stopped fighting, he gave it another couple of minutes, then released the air from his grasp. He chuckled quietly to himself, *Well, there is going to be a vacancy on the council,* he thought, then sent word for his apprentice to come and dispose of the body. If his associate would've been more powerful, he would've been able to do this to the king and queen and not empty the whole room. That would teach him to send lesser sorcerers to do a master's job.

THEY ALL MET in the council chamber, and only Karsis thought that the torches were a bit much. There weren't usually this many and it wasn't even dark yet. Something about that nagged at him deep in his memories, but he had to focus on the councilors as they came in.

He had information from Fenton and some of the other pages, and if they were right, he might have a clue as to who was in on this conspiracy. Most of the council was there now, looking at what lay on the table wondering what in the heavens it could be. Except Ralavin. Ralavin was asleep, by the grace of his god. How that old man could stomach all this intrigue at his age, Davalar only knew. Karsis looked over at the queen and had to smile. She had dragged a heavy rug all the way to the council chamber and placed on the great table. He knew that the body of the assassin was wrapped therein and couldn't wait to see their faces. Particularly the one that knew him. Expressions were the bard's forte, that and charming the pants off of people. Arian finally came in and looked around, trying not to laugh at the huge rug on the council table.

"Okay, it seems we are missing Alyssa and Othren. I see that Othren has sent a representative. And you are?" The king seemed suspicious of the missing council members, and narrowed his eyes at the young man seated in Othren's chair.

The young man visibly withered at his king's stare. "Yo— your highness, I am Grason Eastlake. Othren sends me in his st —stead, to cover for him. It seems that he has taken ill after having so—some bad food." He couldn't look at the king anymore, that stare was boring into his very soul. He looked down at the table then, and started playing with his fingers.

The king sighed, then took his place at the far end of the table. "Very well, this council welcomes you, Grason, and approves your temporary commission to these proceedings. Anyone know where the merchant councilwoman is?"

Trost, that nervous scribe, was taking notes even now, and Karsis couldn't for the life of Syll figure out where that man kept his backbone. He was shaking even as he wrote, and damned near jumped out of his skin when the king banged the gavel. He finally looked up at the king's question, as if he'd just woke up. "No sire. She was last seen hours ago in the west hall."

"Very well, we will start without her." He looked around the room quickly, to make sure everyone there was paying attention. He lingered his stare at Frenir, the councilman for foreign relations, a bit too long. "If you haven't heard from your spies—I mean sources--there was an attempt upon the lives of your king and queen. Only the pertinent arrival of the high general Carana, and the great bard Karsis saved the day." He saw some shocked faces, and some solemn nods, and it seemed Ralavin finally woke up. "This was the second attempt at a royal death in as many days, and someone is going to answer for them." He slammed his fists upon the table and made the bundled rug shift towards Carana. She smiled. Arian wasn't sure what made them more nervous--the rug, or the fact that Carana was smiling.

"To that end," the queen began, cutting his angry tirade off at the feet, "I have brought you all a present." She stood and grabbed the open end of the rug and yanked hard. The rug unfolded rapidly, and the body rolled across the great table, stopping when Carana stood and stabbed her sword right through it, pinning it to the table. The sword went through the great oak surface, and was protruding at least one foot under. "This!" —Maressa had to shout over all the screaming and shouting— "is the assassin someone allowed into this castle, and by the gods we are going to figure out who they are." She saw Arian's smiling face, his rage washing away at the sight of her unveiling. She looked towards Karsis, and noticed that he was openly laughing.

"What did he attack you with?" Ralavin was not shouting. He seemed interested in the dead body. He stood, sheathing his ceremonial dagger, and poked it with his walking staff, smiling like a kid at a festival. "And what killed him?" Ralavin was the only other person allowed a weapon in this chamber, but only because it was ceremonial and couldn't cut wet parchment.

Trost was mortified. "I can't believe that you brought a dead body into the council chamber!" He was out of his chair and backing towards the door slowly. His eyes kept darting towards Carana and Karsis.

"Well, dear Trost, we brought this here partly to see who would show the right reaction to it, and mainly because it would upset you all." Karsis wasn't going to speak right yet, but something wasn't adding up. Something was itching at the back of his mind. Fenton. He started going through his thoughts out loud just to bring them to the surface. That might speed things up in his mind. "I had the pages tell me what they have noticed around the castle, and went to check on them after the attack hours ago." He stood and moved towards Grason, someone he didn't know, and continued.

"You wouldn't believe what they have been doing. You see, they have been filling silly requests for nobles and council members--including dinner in their private chambers, and even delivering torches..." His face went blank. *By Syll's teats, I missed it. Well too late to sell the cow--looks like we're eating beef,* he thought, as it all clicked in his head. In one fluid movement he spun around in a circle, letting his longcoat fan out and yelled "Arian *down!*" Then he heard the sorcerer try and force the fire in the room to join together. He knew it was a sorcerer, because he used that hated word. Obren . . . *obey.* What did shock him was that it was coming from Trost! That nervous little man now stood perfectly straight his arms spread to direct the flames out to the widest parts of the room.

"Obren fire, join and burn this room!" Trost screamed it, knowing that his cover was gone. Hells, it was gone the minute that bard came to the castle. He had heard the stories; that's why he laid this particular trap. Not for the king, that would be a bonus, but to turn those auburn curls to ash. However, what Trost apparently didn't anticipate was how good Karsis was with magic.

The lithe bard spun as he shouted a warning to the king,

then he went into a trance and threw his arms out at the two nearest torches and spoke in elvish. *Oh, by the gods I could be doomed,* he thought as he backed towards the door quickly.

Carana grabbed the queen and shoved her into a corner, protecting the royal with her own body as if she knew what was coming. The king swirled around and down, covering himself with his great cloak. The room then burst into flames, setting the rug and the dead body alight and even igniting the thick table. Grason was covered in flames and Frenir's cloak and shirt started to burn. The councilor from G'harr shouted, commanding that the flames treat him as their friend. The fire around him subsided, but not fast enough for him to escape harm. Karsis, on the other hand, was smiling.

"Ash'anti fir, sistren wa halven alar!" Karsis urged the flames to draw back. He couldn't ask nicely when the element had already been compelled by magic; that was the real problem with the war of the elves. No, he had to wrest it away from the sorcerer, little by little and by force of will. Sweat dripped down his face from the exertion and heat. The side of the room he was on started to cool, then the torches behind him went out. Slowly, around the torches at first then the wall, frost appeared. It lasted less than a minute, but the contest of wills seemed like hours. The great bard could hear Arian screaming for his wife, but Karsis couldn't see the girls from where he stood. If he lost concentration, Trost would ignite his side of the room and he would be in a world of trouble. This guy was good.

And that was when Ralavin slammed into Trost with his ceremonial dagger wielded in two ancient hands. He wasn't burning at all, and rather seemed like he was coated in a soft glow. Karsis couldn't exactly be sure, since most of that side of the room was in flames anyway.

Trost took the hit and then brought the fire in close, focusing it on the old priest. The glow shuddered and collapsed as flames covered him instantly; still he pushed that dagger deeper into the sorcerer's chest. Trost gasped weakly then collapsed, taking the burning old man with him. Everyone had dismissed the old councilman, and as he and Trost fell to the floor Karsis flexed his will and grabbed the fire from the dying sorcerer. The room instantly grew cold and frost covered the walls and any furniture that wasn't already ash. Karsis fell to his knees and breathed in the cool air.

Damn that took a lot out of me, he thought as he tried to struggle to his feet. He had to check on the king and queen. He wasn't worried about Carana. He was sure the fire would simply cleanse her wicked soul.

Frenir was the first to the queen, pulling Carana back and checking for a pulse. Carana was covered in burns, but she was breathing.

Maressa coughed then and Arian called her name. "Mar! I'm coming!" He threw chairs out of his way to get to her. He wasn't burned, being right near Karsis, but the smoke still got to his lungs.

"Arian! I'm okay. Gods above! Someone help Carana! Ralavin! Please!" She hadn't seen the old priest's valiant attack, so didn't know that he had gone up in flames himself. Arian slid to his knees, pushing Frenir out of the way to wrap his arms around his wife.

"Frenir, well done, man. How's Grason?" Karsis only asked to draw attention away from the king and queen. He still didn't completely trust the man, but for the moment he had nothing against him. The guards came rushing in and were waved back by the king. The council chamber guards outside the door must've been slain, because these were royal guards. They must've run like the wind to get here that quick.

"Aye, the lad's gone." He walked over to Trost and Ralavin, kicking the sorcerer off of the priest's body and rolling the old man over. He placed his hand over his heart gently and looked up in astonishment. "Karsis! He lives!" He looked down again, tears falling from his bearded face. "Hang on you old coot. That was the bravest thing I've ever seen, don't leave us now."

Karsis leapt up and over the burnt table, landing near them, and threw wide his coat. From an inside pocket he produced a tiny vial of deep red liquid and uncorked it. Tiny motes of sparkles fell all around his hand as he held it. "Ralavin, take this in the name of Irilyn, Queen of the Faeries, and may you live to greet her in person for this deed." He tipped the vial to the old man's burnt lips and poured it gently. Instead of a liquid, it came out like a fine mist, winding its way into the mouth all on its own. Karsis never thought he would use this; it was the most powerful item he possessed, and was a gift from the faerie queen herself. He corked the empty bottle and reverently placed it in his coat pocket once more.

"What in all the hells was that!" Frenir's eyes were wide and his mouth was open. The body beneath him stirred, then twitched, and made the G'harran councilman jump back. "Ralavin!" He could scarcely believe his eyes, and he had seen a thing or three. Ralavin's skin was healing rapidly, turning a nice shade of pink, then back to his normal color in a matter of seconds. His clothes, not so much. In a minute he stood, and everyone in the room collectively gasped upon seeing him--everyone but Karsis. He knew what was coming. Standing before them was Ralavin, healed from the brink of death and cured of all ailments; including the detriments of age. He stood there in his prime— around twenty and five winters—and was completely naked.

"Why, hello priest." Carana said weakly. She had stood finally, her burns healing faster than a mere mortal's. Thankfully for Karsis's little stunt, no one would notice. She moved out of the way, allowing Maressa and Arian to rush to their old friend's side unhindered. If she could leave the room without anyone noticing, then she could blame it on a potion she had in her room, or something.

Ralavin stood awkwardly, not used to these bones and muscle anymore. "What did you do to me, bard?" He asked in awe. He remembered whispering a prayer to Davalar to protect him from flames, and even recalled grabbing the ceremonial dagger and lunging at Trest, that nervous little traitor. He may be old, but he still had some of his strength, and now it was all back.

"Ralavin, I did what anyone in this room would've done, had they possessed that vial. I happen to be the only one with it. It was a gift from the faerie queen ages ago--and no, I won't tell you how I came to be gifted with it." He looked around the room and noticed Carana was heading for the door. "Lady general, wait. Let us help." He moved to see if she was alright, but Ralavin was quicker. He tried to move as he used to, but stumbled and caught her arm more forcefully than he intended to. He was shocked that she didn't even budge, never mind pull away in pain. He didn't waste time thinking about it; he closed his eyes and recited the prayer instantly, having decades of practice. The healing energies flowed through him into her, and he smiled to see her in shock.

"Damn Ralavin! I've never seen a priest heal so much in one shot. Were you this good when you were younger?" She wasn't placating him; she was fine, and it was mostly him. The faith this man had in Davalar must be astounding.

Arian was there then, clasping his old friend's shoulder. "Well now, I'm the old man around here it seems." He saw the priest blush a little and laughed through the coughing fits; the smoke in his lungs had not quite dissipated. "It's fine Ralavin. I know you--you're thinking that you don't deserve this, but by

Davalar you do!" He moved a little so Maressa could get in and give the man a cloak to cover himself up.

"Well, I say we all retire and recoup. This brings a lot more questions than answers. At least we now know who the traitor was that hired those assassins." The queen was still hurt, limping and cradling one arm, but no one dared say anything to her. They knew better.

"Yes, let's take a day or two and talk this through, then I have to be off to the Misty Woods." Karsis didn't explain his errand, nor did he bring up the fact that G'harran assassins came in fives, and that made four. He liked to think he was wrong, but that hadn't happened in ages. With any luck he would be back at the castle with Rhoe and the princess in no time, then they could plan their next move.

An hour later, Karsis and Maressa lounged in her private quarters, her arm in a sling and a frown on her face. They were comparing notes on what they had learned, and she was upset that Karsis had gotten the better info. "So, you're saying that the pages told you?" She still couldn't believe that she missed that.

"Well, not in so many words, but yes. You see, they see everything but dare not tell anyone because to speak against nobility is considered treason, by your own decree."

"Not mine."

"By association, my queen, but that's not all. They also have the added benefit of being practically invisible. How many pages walk by and no one even cares? You could send them into places to hear what you would never get a chance to." Karsis sat with his feet up on a small table, delicately munching on cheese.

"So, they delivered the torches on his request. I got that, but what did they hear when they delivered him his meals?" She was trying to understand everything, but it had been a long couple of days and her mind was spinning with it all.

"They had brought him his meals in his chambers. In fact he

wasn't the only one, but they had seen him walking with Alyssa's body, and with her disappearance, we can now assume he arranged for her death. I just wish I knew why." That one was bugging him. *Was she part of it? Or did she find out who he was?* His thoughts were clicking so fast that his head was starting to hurt.

"I'll have the guards start looking room to room for Alyssa now that we suspect her demise. With that decree, no one can keep them out, even the lords." She finally smiled. That notion made her heart sing. "I'm glad that you figured it out before he went through with it on his terms. He would've had us."

"You. He would've had you. I would've been fine." Karsis lied, but he had to keep up his facade of arrogance; he had an image to maintain. "But I digress. I also think that Trost had tried to poison Othren, using the pages to deliver the food." He made a mental note to check on the man before he left.

She had to laugh. Gods above how she missed this devilish man and his obscene arrogance. But she had seen him in action, and he had saved Arian. She owed him her life for that one. "I'll send someone to make sure Othren is okay. Meanwhile, Arian is visiting the slain guards' families. They died in service to the throne, and as such will be buried with high honors." She hung her head, remembering the shock of seeing their bodies slumped against the wall, their throats crushed.

"I should've seen the signs when we entered the chamber; those guards died because I missed something." He stopped smiling, remembering their faces, and filing them with the host of others that had died either because of him, or his plans. "I'm glad that I had that Vial of Eternity. That crazy old man did the bravest thing I have ever seen." Karsis shook his head, regaining his trademark grin once more. "Attacking a sorcerer with a ceremonial dagger. That thing isn't sharp enough to slice through fog!" He laughed so hard he dropped his cheese. His laughter was so infectious, that she joined right in, not knowing that the laughter was the thing she needed most right now.

In a room not so far away, while the two bards had their discussion, Ralavin paced back and forth. He wasn't exactly upset that he was young again. Not at all. But still, there was a nagging feeling that he was now... unnatural. *Dear Davalar, what has happened to me?* He stopped, looking around his room with new eyes. It was Spartan, not having many knick knacks or paintings to speak of, except the tapestry of Davalar's choosing. He paused in front of it and reflected again. The tapestry depicted the god of life and protection choosing a new incarnation, after his original was slain. He hovered over a tiny farming village and the girl he was blessing looked ordinary. "What can I learn from this?" He asked himself out loud, not even realizing that he had done so.

"Well, for one thing it was raining, not sunny with a bards-be-damned rainbow," Carana said from the open doorway. She came in and shut the door behind her, her face a mask of calm. "Other than that, the only lesson I learned that day was that He cared for everyone, no matter their class or station."

Ralavin was in utter shock. He leaned against the wall and took several deep breaths. The high general of Everknight was saying that she was there... that she... *was* Davalar's incarnation.

It all sort of fell into place right then, all the things she would say, and do. "So you're the living embodiment of Davalar?" He couldn't wrap his head around this. *Why here, why out in the open? And why in the name of all the hells did she reveal it to me?* He tried to keep his judgments off of his face, but it must've shown, because she laughed right then, as if she could read his mind.

"Oh, Ralavin. I didn't think you would take it so hard." She moved in and sat down, hands out to show she was unarmed. She could tell he was taking up a defensive posture. The slight shift of his feet, a slight turn of his head to look at the back room. He thought she was here to kill him or some such nonsense. "I'm here to tell you that He approves of you wholeheartedly, and any fears you have of this renewal being unholy can be laid to rest." She had heard from Davalar directly once she had made it to her rooms, his thundering voice echoing inside of her head like a team of rampaging horses. *Cara Annalan, I need you to let Ralavin know that he is loved, no matter his form. Inform him of his importance, and reveal thyself if need be.* She knew that she would have to tell him who she was, no way around that one. "You don't know how special you are, do you Ralavin?"

"I know that not many truly hear the voice of our god, and fewer still can ask Him for prayers." He walked over and sat opposite of the creature in his room. For that was what she was, a powerful creature infused with the power of a god. She even looked human.

"Not many? Fewer still?" She started to laugh, then saw his face drop and tried to stop. It took all of her composure. "I'm sorry, but you fail to understand. Ralavin, there are only three of you—that I am aware of—whom are still alive to do so." She waited for that to sink in, for his eyes to grow wide, then continued. "You, Lady Caerlyn, and an elven priest are all that are fit in this world... so far."

"But surely some of the other priests—"

"Titles, given as payment," she interjected. "Makes me sick. Some of the lords do that now, promoting their own acolytes to priest just for the prestige. It used to be bestowed on someone from a Chosen of Davalar." She shook her head sadly at the changing times. "But you three are truly blessed, able to channel some of His power."

"I never knew, couldn't have guessed." Ralavin was shocked to the core of his being. He knew he was special, but to be only one of three people in all the land. Could he even handle that responsibility? "But why did you tell me who you were?"

"Would you have believed me if I hadn't?" She smirked at him. She had always loved his faith, and to see him grow old and fragile had broken her heart. With his renewal, she felt invigorated herself.

"Point taken, lady." He sat back, a great weight seeming to fall off of his shoulders. He suddenly felt His presence, and closed his eyes in acceptance.

"I am not a *lady*, Ralavin. Don't make me hurt you after witnessing that heroic deed of yours today." Which was the truth. She had never seen such bravery from one so old. *Which reminds me, I have to remember to thank Karsis for saving this priest. Maybe I'll give in to his charms finally,* she thought. That would be an interesting night to be sure.

"Apologies, my dear high general; and as an aside, I understand that your secret is your own. I cannot tell you how important it is to me that you chose to reveal your secret to me." He opened his eyes to see her standing before him, a soft look in her usually hardened eyes. She knew he would take it to his grave. She simply nodded and with no further words, turned and left him to his own counsel.

Later that night, walking his horse through the streets of Everknight, Arian searched the night stars for guidance. He had told the three families of their husbands' demise, and even met with the oldest sons of two of the men.

They were given stipends for the rest of their lives, and a personnel medal of service handed to them by their king. But the men were still dead. He left the last house and sent his honor guard home after much arguing. In the end, he was their king, so they left. Now at almost midnight, he wandered the mostly-empty streets. The occasional drunk wandered by, and of course the ladies of the night were out here and there. He chuckled to himself as he strolled by; if they only knew who was watching them.

It was technically illegal to sell sex in Everknight, but as long as they kept it relatively quiet, he let the few brothels there were in the city proper operate. He nodded to the ones that met his eye and kept going, wondering if they still had faith in a king that couldn't protect them. That was the real problem tonight. He felt that he was letting his people down. Did they despise him for it? Did they whisper to themselves that he was a fool? It was then that he heard the clang of metal. He let his hand fall to the hilt of his sword, Chalice, and ran down the street for the alley where the sounds must be coming from leaving his horse behind. As he took the corner, he undid the clasp of his cloak with one hand and drew Chalice with the other. Stunned gasps echoed from the assailants and victims alike as the king stood there, the very image of a hero. Then he realized what he was looking at, his mouth fell agape in surprise, and then he started to laugh.

The half dozen boys and girls in the alley were filthy and dressed in rags. Some were equipped with long metal rods and wooden shields, while still others wore long dirty cloaks. Two of the girls were behind the cloaks, obviously prisoners. One of the 'knights' actually had the strands of a mop on his head. This one stepped forward, and in a shaking voice said as he brandished his rod and defied Arian. "Stop, in the name of the king!" He then whispered over his shoulder, "Guys, run. I'll draw him off. Go!"

Arian thought he was going to cry. Here were street urchins, homeless waifs pretending to be the king and his knights saving the girl. Lo and behold, one actually had the courage to be a real hero. "Stop, you're fine. I have no quarrel with you." He sheathed his sword and picked up his cloak, carefully keeping an eye on the young 'king' as he did so. As he swirled the cloak around his shoulders one of the other children gasped and pointed.

"Lan, look! It's the king's seal on that cloak!" The boy was tugging on the young 'king's' sleeve, marking him as Lan.

"Easy Griff, he could've stolen that from the castle during the attack. The king wouldn't be out here without his guard." Lan eyed Arian with scrutiny, obviously taking in his polished armor, but trying to be level-headed. The others clearly looked up to him. In fact, the others had not even tried to turn and run. They all looked ready to stand with their friend to the end. That was rare to see in street children, to say the least.

"What if I could prove who I was?" Arian asked them, intrigued by this band of misfits. He wasn't sure if it was because he was missing his only daughter, but he wanted to give these children a place and train them, they had real potential. Maressa had her spies, maybe it was time for the king to have his own presence in the castle.

"And how would you do that? Anything you could show us could be stolen property. Besides, King Arian is much taller." Lan seemed to straighten his back a bit, feeling that he had backed the warrior in front of him into a corner.

"Well then, I would have to do something that only the king could do, wouldn't I?" Arian had a few tricks up his sleeve. Hells, he wouldn't still be king if he didn't, now would he? Besides, the boy had never lowered his rod, never fully trusting his opponent; Arian liked that in a warrior.

"Go on then, show us you are Arian Everknight." Lan backed up a smidge and spread his feet apart so he could pivot on the balls of his feet if he had to. His father had showed him that at least, before dying.

Arian lowered his head and held up one hand to the sky. He let his breath out in a long rush, then held it and called to his horse that he had left in the street. "Let no one tear us asunder," he said as he opened his eyes and lifted his head. A horse brayed in the night and they all heard hooves galloping on the cobblestones.

Lan finally dropped his rod and fell to his knees. The others cried out for forgiveness as it became apparent that only the king had the magic to call his horse like that. It was partly true; this was an old gift from Karsis, back when they had adventured together. A silent link triggered by those words.

"Oh please, don't throw us in the dungeons!" one girl cried out. Posing as the king was supposed to be treason, but they didn't understand that what they were doing wasn't the same. At hearing this, Lan lifted his head, a fire in his eyes "No! It was my idea, all of it. They had no choice, it was I that impersonated you, my King."

How old is this boy? Forty winters? He certainly has the manners and courage of those years even though he looks to be only fifteen winters at most. Arian's thoughts were light, but the lad did impress him, how could he not? "Quiet, all of you. None of you are in trouble. Now, it's late." He stroked the mane of his steed as he addressed the children, seeing the wonder in their eyes at such a majestic creature up close. They usually only saw horses like this from a distance. "So I want all of you to come with me and we can discuss what I'm going to do with you in the morning."

"But sire, they did nothing . . ."

"Lan, I said you were coming with me, I did not say as my prisoners." He smiled then, and laughed at their uncertain faces. "I want you to be my eyes and ears in the castle, and I want to see what you all can do, but not here, and after I've slept and broken my fast."

The children burst into excited chatter, all except Lan. The young boy had tears in his eyes as he looked upon his king, and he fought to keep them from falling. He had always wanted to be a knight, but being homeless broke that dream. Until now. "You will never regret this King Arian." He stood and knelt like in all the bard stories, his eyes burning even as the tears finally fell. "I pledge my life to you, to the People, and to the Land."

Arian's mouth fell open, then he quickly closed it lest the boy become offended. That was the pledge that knights took. The boy knew, probably dreamed of this most of his life. *I came out here for a sign, for guidance, searching the stars when it was right here at my feet,* Arian thought, as he felt some of the weight of king lift for a moment.

Davalar works in mysterious ways. He led the children home to the castle. They were talking about what they could be called and Arian had to smile. Carana wouldn't like it, neither would the master at arms, but these six children were going to be his... *My what? They couldn't very well be knights, they were too young yet.* It was then that the children all agreed on something that Arian missed in his contemplation.

"We would like to be called the King's Messengers. Delivering your word to places too dangerous for mere pages, and even escorting people to the castle from the city." Lan had a smile on his face that looked like it hadn't been there for a long time.

"That sounds wonderful. I like it, but the queen is going to be upset." He saw the faces of the children grow worried, some looked back towards the city as if they could still turn back now. It's a good thing he didn't tell them about the high general training them. They may have turned and ran without looking. "She'll be upset because she likes naming things, it's kind of her thing." He laughed as the joke settled in and they started to laugh.

One girl perked up, "It's okay sire, I'll make sure that when we discuss the name it seems like she came up with it." The girl seemed proud of herself, but another girl elbowed her in the ribs.

"Duh, Kari, she's a master bard. You could never pull that off!" She poked her in the forehead and the first girl, Kari, just shrugged, as if to say it didn't matter.

Oh Maressa, what have I done? The king laughed as they approached the gates, well after midnight, and were met by his guard mumbling things like 'never do that again' and 'what are they doing here's.'

"Sire you've had me worried to death! I've tried to remain calm but..." The Master at Arms came rushing to the gates when he heard them enter.

"You couldn't even spell calm, Jervais. Now button it! I'm tired and these children are to be given rooms and clothes. Understood?" The king needed to exert his authority once in a while, and he was just in the mood for it.

"Yes, your majesty, I will get them rooms for the night and clothe them."

"I didn't say 'for the night' did I?"

"Well, no Sire."

"Oh good, I was worried there for a moment. Just get them rooms, and clothes, they will be staying for a while. They are under the king's protection." With that he pushed past his guards and dragged the children behind him by sheer force of will. Towed behind like fish caught in a wake, they all smiled at the Master at Arms as they passed him. All except Lan.

Lan stopped in front of the man and bowed slightly, then turned and bowed to the knights as well, before quickly hurrying after the king. The king's guard stared mutely after the young man, scratched their heads and went back to their duties. That had been a knightly bow, but there was no mocking gesture to go along with it. The knights decided to forget about the whole night and maybe think of something else for a while.

❧

KARSIS STROLLED THROUGH THE HALLWAYS. He hated leaving his friends when there was one more assassin in the castle, but he had to meet Rhoe when he came back with the princess. The book said: "And the fool will lead the chosen across the waters and into the house of everlasting faith."

There was no other fool bigger than he, so that meant he had to catch them before they crossed the river. He had a couple more days, but it wouldn't hurt to leave early and get a good head start. He turned the corner and started toward his room, ready to go over the book one more time before sunrise, when he saw Carana standing in front of his door. "Well, well-- if it isn't the high general. What may I do for you, beautiful and deadly creature?" He wasn't really shocked that she was here.... he was more shocked that she had that grin on her face.

She walked slowly towards him, trying to make him feel uncomfortable. It wasn't working. *Does anything shake this man?* She thought, as she neared him. She was wearing almost nothing. She had on breeches and an unbuttoned shirt, with her hair down. She smiled at him and eased into his arms. She kissed him fiercely and pulled him backwards into his room. The door closed all by itself, and she felt her shirt move as if someone were taking it off. "My, my--you're full of surprises bard." She said as he still looked unfazed. It had been a long time since she was the one that felt like a fox in the hunt. *And I even went on the offensive; how did he do that?*

"Well, my dangerous little minx, you haven't even seen the best tricks yet. I hope you don't like sleep, because you may not get any this night." He whispered to the candles to ease off their flame and dimmed the light in the room, then smiled his own devilish grin and went after her. It was going to be a good night before he left, and that was a surprise. He would peruse the book on the road. They fell together then, and all thoughts of darkness and evil were left behind for one night.

Eastern Lythinall; Hidden Vale

THEY HAD SLEPT ON ROCKS, she knew it. Allissana--or Liss as she was going by for the moment--was cranky. Her hair was a mess and her boots had some sort of fungus in them. They were on their way to meet the faerie queen, and the forest was getting close. People didn't come here, nor were they wanted apparently. The night was spent sleeping on the ground with a tiny flame—nowhere near any sort of campfire she had ever seen— and listening to Liana tell ghost stories. They weren't scary, but listening to her definitely put one to sleep. Until she woke you up with her shrill screams of terror. How Rhoe had slept through it all, she would never know.

"Copper for your thoughts?" the young warrior asked, sliding around a tree to catch up to her side.

"It's nothing Rhoe. Just a small boulder lodged in the small of my back." She couldn't believe that his hair looked that straight and clean after what they had been through. Not that she was staring at him. *Focus girl, not now.* She reined in her thoughts quickly.

"It can't be that much farther. Maybe they have a nice bed of leaves we can sleep on tonight." He felt refreshed and hopeful that this queen would know how to help them find a way home. After all, that faerie knew Karsis. He had asked Liana that night around the fire, tiny thing that it was, and she had offered the tale without so much as a breath. It seemed that years ago--how many she was unsure, as time turned for them like so many stars in the sky--that a wandering bard had come into their forest and came upon the queen in her glade. She was being attacked by a group of Korreds and so he came to her aid. He slew their leader and scattered the rest with his mighty magic.

The queen used her own magic to grab the life essence of the leader and bottled it up. This she gave to Karsis as a thank you at that night's Revel, and for a year and nine days they held court together. One day a dark wizard came upon them and unleashed his shadow upon the woods. Karsis battled him upon the high trees, throwing him down and encasing him in the earth amid the roots. Liana went on about meeting Avaryn and saving the princess and queen, but Rhoe had stopped listening by then and was fast asleep by the next sentence.

"Sharing a bed of leaves sounds like heaven right now." She looked right at him when she said it, and they both felt the heat rush to their faces. She looked away first. "I mean, anything is better than that ground." *Stupid, stupid, stupid, why did you say that?* She was out of her element, lost in the wilderness and couldn't find her balance. She needed the familiarity of home, and soon.

"No, I know. Not that it would be bad, but... wow. I actually am bad at this kind of stuff." He stopped and Liana flew right into him.

"Hey, I wasn't listening! It's not my fault!"

"Liana, what did we discuss about personal space?" Liss was smiling, glad for the intrusion before it got *truly* awkward.

"I know, but you two are so interesting!" She flitted about them, twirling amid the breeze, then settled on Liss's arm. "*Oh!* I didn't see that before, Is that your ring? I mean, you're wearing it, but I don't remember seeing it on the beach."

Liss looked down on her hand, and her heart stopped beating for a second or two. It was her father's ring! She held it up, almost in horror. *How did this thing get on my finger? How did I not notice it?* Her thoughts went back to how she wasn't even scratched on the beach from their wild trip down the river. *The ring was always on his hand... what if something happened?*

"What's the matter Liss? You look like you've seen a ghost." Rhoe hadn't noticed the ring until Liana had mentioned it, and she was right to look shocked--there was no way anyone would've missed this ring. It was a solid gold band, etched with snakes intertwining all the way around and set with an onyx stone. It was definitely a man's ring, although the minute he thought that, the ring seemed much slimmer.

"This was my father's ring, I don't know how it got on my finger, or why I didn't notice it." She had calmed a little, but only a little.

The ring is magical, and seems to be tied to you. Powerful magical tools like that always have to be given or they find their way back to their owners. Avaryn spoke in her mind, then walked up and nudged her empty scabbard with his horn. Sparks flew when he touched it. *Likewise, your sword must be enchanted too, for the scabbard calls to it even now.* He turned to Rhoe as well, and stomped the ground a little. *Like the ring you wear on your belt. That one is very strong.*

Rhoe looked down and was surprised to see a ring hooked onto his rope belt. Not just hooked, but the tiny clasp was like a clawed hand, grasping the belt like a bird of prey does its meal. "Well now, where did you come from?"

These things also have a clouding aur, so as not to attract attention from others. I'm not sure why they became visible at this time. For once the unicorn seemed generally unsure, but Liana came to the rescue.

"Sillys! It's because of her." She pointed to the trail ahead and there standing in the trail was a woman, about five feet tall with glorious gossamer wings folded down at her sides. She wore a thin gown that grazed the ground, and her feet were bare. Her long flowing golden hair seemed to move as if there was a light wind. Liana flew quickly to the woman's side, and the woman greeted her with a bow.

"Well, come Liana. Are these guests to the queen's court?" Her voice was melodic, and she seemed majestic and regal. She bowed in turn to each of them as she walked up, her gown never catching any of the dirt on the trail. "My name is Irilyn, and I formally greet you in the name of the faeries." She seemed to be taking them all in with her eyes, not missing any details and seeing into their very souls.

Rhoe kept watching. Her eyes kept coming back to him as she looked over everyone, making him feel uncomfortable without knowing why. "M—my lady." He bowed deep, not knowing what he should do. Apparently, he didn't do it right because Liana started laughing.

"We don't bow silly!" She fluttered around to his face and laughed again. "Watch me." The little faerie turned in midair and spread her arms out wide, exposing her chest to the woman. "See, we show that we have nothing in our hands to harm one another, and nothing over our hearts to protect us from another."

It was so simple, yet sincere that he found himself smiling. *You would never catch merchants doing this,* he thought as he mimicked her movements perfectly. The woman had a smile big as the sky at this and she shook her head at him.

"It is rare for those of elven blood to show this much respect; I appreciate this young one." Irilyn looked a little shocked, but kept it mainly to herself. He didn't have the ears, but plainly had the hair. Curious to say the least.

Liss caught Irilyn staring at Rhoe, and even saw the look of shock cross the small woman's face if only for a second. *Thank you, mother, for making me sit through all those council meetings. I would've missed that if I hadn't.* Her thoughts were distant, and so she only caught half of what the faerie said about Rhoe. "Wait! What did you say? He's elven?"

"No, I'm not. My parents were both human." Though even when he said it the conversation between Karsis and his parents played over in his head.

"My pardon then. You have the hair of an elf, though admittedly not the ears." She walked up to him slowly, like she was approaching a wild animal. "Your eyes are human as well, and here." She moved back his hair from his neck and draped it over his shoulder. Yes, touching it confirmed what these two children would not know obviously. His hair was silky smooth to the touch and angel-thin. "Here is the weirdest part." She moved his hair so everyone could see, and there was... nothing. Liss was confused on so many levels that she didn't know where to turn. You may as well gag her and throw her into a shouting match. The minute the faerie woman touched his hair she felt the oddest feeling. She did NOT want her touching him. *Where did that come from?*

"What? What's there?" Rhoe was trying not to panic, but it had been one hell of a couple of days. "Someone tell me what I have on my neck before I jump off a bridge." He saw the look of terror on Liss's face and couldn't help but laugh a little.

"Not funny Rhoe." Though in truth, it kind of was. Then she started laughing as well. The others had no idea why it was so funny so they tried to ignore the two. "Okay, so there is nothing on your neck, relax." She turned to Irilyn, as if she were ready to claim her property from those delicate faerie hands. "What is supposed to be there, or do you see something we don't?"

"What is supposed to be there is a house insignia. Every elf is born with one, a birthmark if you will." She let his hair go, never taking her eyes off of Liss. "So it is most confusing. Your hair was like this at birth?"

"Yeah. The acolyte at the temple whispered that I was diseased or something." He had never thought anything about it, until now.

"Well, this is not the place for this discussion anyway." She reached into her gown and the tiny hand slipped into a hidden pocket. She smiled at Liss then pulled something long out of it. Not just long, but almost as large as she was. It was a sword.

"Deathsong!" Liss couldn't believe her eyes. Not because the woman had pulled it out of thin air, but that she had it at all! "Where did you come to find that?"

"These things cannot be lost if not freely given, and it is powerful indeed. It was found not far from the Council Tree, sticking out of the ground as if it had fallen from a great height." Irilyn bent her knee and offered it as though Liss was some sort of proud knight.

Liss felt something then--maybe the weight of fate, or the pull of destiny; with her luck it was her empty stomach. She took the sword and bowed her head, then replaced it in its sheath. The sword rang when it slid home and Liana flew in crazy circles around her waist.

"Didyouhearit? Didyouhearit? Theswordspoketome!" She was off the deep end now, and no one paid any attention to her. It was best that way sometimes.

"Wait--I wasn't given this sword though." She realized after she spoke that she didn't want anyone here to know how she came to have the sword, let alone who she really was.

"Dear one, there is a lot about giving that you may not realize, but come, come. Let us away for now to the Council Tree. There are some dark things we must discuss and it never bodes well to do that out here." She turned then, and started to glide away. Even though she had bent her knees, her dress was still pristine.

"After you, brave knight." Rhoe flourished his arm out for

Liss to go before him, only half teasing. He remembered her grace while fighting that thing on the bridge. She was a canny fighter and he had never seen moves like that, even from his father. He truly admired her skill, and besides, he couldn't keep his eyes off of her. *It's not the first pretty girl you've ever seen, keep your head on man!* This wasn't the first time these thoughts had crept into his head. He didn't know why he was so attracted to someone he just met. He locked down those feelings for another time, maybe when the Dark One's own wasn't right behind them.

Avaryn watched the whole exchange between Irilyn and the curious humans and kept his own councils. These two were rooted deep in destiny and he just knew that meant trouble for the forest. He also could see fate pulling them closer together. He shook his mane as he followed them to the Council Tree. For the gods to involve mere humans—or whatever this young boy really was—in their schemes and not the incarnations was baffling. *I'm getting too old for this,* he thought, and lowered his head as they walked. He knew something bad was coming, and here in these woods, there was always a balance. To stop great evil, good must be sacrificed... he hoped that the price wasn't too high.

The Far East of the End of the World

DAR'KRIST PULLED himself up once more, his fingers bloody and aching. He had climbed over a hundred feet already but it finally it looked like he was almost there. He hadn't been this furious in a long time, and looking down at the river far below made it worse. How that young whelp had managed to thwart him thus far was unknown and unfathomable! He had been washed miles down the river before he had fought off the forces pulling and holding him. After a while they grew bored and no longer wanted the struggle. That was the only defense against wizardry like that--get out of range and the elements grew bored without direction. It was a good thing he could hold his breath that long or else he would've perished. As it was, the struggle was tenuous at times. Finally, he had grabbed a handhold on the sheer cliff hugging the river before he went over a huge water-fall. Now he was close to the top and cursing that boy under his breath every ten feet. At last, with one more pull, he saw the edge. Using all his strength, he surged up and over the rim and lay on the grass.

The green blades withered in seconds, mainly because of his anger, and even the rock was starting to crumble on the edges. He rolled backwards just in case and got to his knees. He stood shakily, looking at what was around and was taken aback. The long mountains stretched out before him as far as the eye could see, and the grass went on about half a day, about waist-high in some places. He sent out his *sight* and was amazed how far he had come. He *saw* a forest in the distance and knew that was his destination, but these mountains were going to slow him down. *I can run quickly when I'm determined, so sleep tight boy, for your reckoning is approaching.* He pulled his *sight* back and started running, his fingers already healed.

The tall grass was withering before he even touched it, such was his ire, and every animal within a mile took flight at his coming. As if the gods heralded his passing, the wind changed direction and blew before him, scattering the ashes of the dead grass to the ether, and still he kept running.

The Council Tree, Hidden Vale

THEY WALKED into a massive clearing filled with all manner of sylvan creatures. Faeries, pixies, sylphs, and dryads flanked the clearing; and in the center stood a massive tree. Its canopy covered the entire area and the sun peeked through here and there in bright beams of light. Buzzing faeries of all shapes and sizes flittered above their heads, and one of remarkable beauty sat upon a throne of gleaming wood at the base of the tree. Rhoe was in awe at the wonder before him. He had grown up reading books on some fantastic places, but none of them even compared to this. The woman on the throne stood when they neared, and her wings unfolded. She looked younger than the graceful faerie woman that greeted them in the forest, yet reminded him of her nonetheless. She was lithe and graceful and wore a crown of leaves upon her head.

"Greetings newcomers. You stand under the protection of the Council Tree, and are welcome to this place. I am Lurien, Queen of the Faeries." She cocked her head at Rhoe, and glided closer. "An elf has graced us after all these years?" She seemed in awe herself, and lost all composure at seeing him.

"No, my daughter, he is not elven." Irilyn said as she stepped with them up to the queen. She laughed easily at her daughter's lack of grace. She had never seen an elf and was still so eager in her youth to meet one.

Liss stepped up and stared at the queen as she glided closer. She could see the resemblance now that Irilyn had said it, and smiled at the younger faerie's smile. She took a brave step forward and spread her arms wide, conscious of Deathsong resting in her scabbard. "Greetings Lurien, Queen of the Faeries." She stepped back and bowed low, bending her knees and keeping her head up as they did in the king's court. "I am Liss, warrior of Everknight, and I thank you for your welcome."

Lurien stopped her advance and turned her full attention to Liss. "Liana has taught you well," she remarked, upon seeing the tiny little faerie hovering behind the human. "Though I have never heard of this 'Everknight.'" The young boy forgotten, she turned back and sat upon the throne. Avaryn walked over and placed himself behind the throne and grazed on the verdant blades of grass with his mane teaming with faeries. Liana was flying at them all claiming ownership of the glorious creature and chasing them away, which they treated as a game. The unicorn just shook his head and snorted in laughter.

"Your majesty? There is something we need to talk about. Is there somewhere private we can go?" Rhoe didn't want to alarm all these good creatures or cause a panic. If the monster came here and destroyed all of this because of him, he could never forgive himself.

"No young one. We discuss everything here, so all can hear and voice their concerns. In the end the choice, if any, is mine, but no one can say they didn't hear about it. This is the way of the Council Tree." The queen sat a little straighter, concern lining her young face. "Avaryn has told me of the darkness coming, and I will share with the Council in a second."

Rhoe couldn't stop himself. "Your majesty, this evil is powerful and if he gets here—"

Lurien stood even as he stepped forward. "Peace!" she said, her voice booming over his with a force that must have carried for miles. She waited for all there to cease their conversations and focus on her. The humans were shocked into silence, but the young boy had his head cocked to one side. Likely that Avaryn was communicating with him the importance of this meeting.

Don't worry young one. I know what an incarnation is and how powerful it is. I sensed it as well, and have warned the queen how bad this is. Avaryn hadn't moved but he turned his head towards the young boy as he spoke to his mind, and what a focused, strong mind it was. He hadn't noticed on the beach, mainly because Liana was a distraction whenever she was near. He continued as the queen walked slowly towards the humans, eyeing the faeries present. *Let the queen tell the faeries what comes and see how we deal with problems here in this world. The Court of Trees may just surprise you.*

The queen strolled forward off of her throne, and looked at all in attendance as she went. "A darkness has come to the forest once more, and we have to help these brave warriors to find their way home so that they can deal with this evil in their own way." She paused, beating her wings, lifting up into the air, and spinning to look at everyone as she continued. The air of tension grew thick and everyone was intent on her every move. "Someone will have to lure this evil away, and save the Court." She hung her head as she floated back down, her voice magnified still, even though they couldn't see her face. "I will not lie to you, I never have. This will be the most dangerous thing we have ever faced, and I cannot order anyone to do this."

"I will do this!" A voice rang out in the crowd behind Liss and Rhoe. The woman that met them in the forest walked forward and the crowd of faeries all gasped in unison.

"No mother, you cannot! Another will step forward and be brave--your place is by my side." The royal's voice was strong, but it held a quiver that was fighting to get free. "You are a former queen, and as such, cannot leave the court." She could not lose her mother to this evil.

"Child," Irilyn laughed, "there is nothing you can do to prevent me from doing this. I hold no position of importance, and I have lived a long and full life. No one else here has more experience in evil like this, if even I do." She walked forward and others stretched out their hands to touch the former queen.

Liss had tears in her eyes for no reason she could name. The sacrifice that was being made here was profound. She could see the faces of the faeries and they all held relief that they wouldn't have to face this evil. She looked away and saw Rhoe staring at her, his hand out to comfort her, but frozen in doubt. Her resolve broke and she rushed into his arms and cried. This could've been her mother.

Rhoe was torn. He could tell she was hurting over the former queen's resolve to fight the evil alone, and he reached out but stopped. *I can't, she would probably slap me for being so forward.* Then she saw him. She was in his arms in a second, sobbing into his shoulder. He was a little remorseful himself. After all, his own parents had done this very thing. He held her close, whispering in her ear that everything would be okay. He almost believed it himself.

The queen was broken, her eyes showed it. "Then... by the queen's decree, Irilyn shall face this evil and save the court." Her tears were falling, and tiny sparkles flew up where they hit the ground. A light rain followed shortly, and no one seemed impressed that it mimicked her emotion.

"Daughter, my Queen. Hold goodness in your heart that I will prevail against this evil, and even if I don't, my spirit will bond with the Council Tree as a former queen." She embraced her child, and even Liana was crying freely now.

Every faerie was trying to hold back their tears, trying to be brave, and one by one they bowed their heads in respect. "Now, let us all go to Revel and celebrate the freedom we will have shortly from this evil." She let go of her daughter and stepped back, allowing Lurien to gather her own strength and straighten up. "As for the newcomers, Avaryn will take you to where you can pass freely home in the morning. Eat at Revel and sleep content that you brought no harm to us in this."

Rhoe nodded for the both of them, then moved Liss over to the side near the throne. It was like she had read his mind. He felt guilty that he had brought that thing here inadvertently. The faeries were in a bustle at the mention of Revel, and Rhoe could only guess at what it may entail. "Liss, are you okay?" He didn't want to let go.

"Yeah." She sniffed and tried to compose herself. *Way to go stupid, so much for being a warrior woman. I broke down crying at the first emotional thing I heard.* She was being hard on herself, she knew it, but she had to--no one else was going to out here. *Gods, I miss Carana.* She blinked at that, then smiled. "I'll be fine. Thank you for being here." She backed up and realized that he wasn't letting go. What was worse, she didn't want him to.

Young ones, Revel is soon. Come, let us get to the festival and see about some food for you. Avaryn's voice broke the tension and they drew apart reluctantly. He watched them and *saw* that the weave of destiny was thick around them. Something else too. The young boy had something around him akin to a fate charm, but different. Almost prophetic in origin. *Ponderous indeed.*

The queen came over to them after saying her blessings over some of the other faeries. A sobbing Liana sat upon her shoulder. "I'm truly sorry that you have to visit in such dark times. But no matter! Let us away and eat." She patted Liana on the head and patted Avaryn as he stood. She led them away from the Council Tree and into the forest for the quick walk to where they would hold the Revel.

She explained along the way that the Revel was a time to celebrate the courageous actions of their people. Drinking and dancing was a must. Liss worried that she might lose herself in this Revel. *And would that be a bad thing?* She thought. She shook her head trying to forget the feelings that she had about Rhoe, and to focus on their way home.

BEHIND THEM, watching from the shadow of the Council Tree, the little Korred laughed and ran his finger through his tangled hair. The mess of hair reached all the way down his back and he was covered in leaves. He followed them here from where he saw them in the forest, and now that he knew of this evil... well, he had an idea that could help him get his revenge upon this whole charade. He faded away into the woods, back the way he came, and ran for the edge of the forest to where this evil would come out of the mountains.

❀ 9 ❀

WHAT WE FIGHT FOR

"Y̲ou want her to train who now?" Maressa asked her husband. His brilliant idea of recruiting children was bad enough, but to have Carana train them? That was cruel. "Are you out of your mind dear?"

"She trained me as a child, and Allissana as well. She works well with children." He was confused about why his wife thought this was a bad idea. Sure, she could be rough and demanding, but it did build character. He always thought that was something adults made up until he became one himself.

"She trained *royalty* dear. It is expected, but these kids..." She was at a loss on how to explain it to him. He was stubborn, and when he got an idea in his head it was nigh impossible to dislodge it. "Well, no matter. You'll have to find her first. I've looked everywhere this morning for her, to no avail." Maressa wasn't looking hard, but still it wasn't like the high general to be absent like this.

He smiled, thinking he had won a minor victory, when he should've seen that he lost the field instead. "I will. She will do fine with them, and speaking of the children..." Arian turned so his wife wouldn't see his smile. "There is a girl that would benefit from your teachings as well. She has a keen wit and sharp tongue."

"Oh Arian! We don't have time for training young ones right now. I'll send Jerina in to see her next week. She is my most competent bard, and she will teach her what she wants to know." The queen turned to the window and stared out at the countryside, past the city beneath them. *Where are you girl?* Her thoughts were on her daughter this morning, which was partly why she was looking for Carana.

"Still thinking about her?" He knew his wife well, and wished he could say something comforting about his daughter, but he couldn't. He was having fears himself. "From what we have heard that boy was with her, and if he is anything like his father, she would be fine."

"Can't you even say his name anymore?" She had known that the rift between Gareth and her husband was deep, but as the years rolled on, it seemed to become even more vast. They weren't even there for each other when they had the kids.

"I don't want to discuss it." The power in his voice, as always with this subject, demanded it was closed.

"Okay. However, my husband--" she began mockingly. It served him right using that tone with her, "--you *will* have to deal with it when they arrive." Hands on her hips, she spun and headed for the door. She knew she wouldn't get that far.

"Here?!" He shouted. He grabbed her around the waist and pulled her back, looking her right into her deep, knowing eyes.

"Yes. What did you expect? You sent a patrol to help them and see if they were all right. Well, word came back that they found them, so I ordered them to be brought back here." She wasn't about to tell him that Gareth almost refused, but Tierra kicked him in his broken ribs till he conceded. "They should be here in another day or so, if the weather holds."

"Why didn't you tell me?" He felt... he didn't even know

how he felt. When he last saw Gareth, the big man was storming out of the court with Arian's blood on his hands. Arian had said things then-- hurtful things that he wished he never uttered. But he had.

"Because you would react like this?" She hugged him tight, knowing how much this must hurt. She wasn't there to see what happened between the two, but she saw him afterwards, and he clearly lost whatever fight they were in.

"Never mind that now. I'll deal with it when I have to." He kissed her on the forehead and backed away. "I need to go check on the kids, one of them has real promise Maressa."

"Speaking of kids, you gave Allissana your ring, didn't you?" She hadn't forgotten that his ring was missing. That ring had kept him alive in the worst of scenarios.

"Should've known you'd notice the little things about me. Yes, I put it in her pack so it will find her finger in short time." He shook his head, he felt naked without it, and that attack in the council chamber could've killed him without it on. "We're a pair huh? My ring and your sword."

"Deathsong." Her eyes smoldered, ready for a fight.

"Yes dear, Deathsong." He laughed at her face. She was so adamant about that name.

"You don't seem to understand, husband. Its name is Deathsong, and it is the only reason I'm still here and not chasing her across the world." That sword would keep her alive, especially with her training and skill in the blade.

He smiled that diplomatic smile that said he didn't understand at all, but he agreed. He kissed her on the lips, then hurried away to find the street kids. He was amazed there hadn't been any altercations yet.

Maressa rolled her eyes, then looked for a page to go find Carana. Then she smiled. Leave it to Karsis to teach her something. "Page?" A small boy came walking in from the hallway.

Where do they come from? It's like they just appear. She laughed at her own thought as the boy bowed to her, waiting. "Fenton is it?" The boy nodded, clearly uncomfortable. His eyes were downcast, staring at her legs, and his feet shifted slightly. "I need you to answer something for me. Do you know where the high general is?" She was going to have to memorize their names from now on. No more thinking that they were just servants.

Fenton blushed, then looked down before answering quietly. "Yes, your majesty."

"Maressa."

"Yes your...Maressa" He cleared his throat and looked at the queen, who was staring intently at him. "She, well... she is in the guest room. The one you assigned for Karsis." He shifted his feet nervously again.

"Oh!" Maressa suddenly knew why the page was nervous, no embarrassed, about this question. Then she smiled, feeling devious this morning. Her husband had gotten her in the mood, and she was going to have fun. Besides it would keep her mind off of her daughter. "Take me to her."

CARANA LAID THERE WATCHING Karsis dress. Something about this dandy was nagging her, and she couldn't put her finger on it. Like an itch you just can't scratch... and she had scratched all night long. He had a style that was outdated, but no one would know that, except her. She had seen that style about fifty years ago, but he wore it well.

His black silk breeches were snug, and his high black boots were polished to a shine. He had a white ruffled shirt, unbuttoned in the front about halfway down, and his burgundy longcoat seemed almost magical.

"Enjoying the show my dear?" He seemed refreshed, even

though they hadn't slept one bit all night long. It was his little secret. He didn't sleep that much anymore unless he had to. He had to get going this morning, but he had to admit he was tempted to stay.

"I got to see the main show up close, right near the stage, and it was everything that was promised and more." She hadn't had that much fun in decades, and he seemed to enjoy it almost as much as she did. He was as good as the stories made him out to be. She got up and started getting dressed herself.

Karsis skipped over and kissed her lightly before springing away, "I'm off, lovely. Do make sure the king stays alive before I return with his daughter." He laughed as she tossed a small lead statue at him as he skipped out the door. He skipped all the way down to the king's stables and met the head groomer with a flurry of rumors, hints, and even some accusations of infidelity. The head groomer agreed that he could have the fastest horse in the stables just to get rid of him. His plan worked brilliantly. He rode out of the city singing a quaint old tune and not the least bit sorry that he didn't get to read at all last evening.

Carana had put on her breeches and was reaching for her shirt when she heard clapping from the doorway. She turned, not even bothering to cover herself. It was her experience that women's breasts distracted people, and if she needed the distraction to get the upper hand in a fight, she would take it.

"Well, now I see why Karsis would entertain you most of the night." The queen had a smile on her face, and was trying not to burst out laughing. The poor page next to her, however, was trying to look anywhere but at the high general. Poor little kid. "Seriously though, I thought you knew better than to shack up with bards. Haven't you heard the stories about him?" Maressa walked in and found a comfy chair to sit in. She noticed the poor page then and burst out laughing. She had to stop forgetting about those kids. "Apologies Fenton, you may leave us. I'm very sorry to have kept you." He bowed slightly, and turned and bolted down the hallway. He knew he was going to regret helping the nobles, but it did feel good to be seen for a change.

"May I get dressed now your majesty, or would you like to look some more?" Carana was feeling good, mainly because she got rid of most of her stress last night. Okay, all of it. She grabbed her shirt, put it on, then sat without buttoning it.

She felt comfortable with the queen--plus it helped to keep even women off guard, especially master bards. "So, what brings you Maressa? This can't be business." The queen looked disturbed under that smile; it must be worry over Allissana.

"I was looking for you to see if you knew what was coming next. Karsis says he is going to meet the kids and bring them home, but then what?" Concern lined her face then, the smile fading.

"Ah, well, there's the problem Maressa." Carana sat up a little straighter, knowing that it really was business this time. *Damn all nobles to the hells, I was looking forward to kissing and telling.* Carana smiled at her own thought, and continued. "I wrote that book, 'tis true, but I was helped by Davalar. You see at the time I couldn't read or write, I was just a simple farm girl. When he chose me, he insisted that I write this book, and when I told him that I couldn't...Well, he kind of just *made* me do it." She stood up and walked around the room. She had never talked about this to anyone; the closest she had ever come was the priest last night. She suddenly had tears in her eyes at the memory of that awful rainy day.

"How did he make you read and write something in an ancient language?" Maressa could tell something was going on. More than just a story, or reflections of a story. No, she was reliving something and it didn't seem pleasant. Maressa could relate to something like that.

Carana turned and looked at the woman with an incredulous look on her face, then started laughing. Not just a giggle, no. She had to lean on a book shelf to keep from falling over she was laughing so hard.

"Ancient! Oh my, Maressa," she breathed, trying to stop herself so she could talk. "The Auld tongue *was* my language back then. It is a mixture of elvish and common, though more towards the elvish." She went into another fit of hysterics, and this time the queen followed her.

After they had a good laugh, Carana sat back down and cleared her throat. "You see, he kind of took me over, imparting the knowledge of literacy to me. He then sent me visions of what I was to write, and I did so, sometimes talking out loud as I did. No one could see Him, so the villagers whispered amongst themselves. She paused and looked down at her hands, all traces of mirth gone from her face. "They came for me eight hours later. I had gotten halfway through the book and they burst in with torches and rakes, just like the stories they pass around the campfire." She breathed in deeply and tried to steady her voice. "They burned me at the stake in the rain. Me! They raised me, and taught me everything I knew about living and they burned me just like that."

Maressa felt like she shouldn't be hearing this. "Carana, you don't have--"

"They watched as I screamed my life away. When I realized that I wasn't going to get them to stop, I screamed Davalar's name, and begged Him to save me." Carana put her head in her hands, and took another breath. "He did."

Maressa held her breath, stories of the gods coming down were just that--stories. Yes, some stories were based on truth, but as a master bard she knew which ones were and which ones weren't. Here she was hearing a firsthand account of it happening and it was awe-inspiring. It had been a long time since she was on this end of a story. "What did He do?"

Carana looked up and smiled through fresh tears. "He opened the clouds and came walking down on steps of light."

"In the flesh?!"

"No!" Carana said sarcastically. She almost laughed, if the memory wasn't so painful the look on the queen's face would've been priceless. "He did something much worse. He bent his will upon the town and... spoke to them."

"That's it?" Maressa couldn't believe that they got a slap on the wrist for burning his chosen vessel.

"*It*? Oh, Maressa think on this for a minute. The entire village heard the voice of a god--not a passage from a book, but His *actual* voice." She took a deep breath, recalling that fateful moment before continuing. "He told them 'You are hereby judged by the will of the gods.' That voice was never meant for mortal ears. They screamed their sanity away; most of them died from the shock. Those that didn't pass right away went into terrible fits and laid down weeping. They all died in a matter of hours."

"How did you escape the flames?" Maressa was fully into it now. If Carana were an actual bard, she may be weeping as they spoke. She would memorize this story, even if it was never to be told.

"The rain that had been falling all day picked up in intensity and put out the fire, almost as if by magic. I healed quickly and realized that because of me, that entire village had perished. I was alone." She looked at the queen with eyes so intense that Maressa tried to sink into the chair. "Even the children Maressa, from the littlest to the oldest, were dead and gone. That was when I started to fear the rain."

"Oh Carana, I'm so sorry." Maressa didn't know what to say.

Somehow, her own worries about Allissana seemed insignificant. "I shouldn't have asked about the book."

"No, no, it's okay." Carana got up and walked around, finally buttoning up her shirt. "I wanted to talk with you; granted I thought it was going to be details of last night, but I needed this." She looked at the queen over her shoulder and smiled. "I don't get a lot of girl time, so I like to grab it when I can."

"When was the last time?"

"Oh, about fifty-five years ago." Carana smiled and went on. "With the book, it all came to me. I've read it over the decades, but without the original visions to go off of, I'd be guessing like anyone else. Some things were a given, like helping Allissana, but others are cryptic."

"Okay, so you don't know exactly what's going to happen, but is there anything that could help?" Maressa was desperate to do something, anything, to prepare.

"Yes. When they get here, we have to find a new king, one that rides upon a golden squirrel." She ducked as Maressa threw a pillow at her, and they both laughed. She wasn't about to tell the queen that the kids would have to leave again, and there was no way she would believe where they would have to go.

"Oh, and by the way--Arian would like you to train those street children he brought home." Maressa kept her face straight, not wanting Carana to get the wrong idea. After all, she wasn't noble either. *No, she's simply immortal.* She quipped in her own head.

Carana sighed and shook her head. "The king orders it so I obey, but I will give them my own test to see if they are worthy. He won't like it though." She got up and bowed to the queen. "I take my leave my lady. I have to go get the right clothes for this little meeting."

Maressa watched her go, and looked around the guest room

noticing the wreck for the first time. *I think they had more fun than I did the other night.* With that thought, she got up and left, walking the halls and wondering if they would all get through this.

RALAVIN HAD GONE for a walk and ignored the stares of all who passed him. He was given a fresh outlook on this gift, and no one would ruin it. He had thrown on his robes and tied them with a golden cord as fitting his station, no longer feeling that he was in another man's skin. He lost himself in the halls of the castle, walking with no known destination, going where Davalar took him. So it was with some surprise that he wound up in the lower levels of the castle, near the training area. There, practicing with various weapons and tools, were a bunch of street waifs.

"Hello priest!" One of the young girls exclaimed, making him turn his head in her direction. She had on a nice dress, but wore it like a street child.

"Why greetings children. And how is it that you have come to be here?" He tried not to sound accusing. His was not the voice of discipline, but of direction.

"We have permission." The young boy, almost a man by the straightness of his back and pride on his shoulder, spoke. "The king has taken us in as his personal messengers. My name, good sir, is Lan." He bowed in the way of the knight, as if he had been doing it forever.

"Ah, I had heard something of that. Well come to castle Everknight then, and may you thrive in the will of Davalar." He saw one boy perk up at the mention of the god of protection and walked over to the boy after bowing to Lan. "And you are called?"

"Griff, sir. Are you one of the head acolytes?"

"Heavens no! I haven't been that in a very long time. My name is Priest Ralavin, and I am the head priest for the all of Everknight." He watched the bored expressions of almost all of the children, all except Griff. The kid's face lit up like a fireworks display. Ralavin saw something then, a glow around his head like an aura. Ralavin knew the hand of his god when he saw it.

"Um... Did I say something wrong, sir?" The boy saw Ralavin looking at him and drew back a bit from the man. He was tingling all over and didn't know what the man was doing. "Stop doing whatever you're doing... it feels funny."

"Son, that's not my doing... it's His." Ralavin held up his hands to show that he was empty-handed. He hadn't fought in years, although he seemed pretty good with a ceremonial dagger. He chuckled at that, and the children thought he was laughing at Griff.

The Priest cleared his throat to stop from laughing, and looked around at the children, then back at Griff. "You see Griff, it seems like you have been touched by Davalar, and no, I don't know what that means as yet." He walked closer to the boy and closed his eyes. Yes, the boy had some of the gift of the calling, he could feel that at least.

"Does this mean I will be able to heal people?" Griff couldn't believe that He had chosen him! He had worshipped Davalar in secret for years, ever since his mother was beaten to death by his drunk father. He shook the bad memories out of his head and concentrated on the priest.

"If you would like me to help start training you, I can certainly do that, but you will need to go to Caerlyn Hold eventually. The Lady Caerlyn trains all new acolytes." Ralavin smiled at the thought of seeing Lady Caerlyn in this new body; he had always wanted to shock her a good one. The other children grew bored and went back to their practice since they weren't in trouble, and even Lan went about his lessons, trusting that Griff wasn't in any danger. "Let's walk Griff, I'll show you the temple here and we can meet some of the other acolytes." He reached out to the boy and felt a warmth come from him.

Oh yes, you've touched him all right. What path will he walk though? He thought, as they left the training area behind. They hadn't gone more than a couple of steps when the king came strolling up the hallway towards them.

Ralavin bowed his head to the man he had known since he was born, and smiled to himself. *What a fine young king he has tuned into.* "Your majesty, what brings you down here this morning?"

"Oh Ralavin, I thought that was you. I was coming to check on my new recruits, when I got sidetracked. Seems they found Alyssa's body this morning," He looked down at the boy staring at him and remembered him from the alley. "Oh, hello Griff. Learning the path of light and hope?" He remembered the teachings of Davalar from his youth and all the classes he had to sit through.

"Yes sir. At least I think I am." He smiled nervously. He still couldn't believe that the king wanted them to help, when every other adult thought they were nothing.

"Well, I've got to check on the others. Should've been down here hours ago. Have fun you two." Arian walked on, shaking his head at the thought of Ralavin being so young again. He remembered him from his youth, and it freaked him out to see him like that now.

The figure in the shadows waited for the Priest and the little boy to move further down the hall and pass out of sight. It wouldn't do for that one to involve himself in this upcoming fight, there was no telling what he could do in his newly-restored condition. The figure counted to fifty, then crept slowly down the hall, waiting for the right moment to strike.

Arian turned into the room and saw the children practicing and was in awe. They were focused and were doing quite well. They weren't actually fighting as such, but they were getting used to what weapons they had picked, and seeing what fit them best. Hard to think they were all street thieves a couple days ago.

"All hail the king!" Lan called to the others when he saw him standing in the doorway. He dropped to a knee and bowed his head. The others weren't so quick, but still followed suit.

He was going to tell them it wasn't necessary, but thought twice at seeing their dedication. "Rise. I came to check on your progress and see how you're coming along. Are you comfortable in the quarters they gave you all?"

"Yes sir. I've never had my own bed before." The girl was clearly in awe of the castle, and had chosen the jo sticks as a weapon to train with. She had long brown hair, tied up in twin braids, and even had placed red ribbons in her hair. She didn't look like a street child anymore.

He searched his memory for her name, and it finally came to him, "Kari, I'm glad you like it, those are nice weapons you found there. Why did you choose those?" He looked at the others as they gathered around to hear the king.

"I chose these because they only look like sticks. I can paint them and decorate them to look ornamental, and no one would know I had weapons ready." She spun around in a circle and tucked them into her belt behind her with a flourish, her ribbons flying in the air.

"Well, very good! I see you've all found something to practice with until I can find you an instructor." He noticed a little girl in the back that he didn't know yet. She had to be all of eight winters old and had no weapon at all. "What's your name, little one?"

She looked up and smiled at the king, bowing deep and

blushing. "I'm Sprout, your majesty." She was only four feet tall. Her short blond hair was still dirty despite having been washed, and her skin was a dark tan from being on the street all the time.

"Nice to know you Sprout. Is that what your parents called you?" He didn't want to be nosy, but it was an odd name. How could one so young be all alone out there?

"Yes sir. If I have a real name, they never told me. They were taken by bad men one night and I've been by myself ever since." She didn't tear up--wouldn't tear up--in front of the king.

"Well, I like it. It suits you perfectly. Sprout. Kind of grows on you." He laughed at his own joke, and the children tried laughing, but just because they had to. He could tell. "Okay, no more awful jokes. What did you find for a weapon, Sprout?"

"Nothing your Majesty. You see everything is too heavy or needs big muscles to use. So, I just started using my arms and legs and tried to kick things. I'm awfully good at kicking things." She craned her neck around the king and looked at the man in the doorway. Before she could ask if he was a friend of the king, the man lunged at them.

Arian felt a train hit him in the small of the back as the children all yelled warnings. He tried to roll with it, but his assailant followed him as he went down and forced him to the side with tremendous force, spoiling any controlled fall. "Run, children!" he yelled before his temple was bashed by a pommel. His vision blurred and he barely held onto consciousness.

"Majesty!" Lan drew his practice sword, aware of the feeble weapon's inability to hurt an attacker--but when the gods will, the brave must rise. He didn't rush, but rather advanced quickly on the balls of his feet. He had to draw the attacker away from the king. He saw the others all advancing cautiously, pulling out whatever they had found to practice with, except for Vance. He was a slender boy, ten winters old and exceptionally good with a bow. Unfortunately, there weren't any bows in here, so he had been throwing knives at the practice dummies. Now he and Sprout were going around the left side trying to stay out of range of the wicked looking dagger in the attacker's hand. Kari had pulled her sticks out and circled around the right with Tomas. Tomas was a big boy for only eleven winters, and growing fast. He used a hammer like the one that had been in his hands early in his life, as the son of a blacksmith, and the one he had now looked dangerous even though it was only made out of hardened wood.

The attacker was wearing a black suit and cape, along with a form-fitting mask that left the mouth open. The attacker looked at the approaching children and smiled. Lan was the first up, and the attacker lunged up from the ground and batted his sword away like it was paper. A solid kick to the midsection and he was on his knees, trying desperately to force air into his lungs.

"Run little ones, I don't need you all dead." The voice was husky and dark, like black water.

They all started to tear up, but they held their resolve. The king had treated them like human beings, something no one had ever done, and he needed them. They all looked at each other and nodded. They had always been able to do this, to simply know what each other was thinking deep down. Tomas yelled, holding his hammer high and running like a dumb kid. He was down in a heartbeat, but that's what he wanted.

The attacker hit him low on the knee, spun around, and swept his legs out from underneath him. He hit the ground flat on his back and his air left him in a rush. But he grabbed the attacker's foot at the last moment in his vice-like hands.

"Huh! Not bad boy." And that was all the attacker could say. The others were rushing, with the little girl sneaking around behind and the knife-wielding one circling back to the front just out of range. There were a flurry of attacks, all of them bad. The girl with the sticks came in and got punched, then thrown back behind the attacker, sprawled on the ground moaning. A back hand and the boy on the ground was seeing stars. Even Lan was up and swinging that piece of wood. He was kicked back again, landing on his back with a solid thump. Then everything slowed down. They were the distraction. "Damn."

The first knife hit solidly in the chest, center mass, and the attacker moved at the last moment so the second one grazed the ribcage slightly. *Great, possibly a collapsed lung.* Carana thought, as she rolled off of the unconscious boy and came up to her feet, pulling off her mask. "Stop, I'm the high general! It's okay, you all did great." Then she heard the small whimper from behind where she was. Sprout stood there, holding the knife that was sticking out of her chest, right where her heart was and her eyes rolled up into her head. Kari tried to catch her as she fell, but somehow Carana was still right there. "Don't pull it out! She was smart, hold it there."

The king stood weakly, shaking his head and trying to focus. It had all happened so fast. "Guards!!" He saw Carana and knew what she had done. She must've sent the guards away, and there was no one to save the little girl. "Oh Sprout." He stumbled to her side as she started to fade.

"*Move!*" Ralavin came skidding into the room on his knees, already chanting. He placed his hands on her and the glow that came from them swept around the knife and down the blade into her. Griff was right behind him, tears running down his face the minute he saw her. "We heard the king yell for you to run and ran as fast as we could back here . . . Oh gods!" He dropped to his knees and held her legs, as if that could somehow help.

"I'm sorry, I'm sorry... I didn't see her behind... I mean, I didn't think." Vance broke down and sobbed into his hands. Kari went over and held him tight. Lan stood behind the king, ready to defend him, not knowing what else to do.

"Griff, I need you now." Ralavin breathed deep and steadied himself. "She has slipped too far for just my healing. I need you to join your hands on mine and clear your head." He looked at the frightened boy and smiled. "I know, you're scared, it's okay. We can do this." He didn't need the boy--he had stabilized her quick enough--but he needed to see what the boy could do untrained.

Griff let go of her legs almost reverently, and crawled up to her chest. He looked at Ralavin with questions on his brow, but left them unasked. Closing his eyes, he placed his hands around the knife close to her chest and let go of everything. *Please! Please Davalar save her!* He thought as he squeezed his eyes shut with concentration.

"Easy lad. Not so hard. Ease up on your eyes and just *feel* Him." Ralavin let go of the girl and let Griff continue on his own. The boy had started healing her the minute his hands made contact, although he didn't know it. The young lad was a natural, channeling the power easily.

"Come back to us Sprout..." He said out loud, and then he felt it. His hands grew warm and tingly, and the wound started closing. Then he realized that it was closing around the knife! "Ralavin help!"

"It's okay Griff. I've got it, she won't feel a thing." He gently slid the knife out as the boy closed the wound behind it, and there wasn't even a scar. It would've taken him at least another ten minutes to get that far. He felt everyone staring at them and let out a breath he didn't realize he was holding.

"Is the little one okay?" The king asked weakly. Gods above, Carana hit him hard. He was still seeing stars. He looked over at Carana, and was shocked to see her crying. *By Davalar, I don't think I've ever seen her do that.* He reigned his thoughts in and looked at the children. They had stood by him and were ready to die for him. If this had been a real assassin, they would have.

"Okay, she is stable. Children, I want you to take that small table over there and put her on it, then carry her to my room." The guards came rushing in then, and skidded to a stop once they saw the king was all right. "The guard here will escort you." He looked at Carana and the one with the knives and his eyes softened. "You two stay here, I wish to talk with you both."

"That goes for me as well." Arian said, rubbing his head and shaking the dizziness out. "The rest of you know this: I will never forget that you chose to stand with me this day." He bowed his head to them and they bowed back, clutching their various wounds. After they had left the room, Carana started pacing, all trace of her tears were gone. She wouldn't look him in the eye. "You start Ralavin, I need to gather my thoughts before I yell." The king winked at him, knowing that the high general couldn't see it.

"Very well," He turned first to the grief-stricken boy. "What is your name son?" He noticed that the boy was still shaking.

"V... Vance, sir."

"I'm no sir, young one, and I want you to understand something right here and now." He walked over to the boy and put his arm around him, pulling him in close. "This was not your fault. You were up against someone that I haven't seen lose in all my eighty years." He saw the boys confused look and laughed. "Don't ask, long story."

"But I should've seen her, I should've—" That's as far as he got before Carana slapped him in the head.

"You didn't see her because you threw blind." She was furious, more at herself than him. They weren't supposed to have real weapons; she forgot about the throwing knives kept in here. She tore the knife out of her chest and threw it at his feet. "Don't get me wrong Vance, you threw them perfectly. I almost caught both in my chest, but you threw them without knowing where your allies were. That makes it a blind throw." She saw Arian nod, smiling at her.

Ralavin let go of the boy and walked to Carana, arms out wide so as not to spook her. He'd heard stories about her after a fight. "And you did the same thing, General." He got close and when he didn't get hit, he lowered his arms and looked right at her, placing his hand on her chest and healing her wound. He didn't think she needed it, but it helped.

"Oh? How do you suppose that, Priest?" She wasn't angry at the accusation. She was angry that he was right. At least he had finished what her own body would've healed, that would stop the questions.

"You went in not knowing what the conditions were. You knew you were going to win, so you never planned for what could happen." That was going to get him hit he knew it, but she needed to know, and better it came from him instead of the king.

"I know! That's why I'm so damned angry." She smiled at him, then rested her hand on his shoulder. "It seems even the high general makes mistakes. But if you ever tell me that again to my face, I will make sure you get to meet Davalar in person."

"Can I go now?" Vance was getting uncomfortable with the tension in the room. This fight had taken his cocky attitude and thrown it out the window, then shot it with an arrow and watched it fall into the moat. He just wanted to go and see Sprout.

"Well, I was going to give you a speech about how, when I give you an order, you are to follow it, but I suppose you can go." Arian smiled at the boy's face, then he winked at him and clapped him on the shoulder. The boy didn't exactly run, but he might as well have. "And you." He turned his stern look on his high general and saw that glint in her eye. She was ready to defend her actions, and he liked that. "The next time you plan to ambush me, could you hit me somewhere else?" He laughed at the look on her face as she realized he was playing with her. "Seriously, I'm still seeing stars." The three of them laughed and walked away to go check on the kids.

Carana was truly impressed with the children. She wasn't expecting that kind of loyalty from street kids. "Don't worry, my King. I'll turn them into fighters, even if it kills them."

Hidden Vale

HE WOKE up with a terrible headache. Rhoe barely remembered the Revel, and what he did remember he wished he could forget. He sat up and looked around seeing Liss next to him, her hair a mess of leaves and berries. They were in a hollow tree trunk, and there wasn't much room at all. The night started out fine, with the faeries drinking and singing garish tunes of woe and lust. He had refused any of the drinks, fearing that he would lose his senses, and he had too much control to do that willingly. He did eat some of the food, which turned out to be the same as drinking. So he and Liss danced and lost themselves in the music and singing. He remembered standing upon a rock, holding a stick that he thought was a sword, and pronouncing his undying love for Liss the warrior beauty.

What have I done? he thought, as he tried to get up without disturbing her.

The rest was a blur of kissing, twirling of leaves, and even losing some clothes. In the end, he regained some of his composure and refused to go any further until they were both in their right minds. He didn't remember how well she took that--the rest was a fog of trying to remain in control. The bards weren't kidding when they told their stories; this faerie stuff was potent. "At least I put on my robe before I passed out," he said to himself, as he climbed out of the hollow and felt the fresh air.

"Noyoudidn't." Liana said, as she flew down to him. She had been anxiously awaiting their return to wakefulness and she was all wound up. "I did! And it took me a long time too."

Rhoe sighed and looked up as she came circling down around his head. Of course she did. "Was it you that got us in here Liana?" He didn't think it was, but best feed her ego a little.

"No silly! A bunch of faeries carried you both here after your wedding." She was so happy that these two had found each other on the fateful night, it gave the Revel a happier end. She was still going to miss Irilyn though.

"After our *what!?*" He had to have heard her wrong. Maybe he hit his head and his hearing was all weird. Yeah, that made him feel better for a second. This wasn't happening.

"You got married, remember? The leaves, the wreath and berries. Proclaiming your undying love?" She buzzed around trying to figure out if they hit his head too hard getting him in the hollow tree. Dryads can be so clumsy sometimes.

Liss came awake right when Liana was describing their marriage and she froze. Her memory of last night was literally a dark fog, with only snatches here and there. She did recall the leaves and stuff, her hand going to the mess she wanted to call her hair. Yes, there was the wreath all right. *But why am I not upset?* she thought to herself, smiling happily. Oh, she also remembered the kissing and taking off of clothes, but the most vivid memory was Rhoe stopping. Boys never did that, or at least the ones she had taken time within the city.

She had never had someone look out for her before, and she still felt that warm feeling when she thought about it. *Gods above, I think I actually may be falling for this boy.* Liss got up and then sat back down real quick when she realized that she was almost naked. She had on a leaf skirt that looked like it was made by chipmunks, and what had been a leaf top. It was just two leaves that had fallen to her waist. She grabbed her old tunic and pulled it over her head, then found her other clothes and dressed in the tight confines as she listened to Rhoe stammer about how faerie rules didn't apply to them. Poor guy was really spooked.

She had her armor on in about two minutes, a personal record in that small hollow, then climbed out. She didn't even think she was hung over, until the fresh air hit her. "Oh, sweet heavens, what hit me?"

"Liss! How do you feel?" Rhoe started to go to her, but her look said he better stay right where he was. "Oh, never mind, I'll stay right back here until you're ready to not kill me." He saw her smile, and suddenly he didn't care about stupid faerie rules. *Is this what my mother and father feel when they look at each other?* he thought as the warm feeling spread into his chest.

"Just find me my sword and I'll feel much better." No sooner than she had said it then Avaryn cantered into the clearing near their hollow with a bundle. "You can read minds, can't you?" She teased the magnificent beast. This was such a magical world that she still thought that she would wake up in the cabin any moment.

It is time. We have to leave soon if we are to get you back. Avaryn projected this to both the boy and the girl, and he tried to make his thoughts relaxing. He was anything but relaxed. His oldest friend was going against the most powerful creature he had ever *sensed*, and he wasn't going to be there.

"Is Irilyn going to stop that thing?" Rhoe still couldn't believe that she was doing this alone. He had fought it and knew how skilled it was. Not just powerful, he was that too, but even without being an incarnation, Rhoe had the feeling he would've still been outclassed.

Young one, she is giving her life for us all. She goes with the power of every faerie that was at the Revel, that's why they all shared the bowl of faerie wine. She will use that power to face him, and hopefully banish him from here. Avaryn felt a tear run down his cheek through his fur, he had to hurry if he was to get to her in time. *Now let us away, time is growing short.* He nudged them forward and then led them away from the tree.

Eastern edge of the Hidden Vale

SOME MILES AWAY, far from the Council of Trees, a figure was hurrying towards the edge of the forest. He was coming to meet this dark being to see if an alliance could be formed. He had brought the two highest ranking members in the Court of Shadow, and together they would convince this thing to help them take down the queen once and for all.

"We shouldn't be out here in the open." Dravin said. He was the most paranoid dryad in the Hidden Vale, and wasn't too keen on the plan to begin with. He should be back tending to his tree, not gallivanting.

"I saw the strangers come. They will help the queen no doubt, so we need what they fear." The figure was called Bron, and he was the meanest korred in existence. He was going places in the Court of Shadow. If he pulled this off, they would elevate him for sure.

"Well then, let us have done with this." Sherrent was a gorgeous nymph with golden skin and leaves in her hair. Barely clothed, she flipped her head at the border of the forest. "You sure he's coming this way?"

"Yes, I heard the unicorn say that he was coming this way, and quickly." He squinted against the rising sun coming over the horizon. "Wait! I see something!" He felt his body quiver slightly, but thought nothing of it. Then Sherrent screamed and Bron looked over to see her skin blistering rapidly. Dravin turned and fled towards the nearest tree, but was on his knees in seconds trying to make his rotting lungs work. Bron was going to ask what was happening, but his throat was dry and dust filled his lungs. He looked at the figure that was running at them, and noticed that the trees were starting to wither.

Dar'Krist slowed at the edge of the woods and reigned in his anger. He noticed that the forest was extremely resilient to his power, being one of the oldest around, but the three bodies at its edge weren't so lucky. He was breathing hard at this point, having run all day and night. He took a couple of calming breaths, then straightened his form and walked slowly into the trees. He walked over the bodies without a second thought and strolled calmly after the flickering power he *sensed* in the forest. The boy and the girl were that way, and when he caught them... well, they would not escape him again. And so ended the Shadow Court, its only two members of good standing killed without knowing why. The court was mostly smoke and mirrors, and held its numbers in theory only. With these two dead, the others would grow weary of the games and move on...

Hidden Vale

THEY HAD WALKED for about an hour, and still hadn't said anything about being married. Rhoe didn't even know how to bring the subject up, as his experience with women came down to fooling around with farm girls behind the church. He noticed that she was having a hard time with the roots in this ancient part of the forest. They came up everywhere making footing difficult, if you weren't a warrior with bare feet.

He stepped from root to root, like he was crossing a local stream over the wet rocks, and saw that she was getting angry. The unicorn knew the forest like the back of his mane, so he was effortlessly navigating the path. "Liss, why don't you ride for a while? Give your feet some rest." He wasn't sure if she would take that wrong or not. His dad often said stuff like that and got punched for it.

She can't, Avaryn interrupted before they started bickering. He could feel her frustration. It was coming off of her like her sweat, and what the boy said was probably going to send her off the deep end.

"I'm *fine* Rhoe. And what do you mean, I *can't*?" It would've irritated her that he told her to ride, even more so that she was thinking it herself, but it was the way he said it. He generally did want her to rest. She didn't know why she knew this, but she did. "You offered to carry us on the way to the Court, didn't you?"

Not both of you--just him. I could even let him ride now, just not you. He is still pure. Avaryn mentally slapped himself. He was so intent on Irilyn's fate that he navigated through this debacle in the worst way possible. He may have as much as pushed them off a cliff. Thank the Trees they were almost there.

"What do you mean he's—" She stopped mid-sentence at the look on Rhoe's face. He was horrified. "Oh Rhoe, I'm sorry! I mean, there's nothing to be sorry about." She stopped again, feeling herself turning red at how embarrassing it was for him.

Way to screw it up girl, she thought as she looked down at her feet. Good thing too, as she almost fell over a root.

Rhoe was mortified. Here he was, traveling with this gorgeous warrior woman, and she finds out he has never lain with a woman. "No, I know. It never seemed... I mean I never have..." Then it hit him. Maybe it was an inspiration from his uncle Tanan, or even his time with Karsis, but he stopped, turned to her and smiled. "I was saving myself for you." He didn't expect the line to actually work, but he didn't exactly see this coming.

She fell down to the ground laughing; she couldn't even catch her breath. He started to feel horrible again, but then he smiled and started laughing with her. He helped her up and they walked snickering at each other the rest of the way. *How is it I'm so comfortable with her?* he thought. He looked around. Avaryn had stopped up ahead. The unicorn was prancing uncomfortably near a ring of large mushrooms in a grassy glade, almost like he wanted to bolt.

We are here. Step into this ring and it will take you to a similar ring in what you would call the Misty Woods. He moved off a little ways, hoping that they would jump and be gone. It was such a long way to where Irilyn was he would have to run faster than he ever had. But of course, these humans wouldn't be that easy to get rid of.

Rhoe made his way over to him, and wiped a tear from the unicorn's face. "Hey, it will be all right Avaryn. She'll stop him, and I'm going to find a way to destroy him, I promise." He wrapped the huge beast in a great hug and then made his way back. He grabbed Liss's hand. They checked for their stuff, then stepped through. Avaryn turned and galloped away through the forest at speeds that most faeries would call impossible. Unicorns could teleport, but he couldn't until he *saw* where he was going; he had to be close. He was the last unicorn and nothing would stop him. *I'm coming Irilyn, hold on.* But would he be in time?

Grove of Woe, Hidden Vale

SHE HAD WALKED for a couple of hours now and had arrived where she wanted to meet him. It was here that Karsis had thrown down that dark wizard many years ago, and nothing was ever right with this grove since then. It was renamed the Grove of Woe, and if her plan worked, and she was hoped it would, she would make it back to hug her daughter again. The power of dozens of faeries flowed through her, and the special flowers she had made her cloak out of would protect her as well.

She looked around to make sure that everything was in its proper place, and then she Felt him. Her head snapped to the east and sure as the leaves fall in autumn, there he was. He was walking slowly at her, draped in a flowing black robe and cloak, and she could see the cloak moving. There wasn't any wind. "Ithin Mecirian Basenial! Beast, you shan't gain passage here!" She spread her feet apart and readied herself for the fight of her life.

He saw the lone girl--nay a faerie--and almost laughed at the absurdity of it, until she said *those* words. Those words were ancient, and powerful. They were meant to ward off evil and would've worked had he been anything other than what he was. As it were, he had to walk towards her like he was fighting a strong wind. He closed his eyes and drew power from the ancient trees around them. The trees would've resisted him, but they were weakened by his power already.

She saw him straighten and knew that she was in trouble. If

he could power through those words, then he was more powerful than she imagined. Those words were old, older than the trees themselves. They were handed down from the goddess Syll, who held dominion over magic and nature. The faeries were like her children, and as such she wanted them protected from the evils of the world. If they weren't even slowing him down--well then it was time to switch plans. As he walked a little faster towards her, she backed up hastily, tripping and gasping like she was caught off guard. Now if only he would fall for it.

Dar'Krist grinned when she started her retreat. He could hear her gasping for breath and tripping in her haste. He took two large steps and lunged, and that was when she opened her cloak. The smell hit him like a hammer--that fruity fragrance of the Bloodvine flower! She was covered in them! They wouldn't actually hurt him, but they would protect her from his powers for a while. They did make him sick to his stomach though.

By all the death in the world I hate those flowers, he thought, as he advanced once more, this time cautiously. *I must remember to wipe them all out of existence this time.*

"Leave this place Dark One, you have no power here!" Irilyn barked, moving around the trunk of a tree to keep something between them. She wanted him to come at her on her terms; only then would she have a chance.

"Oh, little one--whoever sent you out here wanted you to die. You can't possibly stand against me." He walked around the tree as he talked, and suddenly reached out to grab her by the throat. Her hands came up and caught his, and she threw him into the tree. The great tree cracked, being already weakened by his rotting disease, and Dar'Krist stumbled a few feet to keep his balance. Why did he keep underestimating everyone that came against him! He stood again and sent out a blast of his power, feeling everything around him start to wither. He walked towards her, death in his eyes. No more games, no more playing with his prey. That was his problem--he was trying to have fun. Well, no more.

Irilyn felt his power wash over her, and her knees buckled. She leaned upon a tree for strength, and stood again, trying to make it to where she needed to be. Just five more feet. "I have the power of all the faeries coursing through my veins creature; I am more powerful than you know." It was partly true, but she could feel herself fading even now. The flowers were helping to keep her alive, and her power was keeping her upright, but it was only a matter of time. *Forgive me daughter, I fear he will be the death of me.*

He came like death, walking to her like an inevitable force. Now that he knew she wasn't a weak little girl, he would wait till she fell, then tear her apart limb from limb. Then he stopped. Wait, she was leading him. He sent out his *sight* just around them, and *saw* where she was headed. Right in front of her was a faerie ring! So that was her plan.

He jumped the last few feet and grabbed her, keeping her away from the ring of mushrooms, then drew up high with his great strength; she kicked her feet uselessly. He watched as the life started to fade from her dull eyes. "Thought to banish me to somewhere far away? Not a bad plan at all young faerie, but it would take someone much more skilled than you to best me." He saw her lift her head, amazingly still alive, then she smiled.

"How about--" She managed to say with what breath she had left. Her flowers had almost rotted away, and the faerie power was draining fast, but the sight she saw bolstered her resolve, and she braced for the impact with what muscles she could still work.

Me! Avaryn charged in, never slowing at all, his hooves making barely any sound across the damp ground. He had used all his power to teleport himself as close as he could as he raced towards them, and now he hit the man straight in the back, his horn piercing his flesh and sending Irilyn flying towards the ring, her form disappearing in a flash.

The pain exploded in his back, and he stupidly looked down at the bloody horn sticking out of his chest. He had never even heard this beast coming. He tried to turn, to get a grasp on anything, but he couldn't. He sent out a burst of power, hoping to reduce this beast to ash, but it only weakened it a little. He screamed then, more out of frustration than pain, and felt the creature start to lift him. *Oh great-- beaten by a horse,* he lamented. If he lived through this, there would be hell to pay.

Avaryn held the creature high in the air for a second, his neck muscles bulging with effort. *I am not a horse!* Then he lowered his head in a great throw, sending the thing into the ring after his oldest friend. The Dark One disappeared as well, the flash leaving a smell in the air. *May love find you Irilyn.* He took a second to catch his breath, wondering why he wasn't dead. He felt the power hit him, and he probably would feel it for many years to come.

After a couple of minutes, he scattered the mushrooms and stomped them into the ground. He wouldn't be able to come back even if he knew how. Then he made his way back to tell Lurien, though he feared she already knew.

The Faerie Ring

HE HIT THE GROUND HARD, rolling onto his knees reflexively. He was losing a lot of blood, but he would heal quickly. Then he felt something hit him in the back of the head hard enough to rock him forward into the earth. Screaming in frustration, he rolled over and over, back onto his stomach. Once more he got hit in the back of the head, then in his back. Dar'Krist screamed in pain. He pushed himself up to his knees and lashed out, connecting with something that he couldn't see, then he got hit again. He went down and turned onto his back, just in time to see a huge branch come streaking towards his face.

She had waited for him, and she was going to go down fighting. She gathered her strength and found a branch; when he appeared, she went at him. She had hurt him, she knew that kind of scream. She had a fleeting thought of making it out of this, when his hand reached out and hit her in the side. She felt her ribs crack and break, and she knew she had to keep swinging. She saw him roll over, but when she came down in a vicious arc, he kicked her square in the face. She hit the ground on her back and her last fading strength drained away as his power took her fully. As her form rotted away, her last memory was one of victory, for she knew where they were. Then she heard the quiet voice of Avaryn saying goodbye.

May love find you Irilyn, and Irilyn of the faeries passed into the next world.

Council of Trees, Hidden Vale

LURIEN STOPPED dead in her tracks. A cold feeling settled over her and she knew what it meant. With tears in her eyes she half ran, half flew over to her throne and opened the secret compartment on the side. *Mother why did you go? Why did it have to be you?* Her thoughts were a blur as she set the bottle on the throne and tried to remember the words. She only had minutes to get this right if she were to salvage anything of her mother. This was the secret of the queen. It wasn't hidden powers or secret traps in the forest. No, it was the secret of the Llirest. The Llirest was a mythical potion rumored to bring those back from the dead. Other rumors say that it can cure anything from blindness to lost limbs. They are all close. The potion is the dying essence of faeries, captured and kept for dire emergencies. It wouldn't bring you back if you were fully dead, but if there was anything left--anything at all of life in the being--it would fully heal you. The bonus effect was that it also cured all maladies known. Lurien closed her eyes and murmured the incantation, which was far older than most of the trees here in this ancient vale. When she was done, a fine mist rose from the ground and wound its way into the bottle, bringing with it sparkling motes of light. These motes danced around the bottle as the mist settled into a deep red liquid. Lurien corked it with tears falling from her delicate cheeks, then hugged it to her chest.

What did Karsis used to call it? The Vial of Eternity or some such nonsense? She smiled at the thought, then looked to the trees. "Go with love mother, and know that you will save someone someday, like you've saved us all today." She hid the bottle in the throne once more, locked it and then went to find Avaryn and lean on his powerful shoulders for a day or five.

Liana watched her best friend walk away and cried herself. She knew what Lurien's tears must mean, but didn't want to intrude just yet. A deep sadness weighed her down, and her wings didn't feel like working. She sniffed and went to go find someone to cheer her up as well.

Central Lythinall

HUNDREDS OF MILES AWAY, another felt the death of Irilyn as well, one who felt it more keenly than even her daughter. Karsis cried out in shock and pain, falling off his horse while riding at a good clip. He never felt the ground, or the rocks for that matter-- only his wife's pain and anguish. "*No!*" he screamed as he felt her spirit leave. He knew she had sacrificed herself and that it was against the incarnation of death. He felt none of the emotions of betrayal or surprise at her death, so she went to this fate willingly, but that didn't lessen the impact on him. They had always joked about being married, as it was a complete accident at the time anyway, but they had grown fond of each other nonetheless. He had visited her over the years, and it was she that gave him her bottle of Llirest that had saved Ralavin. "Oh, Irilyn what have you done?" he asked the sky, as he lay there once the pain had subsided.

He couldn't imagine what Lurien was going through, especially if she had to capture her mother's essence herself. *Well, nothing to do about it now*, he thought. He had to find Rhoe and Allissana and lead them back to the castle so that they could all decide on how to stop Dar'Krist. He shook his head sadly and remounted his horse, which was looking at him like he had three heads--and they were all blue. "You'll say nothing about this, or I'll mate you with a unicorn I know," he said jokingly to the horse. He would never do that to Avaryn anyway; he liked him too much. He rode on through the night towards the Whiteleaf River and sang songs of the faeries all the way there. If he shed a couple of tears here and there, no one noticed in the dark.

Misty Woods

Rhoe stepped down on mossy grass and tumbled head first after appearing out of thin air. His balance was completely thrown off and his head was spinning like a hawk with one wing. He heard Liss cry out as she appeared, then felt her land on him.

"Soft landing at least," she said, as she looked into his eyes. With Rhoe she felt like it was all a dream, and one that she would love waking up from next to him. "Know where we are?"

"No. Besides a forest somewhere, but that would probably get me smacked." He smiled as she lay there, and wished he could hold here there for a couple more hours--or years--whatever came first.

"Probably?" he said, as she smacked his chest as she got her feet under her. Her head was throbbing and she tried to focus. She grabbed Deathsong and pulled it with a ring that echoed through the dark trees.

Rhoe marveled at her stance, seeing that she was ready just by standing up. Whoever trained her knew what they were doing. He thrust his legs into the air and pushed off the ground, leaping from his back to his feet in a single motion, then looked around himself. The forest was dense, barely letting light through the canopy. Was the sun setting? Or was that the sun rising? He hated being lost. It was then that he heard the sound of water.

"This way." He whispered, hoping that she understood that he wanted to be cautious.

She nodded and followed, keeping Deathsong out at the ready. Around the ring of mushroom that they fell out of, she noticed that the moss wasn't as abundant as the ferns. *I'll think about what we just did a little later when I don't need my sanity,* she thought. The canopy overhead was so thick that she could almost see things moving within it. She shook her head to clear it and focused on Rhoe's back. They came upon the river a couple of minutes later. While not as wide as the one they fell into, it was moving quite quickly. The edges were littered with debris, probably from the rains the other day, and she could even spy some pieces of the bridge.

"Rhoe is that..."

"Yeah, I was looking at that too." He saw the wood she was talking about. It wasn't dead wood; it was cut and formed. He looked at the trees again, and noticed the moss growing on them. He turned slowly and oriented himself, closing his eyes. *What was Karsis talking about when he mentioned Ether? He mentioned glamour, and other things...*He couldn't think of what to ask for though. Rather than try something foolish, he tried to think about what his father had taught him about survival. Liss beat him to it.

"Doesn't water flow south? We could just follow this and see where it comes out. If it has pieces of the bridge in it, this could be the Misty Woods like Avaryn said." She was proud of herself for not panicking and keeping her head. "It should come out near River Vale."

"Sounds good. More than I've come up with," he admitted, then saw the shock on her face and laughed. "What? I'm not your typical boy, Liss. I know when I'm out of my element."

She stared at him as he started to walk on the edge of the river, then had to rush to catch up to him. Barefoot and in the wilderness, he was still quicker than she was. She had to consciously close her mouth to keep it off the ground. Gods, they were married! "Um, Rhoe?"

"Yes?" He asked, skirting a fallen log and keeping his robe from getting muddy.

"So, we never got around to discussing that we are married now." She felt embarrassed to say it out loud, but never imagined that he would feel that way too. Until he missed a step and fell into the river. "Rhoe!"

He heard her marriage comment, then his mind stopped and his head turned to look at her. At that moment, his foot slipped on a rock and down he went. He grabbed for a root, but it was wet, and his hand slipped until he was in the water. He heard her call his name in fear as he went under, but he couldn't answer. So, he just stood up.

Her heart was pounding. She wouldn't be able to save him... she was going to lose him... Then she saw him stand up. Fear turned to rage, and she picked up a clump of dirt and threw it at him. "Oh you!"

"What? It's only deep towards the middle." He dodged the dirt and climbed out of the water onto the bank. *So much for keeping my robe clean,* he thought. "And yes, we never got around to it. Does it bother you? Being married I mean?" He couldn't imagine that she was happy with a country bumpkin like himself. *I'm just a warrior, and a wizard too, I guess.*

"No, only worried what my parents may say... Rhoe there is something I haven't told you yet." This was what she was worried about. She hadn't exactly lied, but she had never told him who she was. This time he stopped and moved away from the edge of the river, just to be safe.

He saw that this made her laugh nervously and wondered what could be so bad. "Go ahead, lay it on me," he said, then held his hands up like he was shielding himself.

"Well, my name is not actually Liss, per se." She turned around so she wouldn't see his angry face when he learned the truth. "My full name is Allissana, Allissana Everknight." She held her breath and waited for the tirade that would follow.

"So--you're actually the daughter of the king?" Rhoe was smiling, but she couldn't see him. He didn't care what name she went by, he liked her for who she was. He also didn't care who her parents were; they all had secrets and didn't blame her for keeping something like that from him, but he did want to tease her a bit for it. "You mean I've kissed a princess? I've seen a princess with her clothes off?" He started laughing when she turned around red-faced with shock and embarrassment.

"You...!" She saw his smile and knew instantly that he was mocking her. She tried to be mad, but she liked him way too much for that. She smiled instead and started laughing right along with him.

"Sorry, I expected that you would be mad and not want anything to do with me."

"How can I be mad at you for that?" He was generally lost when it came to this stuff, he wished he knew more about women and how to react to these things. They continued walking, with Rhoe asking about her time at the castle, when he stopped suddenly. "Wait! Does this mean your father was in the Companions of Everknight?"

"Yes. I knew that he may have been, but I also learned that my mother was in the group too. It kind of blew my mind at the time. Deathsong is her sword." She still couldn't get over that. She looked sideways at Rhoe, and thought of all they had done together. She couldn't imagine going through all that without him. She wouldn't have had the strength to do it alone.

"Hey, then maybe they know my parents. They were in the Companions too." Then his smile faded as he thought about his mother and father. They had to be all right. They had to. He looked up at her and she was looking at him with worry in her eyes. He tried to keep the worry off his face but it wasn't working, apparently.

"Who are they? Are they okay?" She didn't know what to say. She had experience with boys, but nothing like this. She was used to the dandies at court or even the swaggering blowhards in the city. This was new to her... did she try to comfort him?

"Gareth and Tierra Whiteheart, and I don't know if they are

all right. Dar'Krist attacked my village after I had left with Karsis and I haven't heard from them since." He looked down at his feet as they walked and tried not to think about that pillar of smoke.

"I'm so sorry Rhoe." She turned and hugged him, not knowing what else to do. She didn't recognize the names, but she could always ask her mother when they got home. She held him for a minute more, then let him go and they walked again in silence for a while.

After they would talk more about how they grew up, now that they were interested more in each other's past, and in no time, they found that they were falling for each other without any form of hesitation. Such were the stuff of stories and legends.

KARSIS LEFT his horse at the edge of the trees and entered the darkened wood quietly. He was still shock over the death of Irilyn, but he was getting better. He wasn't shaking anymore. Karsis looked out through the forest and used his *sight* to peer ahead and find where they would be coming through. There it was--about twenty miles in. He hummed a merry little tune as he walked, and watched constantly overhead. You never knew what one would find in these woods sometimes. He walked most of the day and stopped only briefly near a fallen corpse. It was a huntsman that looked like it had been torn apart by a large creature. Probably a lone wolvren. *Great, wouldn't that just make my day,* he thought, as he started to look for tracks to make sure.

A wolvren was twice the size of a large wolf, and had the temperament of a one-armed, blind beggar on an empty street. They are mean and cruel, and kill more for sport than food. He saw them leading away from the mutilated corpse; they were headed straight for the faerie ring. "Of course, they are," he said out loud. He was worried that if this thing got to Rhoe before he did, he would have to admit to Gareth that he had failed. *Hang on Rhoe, I'm coming.* He called the wind to his aid then, running for all he was worth.

LISS COULD SEE the edge of the forest where the river exited the dark canopy. Moonlight shone brightly over the grass around the river as it kept flowing south. It was then that they both heard the eerie howl in the distance. "What in the name of all that is holy was that?"

"Sounded like it was a wolf, but not one I've ever heard before." Rhoe knew that if it was a wolf and it was in a pack that were following them, they could be in serious trouble. It was also closer than it sounded, he could tell. He turned back to the forest and used his *sight*. He was kind of nervous using it like this again, but he had done it without revealing himself at the bridge. He had to *see* how much time they had. He peered deep in the woods and *saw* it. He recoiled fast before its twisted mind could sense him. It was searching for them, so it was ready. He closed his eyes and gripped her arm in haste. "Liss, run!" He turned and almost threw her towards the field, making sure he was behind her so that when this thing caught them, he would deal with it first. The creature was immense, and seemed... well evil. It wasn't just a normal beast; it was grotesque. Huge spines grew out of its back and its eyes were a sickly red. He had *seen* that its muscles had grown unnaturally, which gave it a lopsided look when it ran. This was going to hurt.

"Why?" She ran as he had said; it was his tone that had convinced her. She hadn't known him long, but he wasn't even this scared when they were fighting that thing on the bridge.

"What is it?" The dew was soaking her leathers as they hurtled through the high grass. It was a good thing that she was in shape.

"It's a very big wolf, but twisted," Rhoe said as he ran behind her. He didn't turn around to keep a look out for the thing, instead he sent out his *sense* to be ready for it. This *sense* wasn't his eyes, but he tried to send his hearing and smell like he would his sight. *With my luck, experimenting like this will strike me unconscious, but why not try it.* He laughed at his own thought and kept running. They only got another hundred paces when he smelled rotting meat. It was near.

KARSIS SLOWED down when he saw the faerie ring and spun quickly, searching the ground for tracks. It didn't look like a fight, but there were definitely human tracks, one of them barefooted. Stubborn warriors and their customs.

Could they have arrived early? He had assumed he would beat them, but it appeared it was the other way around. He noticed that the wolvren had picked up their trail as well and headed after their tracks. This day wasn't going to get any better, and he had the sinking feeling that it may even get worse. Great. Calling the wind to him once more, he ran through the trees, following the river after the tracks. He was so close he could almost follow them by the smell of the great beast after them. If he didn't get there soon, he didn't know what he would find. The kids were good fighters to be sure, and Rhoe was trained by his mother well--plus he had a rudimentary working of magic that may save him. It was the wolvren's ability to warp things that bothered him. If Rhoe tried magic, it could be warped back on him. *Stop thinking about it and just run fool!* he scolded himself.

Karsis focused and dodged through the forest, trying not to think about it at all, and failing miserably.

THEY HAD RUN FOR MILES, and it was gaining all the time. She was tiring, and if she didn't stop soon, she would have no energy to fight the thing. She could feel herself slowing down, and that panicked her more than facing this beast.

"Rhoe, we have to stop, I'm all out of steam." She stopped and bent over, trying to steady her breathing. When the thing howled at the prospect of its meal being closer, she pulled Deathsong in preparation. The sword rang in the night air and turned into a howl of its own.

"Nice!" Rhoe said, as he came to a stop near her. "Maybe that scared him off?" He laughed at the absurdity of his own joke and got ready to face the thing as it came at them. They were near a split in the river as an offshoot headed towards the south west and the main river continued towards the mountains.

"Let's get across the river and make it come to us," Liss said, having a sudden inspiration. *It may be easier to hit it if it's trying to swim,* she thought. She ran the last couple of feet to the river's edge and tried to gauge how deep it was.

"The current is too fast to wade through; we have to go over it," Rhoe said, then closed his eyes, trying to picture what he wanted before he spoke. He thought of how he had the water hold him up while trying to survive the river days ago. *That might work, but can I make it hold both of us?* He had no more time for thoughts as another howl split the night; it was so close. "Ash'anti water, hadar eu ubel." He changed 'me' to 'us' and hoped for the best. No time to worry now. He grabbed her arm and took a step off the bank and onto the water. She pulled back but his grip was too tight. His foot held, now to see if hers stayed as well. "Trust me Liss, I've got you." He smiled at her, standing there on the moving water.

Trembling with fear, she closed her eyes and placed one foot on the top of the water... and it held. She let out a shuddering breath, almost sobbing with relief. "Gods Rhoe, how did you--"

"Not now Liss. Go!" He pulled her arm and ran across the river as he smelled the rotting meat all around them. He heard the pounding of its clawed feet tearing up the earth behind them, and as he stepped on the bank on the other side he let the water go with but a thought, thanking it silently. The beast skidded to a halt on the opposite bank, howling its rage at its prey escaping, then sniffed the water and grinned. Rhoe had never seen a wolf grin. He spread his feet apart and squared his shoulders, ready for the thing to try and leap the river. Gods know it was big enough to try. *But why did it sniff the water?* He felt that it was significant, but had no time to dwell on it.

Liss moved a little ways apart from Rhoe, to give herself room to swing, and tried to imagine what the beast would do. If it came right for them, there wasn't a whole lot they could do. The thing was massive, and if it acted like a wolf did--going for the throat or neck--then even dodging its razor-filled jaws wouldn't help; the thing was too agile. Liss decided on a proven tactic in battle. She bent down, picked up a rock and threw with everything she had. The rock hit the beast right in the head, glancing off its fur and causing it to turn its gaze upon her. Its eyes narrowed and fury lined its features. Snarling, it slowly eased into the water, fighting the current as best as it could.

"Why in all the wide world did you do that?!" Rhoe half screamed at her. He couldn't believe that this trained warrior had gone and provoked the beast.

"I made it angry Rhoe. Now it is less likely to think of plans or other things; it wants to rip me apart." She was smiling at him, not even perturbed by his reaction. She had seen intelligence in its eyes, and as she hefted another rock, she laughed at the simplistic tactic she was using. *Whatever works.*

Rhoe shook his head and smiled himself. He would've never thought of something like that. He looked and found a small rock of his own, and threw it with accuracy gained form years of training with his mother. It landed on its mark, smashing an eye and making the beast howl with unrelenting fury. It surged forward, pushing through the current, and found itself being swept slowly sideways by it. It couldn't quite reach the bottom for grip. But it was still coming.

Liss ran for the bank and met the beast as its front legs grabbed for purchase, swinging Deathsong in a two-handed arc straight down. She landed a solid blow, seeing blood fly on the air as she brought the sword back up, but the thing pulled harder and got another leg up on the bank. A grey blur zipped past her and landed a kick between its eyes, almost going in over the beast.

Rhoe struck true, and the beast rocked backwards, losing its injured leg's hold on the ground. It lunged forward, snapping its jaws down on Rhoe's leg impossibly quickly, but failing to get a good lock on his leg. As the warrior fell back, bleeding freely, it seemed to bolster the wolvren. It heaved itself up once more, finally tasting its prey, and gained ground with both legs. It started crawling up onto the bank, almost out of the water.

"Rhoe!" Liss called out when she saw the thing tear into his leg. Nothing should ever move that fast. She swung across its face, hoping it would pull back out of range so he could turn the swing into a lunge. It ducked instead.

Rhoe saw it all in slow motion. The huge wolf thing ducked its head impossibly low, bashing it into the ground so that her swing cut into its fur but not its skin. It slowed her down enough that he snapped his jaws forward and grabbed her leg in his powerful jaws, clamping down in a death lock and tossing her to the ground.

"*No!*" He tried to get to his feet, but his leg was ruined. Instead, he rolled towards the beast and lashed out with his good leg in a powerful snap. He connected with the thing's head so hard that it made a cracking sound as it spun away from him.

Liss cried out in pain and shock; her leg snapped as Rhoe hit the thing. She was losing her grip on Deathsong, and couldn't find the strength to lift it anyway. The pain was all she knew. "Rhoe!" She screamed even louder then, as the beast grinned at her and started slipping into the water once more, dragging her with it.

"Liss! Hang on!" he yelled as he rolled once more and turned so that he could grab the thing around its head. He found its eye and dug his fingers in, while shouting from the pain in his leg. The beast clawed him as it tried to stop him; it kept slipping further into the water. "No!" he said with finality, "I won't let you have her!" He summoned his inner calm and thought about using the water to help, then stopped as an icy calm came over him. It wanted this.

He wasn't sure how he knew that, but he did. He shook his head and dug his fingers in deeper, blinding it in one eye and yelling at it to let go. He was bleeding all over now, his robe a tattered mess, and still he held on, moving to its other eye. "You can't have her beast... you won't take her from me!"

Liss was on the ground, numb with pain and shock, but still heard Rhoe screaming for her. She looked up through a haze and saw that it had let her go. Rhoe was holding onto its head and blinding it with his bare hands, but the thing had torn him to pieces, almost literally.

"Rhoe... I'm all right! Rhoe.." But she couldn't get the air to fill her lungs well enough to shout. *Don't leave me, Rhoe...* A spear thudded into the beast then, then another, and still another. Men swarmed over Rhoe, pulling him to safety as the others stabbed and stabbed the beast. It slid into the water, howling its last with the spears still in it, and all was quiet.

"Miss, can you hear me?" The voice sounded awfully worried.

"Yes, I think so." Who were these men? Why didn't she hear them coming? *Oh right, I was too busy screaming.* At least she was feeling better, the light-headed feeling was gone, and her leg didn't hurt as bad. It still felt like a dragon was using it as a toothpick, but it was getting better every minute. *Oh, that's right, father's ring!* She had forgotten all about it.

"I'm Aeric Savar, King's Marshal. We were on patrol around River Vale when we heard the howls. Imagine our surprise when we saw it was a wolvren." He shook his head in disbelief. "Your friend is hurt bad, but our healer is tending to him." Aeric stared at this girl, trying to place her. He knew faces, but couldn't for the life of him figure where he knew her from. *And is it my imagination, or was she a lot worse when we got here?*

"King's Marshal?" Liss wanted to laugh at the good fortune. She hesitated though. Would he just drag her back without Rhoe? Would he even believe her? *No, for now keep going as Liss. If he figures it out--well, I'll burn that bridge when I get to it.* She tried to get up, and found that her leg would already support her weight. Painfully, but it held. She limped over to the river bank, where they had pulled him off the beast. 'Wolvren,' they called it: only faint recollections of something she couldn't remember came to mind. Pushing it out of her mind, she concentrated on what they were saying about Rhoe.

Their healer was looking at her with severity in his eyes. "We have to get him to River Vale. I've done all I can for now. This boy is going to need Lady Caerlyn."

"Look at the gashes, he wouldn't let go... bravest damn thing I've ever seen."

"At least he's breathing."

"Gentleman!" Liss had heard enough. They needed to get him to River Vale and save him--now. "If he needs to get to River Vale, then let us go with haste."

"The lady is right." Aeric stood next to her, looking at her sideways. She was so damned familiar. "Get him into the wagon and ready the horses. Veddick, take a horse and run it to the ground to get to Caerlyn Hold. Tell the lady that she is needed desperately." He didn't know if she would come, but he had to try.

Liss saw the worry in his eyes, and knew that the lady may well be busy with other things. She sighed then and straightened her back a little before drawing Deathsong. She drew it slowly, more for show than defiance. She needed them not to panic and think she was attacking. The sword rang though the night air, for miles it seemed, almost like it was a herald. "I am Princess Allissana Everknight. Tell Lady Caerlyn that I need her help personally."

She bowed slightly to the king's marshal as she finished, and his face showed recognition. "If she doesn't believe that you have spoken to me, use the phrase—Caerlyn's touch at midnight —and she will know it is from my lips." Liss hated to sound so official, but they needed to know it was truly her.

"Your Highness, I knew you looked familiar, but I couldn't place you. What are you doing out here?" Aeric was truly lost for words. He needed to get back to the castle and find out what he had missed in the last month.

"Long story, lord marshal. I'll fill you in along the way to River Vale." She bent down to whisper in Rhoe's ear, trying not to touch him too much. Tears fell from silent eyes as she touched her head to his. "Please hang in there Rhoe. I don't want to lose you now that I've finally found you."

He weakly lifted his head, fighting to stay conscious, "Never losing... me... now." He closed his eyes, but kept whispering. Something about the water. They all left within minutes, Rhoe safely nestled in a wagon, and Liss riding a borrowed horse alongside. They would reach the town within the hour and hopefully Lady Caerlyn wouldn't be too far behind.

§&

EVEN ASSISTED RUNNING IS TIRING, and Karsis was absolutely exhausted. He heard the howls and even thought he heard an answering ring as well, but with the wind rushing past his head he wasn't sure. He pulled up to the river fork, and by the sheer amount of blood all over the grass he knew that it had found them. The lack of bodies was promising though.

"Where did you go kids?" He sent out his *sight*, searching the plains for a sign of the kids, and found the caravan headed to River Vale. Karsis breathed a sigh of relief as he noticed the banner of the King's Marshal, but then he noticed how bad Rhoe was. The boy seemed catatonic, at least magically, and that could mean a hundred things. His wounds were grave indeed, but he seemed stable.

His *senses* snapped back to the water then, drawn by something. He stared into the moving blackness, trying to figure out what had alerted him. *Did Rhoe use magic on the water in the fight?* Karsis couldn't stand here and figure it out, he needed to get after that caravan. He couldn't run any more tonight, so he pulled out his harp and walked to River Vale on this cloudless night.

Some hours later, as he neared the town, the sun rose to join him and he saw this as a greeting of things to come. As if it was a sign, Karsis suddenly needed to know where the incarnation was and how close it was to Rhoe. He asked the ether quietly to enhance his *sight*, then sent it straight up, soaring into the clouds. It took him quite a few minutes of searching, but he finally found what could only be the incarnation. Nothing else was that evil. There, almost four-hundred miles north was the form of a man in black, laying in a clearing of newly fallen snow. It would be a long trip, even for something that powerful, to get back to any form of civilization.

Karsis had to laugh. *Leave it to Irilyn to put him where the Court of Shadow had once been.* His thoughts turned towards his grief once more when he thought of her, and he started a sad tune on his harp as he pulled his *sight* back down. He continued his walk towards River Vale, and his smile returned once more, after a time. The Darkness had returned, but with luck, a good song, and some determination, good may well win the day.

EPILOGUE: LYING IN DARKNESS

He stood atop the castle roof and pulled his dark cloak closer to him. He would miss his apprentice, but with his death it took the pressure off him for the moment. With any luck, they would think Trost was the main force behind all the intrigue and he could slip in without being noticed and finally finish what needed to be done.

And I will need someone to train as well, he thought, as he looked out at the city far below. Something caught his eye then. He peered at a wagon coming up the long road to the castle and used his *sight* to spy upon them. It was a patrol wagon and it looked like they had that irresponsible rouge Tanan with them, as well as an enormous man and a woman holding a child. *More refugees, just what this castle needs.* He pulled his *sight* in with disgust, and turned towards the east.

His informant in River Vale had messaged him with the winds that the princess had arrived with a wounded boy. It matched the description of the boy Karsis had traveled with, and if that were true, then they were headed here. Shaking his head with irritation, he readied his own message to his informant and twisted the winds to do his bidding. *Prevent the princess from coming home at all cost. Slay her if necessary, but do not let her reach home.* He sighed and turned towards the rooftop access. Things were still going against him, but if he kept his head and remained calm, he would prevail. If he only knew Karsis's last name, then he could use it to strike him down.

"Another day, another enemy." He chuckled at his own humor, and only the birds could hear him. Speaking of enemies, he thought of the king's new messengers. It was a pity that the young girl was going to live, as they were now on the short list of people that would stand in his way. He walked in and went to his room; it was time to plan for a funeral.

Vale of the Shadow Court, Northern Belt Mountains

IT WAS COLD.

He came to consciousness with that thought, and rolled to his knees slowly, not knowing what had happened at first. He was kneeling in deep snow, drawing in shuddering breaths with still-healing ribs. His robe was caked with both his own blood and that of his enemy's. He looked down at his chest and touched the spot where he was... what?

Oh, right. I was impaled. It was tender but solid. He looked around and saw the shriveled body of the faerie and it all came back to him. That little piece of filth had tricked him--her and that damned unicorn. He bent his head back and screamed his anger out at the sky. Waves of power washed out from him, but there was nothing to decay except the very earth under him, and the mountains he knelt on were too big, too massive to feel his power like that. Dar'Krist took a deep breath and reigned in his anger, knowing that it would not serve him right now. He would save it for when he destroyed that impudent boy and his plaything of a girl.

He placed his face in his hands, trying to force the healing to hurry up with his ribs. He was sick of hurting when he took a breath. That was when he felt the stubble on his face. He needed to shave? *How long was I out?* he thought, *and where the hells am I?* He looked around and didn't need his *sight* to figure out the mystery this time. Only one set of mountains had this much snow year-round, especially in spring. The Northern Belt.

Great. He was so far from anything that it would take him almost two-tendays to get back over flatter topography. In these mountains one mile seemed like five, and he couldn't run well in this terrain. He got to his feet and went to the faerie ring, hoping but knowing what he would find. It was dead, the mushrooms wilted and rotted, probably from his fight with that meddling faerie.

That's when he saw the others. There were at least four other rings around this one, all dormant and still. *Where did she bring me?* He shook his head and tried to focus; he had been healing for gods below knew how long, and now it was going to be months before he could exact his revenge.

He shrugged off the thoughts and gathered his cloak around him. It rustled on its own, and he realized that it hadn't fed since he awoke. That wasn't good. He would find something for it soon enough in these wild mountains. As he made his way, it occurred to him that he hadn't reached the castle yet. He was determined to sit on whatever throne was there and make the people beg him for death. And then there were the faeries and that bothersome bard-who-wasn't-a-bard to deal with. They would all pay. He smiled as conviction replaced anger. It may take him some time to get back, but death was coming--that was inevitable. He staggered up the rocks, found his way south and pulled his cloak around himself tightly. He was coming.

To be continued in **The Darkness Within**

THE ADVENTURE CONTINUES IN
THE DARKNESS WITHIN
AVAILABLE SPRING 2021!

The Incarnation of death has been slowed, but at a cost. Rhoe and his companions must reach the city of Everknight and find a way to stop the Incarnation for good. Yet Everknight is not a safe city. Intrigue and assassins lie around every corner, and the mastermind behind it is eager for Rhoe to arrive. Revelations and long hidden secrets come to light, but will they help our heroes' cause... or tear it all down?

ABOUT THE AUTHOR

Born in the usual way, Michael D. Nadeau found fantasy at the age of 8 with Dungeons and Dragons. He loved being different people and casting magic. By the late 90's, he discovered his love for reading. His favorite teacher gave him her personal books to bring home, and he couldn't get enough. He had even more ways to explore the great worlds out there, and it was harder and harder to come back. When he was much older, and had created and destroyed more worlds than he could count, he decided to delve into the literary realm. He created Lythinall, a place where he could tell epic stories and invite his readers on the journey with his characters. The Darkness Returns is the start of that journey, but certainly not the end. You can learn more about his works at SkullgateMedia.com as well as his personal website, KarisTheBard.Wordpress.com.

 twitter.com/Salen_Valari

 instagram.com/michael_d_nadeau

 amazon.com/Michael-D.-Nadeau

BURIED TREASURE!
CUT-THROAT PIRATES!
SWASHBUCKLING ADVENTURE!

Volume 3 of *Tales From the Year Between* sets sail in the Spring of 2021! Dust off your eye patch, polish your peg leg, and stow away with us for an anthology of high-seas adventures! Arrr!

www.ingramcontent.com/pod-product-compliance
Lightning Source LLC
Chambersburg PA
CBHW071554110726
47908CB00007B/2093